Refuge in Emptiness

Nellotie Porter Chastain

PublishAmerica
Baltimore

First printing

ISBN: 1-4241-7549-6
PUBLISHED BY PUBLISHAMERICA, LLLP
www.publishamerica.com
Baltimore

Printed in the United States of America

DEDICATION

Refuge in Emptiness is lovingly dedicated to my earthly father, Jesse Porter Sr., who was never afraid to preach about the second coming of Jesus Christ—glorious for believers, horrific for unbelievers.

When the rapture occurs, unless I have already joined my beloved family members who are already in Heaven, I will be one of those who disappear in the twinkling of an eye.

If you should be standing next to me, I hope you're ready.

“For the Lord himself shall descend from Heaven with a shout, with the voice of the archangel, and with the trumpet of God: and the dead in Christ shall rise first: Then we which are alive and remain shall be caught up together with them in the clouds to meet the Lord in the air: and so shall we ever be with the Lord” (I Thessalonians 4:16, 17).

ONE

His eyes blinked. The music stopped.

THUD! Thud! Thud! The sound of hymnals bouncing onto the sanctuary's pale, rose-colored carpet caused Jeff Howard's drooped shoulders and head to snap up. His heart jerked painfully when he saw his parents' clothing slipping from the edge of the pew.

"Hey!" he shouted. "Mom! Dad!"

Jeff's words echoed through the octagonal shaped sanctuary of Woodville Baptist Church. The silence of death answered him as his eyes darted over pews covered with clothing of all types. Hymnals and clothing were scattered on the floor. A black suit, white shirt, pink and black striped tie, and black loafers lay behind the pulpit as if waiting to be picked up and worn.

"They're gone," came a hoarse whisper from somewhere near the back of the sanctuary. Spinning around, he saw an elderly man sitting in the next to the last pew. Jeff recognized him as one of the church deacons who had been around since Jeff was a small boy.

"That was a cool trick." Two young men, standing on the east side of the sanctuary where the teenagers usually sat, began to nervously laugh. "Didn't know this was going to be a magic show."

"What's going on?" Amanda, a pretty, blond-haired girl whimpered. "Jeff, what's happening?"

"No! No! Please, no!" Desperate cries that for several seconds had been imprisoned in shock constricted throats, suddenly erupted from two female choir members as they collapsed onto the floor.

Mr. Johnson, the choir's tenor soloist, staggered down the choir loft steps. Jeff watched as he bumped into the pews trying to escape the sanctuary. Although his wild eyes looked at him as he stumbled by, Jeff could see terror in his unfocused gaze.

Jeff sprinted up the center aisle, slamming open the glass doors into the foyer. He searched the long, narrow fellowship hall which held only tables and chairs. Sliding down the stairs into the basement, he followed the sound of desperate crying.

Jerking open the nursery door, what he saw caused his knees to begin to buckle. Sitting in a rocking chair clutching a baby blanket, bottle, baby clothing and a diaper crumpled in her lap, Mrs. Sizemore sobbed. "The babies! The babies are gone. Where'd they go?" Mrs. Sizemore's cries echoed through the empty basement.

Finding it difficult to breathe, he stumbled toward the steps, taking two at a time until he was once again in the foyer where his hands crashed against the doors which led outside. Jeff dashed out to the parking lot to discover that no cars had been moved. They all were still in the same spots they had been parked two hours earlier. He watched Mr. Johnson, who obviously had forgotten his car, staggering down Woodville Road toward Highway 37.

High-pitched wailing seeped through the closed, stained-glass windows, painfully stabbing Jeff's ears. "This can't be real. I've listened to too much of Pastor Don's preaching and now I'm hallucinating."

Slowly, fearfully, Jeff's eyes looked upward, searching clouds which drifted aimlessly across the blue sky that seemed to have lost its luster. His eyes darted quickly to the midnight blue Chevrolet Chevelle parked in his parents' usual place. Jeff ran and jerked open the door.

Leaning against the side of the car, his backside slid down the smooth paint until he was sitting on the blacktopped parking lot. Hot tears ran down his face as the reality of the last thirty minutes settled into his soul.

"Mom! Dad! No. You can't be gone. You can't leave me here!" Not caring who saw him, great sobs erupted from his trembling teenage body.

TWO

Jeff Howard, an eighteen-year-old high school senior, had reluctantly agreed to attend church with his parents that morning.

"I'm just going today because the other seniors will be there," Jeff had told his father.

"Thanks, son, your mother will be pleased." Jeff's dad always encouraged his son to go to church, while trying not to badger him about it.

"You riding with us, honey?" his mother had asked as she walked through the kitchen toward the back door.

"Naw, I'm driving my truck so I can leave right away."

"Okay, son. Your dad and I will be at the baccalaureate service this afternoon."

"I don't know why we seniors have to go to all these church services. Why can't we just graduate and be done with it?" Jeff remembered growling.

"It's tradition, son." His dad had patted Jeff on the shoulder as they each walked to their respective vehicles.

"Whatever," Jeff had muttered. He sat in his red Chevy pickup truck, turning the music up louder than usual. Parked behind his parents' prized, restored car, Jeff had watched as his father opened the door for his mother before giving him a quick wave.

Even after his father's car rumbled to life, Jeff hadn't offered to back out of the way. "'Whatever'? Why did I talk that way to them. After all, they are good parents," he remembered saying out loud. Slowly, he reached over and turned the radio off, opened his door and walked up to his father's window.

"You okay, son?" his father had asked.

"Yeah, Dad," Jeff said. "I just wanted to apologize for my attitude this morning. I'm not crazy about going to church, but that doesn't stop me from loving you."

"Why, son, thank you." Jeff's father had been pleasantly surprised.

Jeff walked around the front of the car and opened his mother's door. Bending in, he had given his mother's soft, warm cheek a kiss, smelling her favorite perfume. "I love you, Mom."

"Oh, Jeff, I love you too."

He then had gently closed his mother's door before returning to his truck. He didn't see the look that passed between his parents or the grateful tears that spilled from his mother's eyes.

He sadly remembered saying, "After today, it's going to be a cold day in…it's going to be a long, long time before I step inside another church."

THREE

Jeff Howard was tall and handsome. His thick, sandy-colored hair lightened to a soft blond during the summer when he worked at the swimming pool as a lifeguard. He could have had his pick of young ladies in his school, but he had chosen to concentrate on his studies and his favorite sports. He had made exceptionally good grades all through school and had been a star on the basketball team since his elementary school days. His summers had been spent playing baseball and life-guarding at the city's pool.

Along with all of the other freshmen, he had been given a special aptitude test during the first week of his freshman year. Six weeks later, Jeff had been called in to the principal's office for a meeting with two impressive looking men.

Both men wore what Jeff thought were weird looking glasses. The lens were somewhat darkened, but they also had a strange shimmer to them, although at that moment, Jeff was more impressed with their uniforms. Having had a lifelong dream of working in law enforcement, their blue jumpsuit type uniforms with gold badges and trim caught his immediate attention.

"Jeff Howard?" The first man reached to shake Jeff's hand.

"Yes, sir," Jeff answered clearly.

The second officer reached over and shook Jeff's hand with an exceptionally firm grip. Jeff looked intently through the darkened glasses into a set of strange looking eyes. A split second of fear nipped at Jeff's heart.

"Please, sit down, Mr. Howard," this man ordered.

Trying to sit quickly, Jeff's foot caught on the chair leg; he awkwardly fell into it. "Sorry," he mumbled.

"Jeff Howard, we have been given the results of the test you took when you entered high school and it looks as if you achieved a perfect score. This is a highly unusual occurrence for high school freshmen."

Terrified that the principal thought he had cheated and had called these special police officers, Jeff thought he was going to be suspended or even arrested.

"I didn't cheat. I swear, I didn't cheat," he exclaimed, rubbing his hands together.

"We're not here because we thought you cheated, Jeff," the first man said with a strangely crooked smile.

"Good, because I never cheat," Jeff said. Although he was somewhat relieved, his shoulders were stiff as he wondered just why he had been called in front of these men.

"We're aware of that. We're here to recruit topnotch students into the World Security Force."

"World Security Force? You mean that's real?" Jeff asked.

As he watched Jeff's eyes closely, the first officer asked, "So you've already heard about W.S.F.?"

"Yes, sir," Jeff said. "My dad keeps up on world news. At dinner every night he tells my mom all the important stuff."

"What exactly do you know about us?"

Jeff relaxed as he began talking about his favorite subject—law enforcement. "My dad wasn't sure if World Security Force had been established yet. He had concerns about a *world* security force."

"You sound as if you don't entirely agree with your father."

"I've tried to find all the information I can on the net and stuff," Jeff said.

"You sure you're just a freshman?" Both men laughed.

"I've always wanted to be in law enforcement, but I don't want to be stuck here in this little town. If World Security Force is real, I'd like to be ready to join when I graduate," Jeff said.

"That's good to hear, Jeff," the officer said. He slid a blue and gold folder across the table to Jeff.

"WOW," Jeff exclaimed.

"W.S.F. is very real. We are looking for intelligent, highly motivated young men and women. Your test scores, along with the information we received from your school officials, tell us that you are a number one candidate for W.S.F."

"WOW," Jeff repeated, so excited he could hardly sit still.

"Are you interested in the W.S.F. recruit training program?"

"Yes, sir," Jeff said.

"Good," the first officer said. "Here's the plan. You take the W.S.F. packet today. Familiarize yourself with it. The last three pages will be the entrance application. Fill those out as much as you can. We will be back to meet with you next week to finalize the application. Two weeks after that, you will begin training."

In awe, Jeff picked up the impressive folder with both hands. "Thank you," he said.

"One more thing, Jeff."

Jeff's eyes darted from one officer to the other. A slight frown drew his eyebrows down. "What?"

"We request that you keep this conversation between us for now. Do you have a problem with that?"

"No, sir," Jeff said. "I understand."

Both W.S.F. officers stood to give Jeff firm handshakes. He left the office trembling with excitement.

For the first time since starting first grade, Jeff considered skipping school so he would have the opportunity to read everything in his new blue and gold folder.

Throughout his freshman and sophomore years, Jeff had joined a handful of other students as they attended a special class. Although the class was considered school curriculum, Jeff and the other students knew it was different. There was never any homework and the school kept no records. During his junior and senior years he had been doing intense hands-on training.

Keeping his secret from his parents had not been as difficult as he thought, even though there were times when he felt guilty. Despite everything else going on in his life, he loved and respected his parents.

FOUR

Watching Jeff's eyes sparkle when he spoke about his dreams for his future brought smiles to his parents' faces all the while their hearts ached. A career in law enforcement was not going to provide financially for their son the way they had hoped a better career would. Their hope and dreams for their son far surpassed his own dreams. And then there was the issue of his mother's fear for her son's safety.

But they kept their thoughts and fears between themselves, not wanting to discourage Jeff or have him rebel and go into that line of work just to spite them.

Neither of Jeff's parents was aware that their son had been recruited into the World Security Force. Every evening as they read the newspaper and watched the news on television, they discussed the soon second coming of Jesus Christ. Terrible things were happening worldwide. Just in the United States alone, many of the freedoms that had always been taken for granted were now a thing of the past.

Churches all across the country struggled to stay opened. Many pastors had been arrested. Christians were no longer free to witness openly without fear of losing their families, their jobs, even their lives.

Jeff's parents were devout Christians, having faithfully attended Woodville Baptist Church since before Jeff had been born. Jeff had basically grown up in Woodville Church, attending Sunday school, children's church, vacation Bible school every summer, and youth group meetings.

His parents worried because of some of the topics of discussion they had heard were going on at those meeting.

Apparently the youth were seriously discussing the authenticity of the Bible. When Jeff's parents heard that the youth no longer believed that Jesus actually said the things that were attributed to Him, they set up a meeting with the pastor.

Pastor Don assured them that there were only two young people who were causing the discord. The youth minister had been keeping him abreast of the situation and they were having special prayer regarding the matter.

Jeff's parents knew their son had received the right biblical training, but to their heart-rending disappointment, Jeff had never made the decision to ask Jesus into his heart.

"Don't wait too long, Jeff," his parents had told him many times.

Those words, *don't wait too long,* now echoed through his mind as Jeff sat on the parking lot sobbing. Life, as he knew it, was over because he had "waited too long."

"What now?" he asked out loud, wiping his face on his sleeve. "What happens now?"

FIVE

Leaning into the car to grab a fistful of tissues, Jeff caught a whiff of his mother's perfume, causing a new round of sobbing. Grabbing the door, he slammed it with such force the car shuttered.

He walked back inside the church and looked around the sanctuary to discover the handful of people who had been left were still sitting as if they didn't know what to do. Their wailing had quieted to soft sobs.

Looking in the direction of the young boys, Jeff saw them going through purses they had found in the pews and on the floor.

"Leave those alone," he shouted. Sprinting in their direction, he continued to yell, "Get out of here! Get out of here or I'm calling the police."

Laughing, the two boys dropped the purses and ran from the building. Jeff turned to walk to where his parents had been sitting. With fresh tears streaming from his dark brown eyes, he tenderly touched his mother's crumpled clothes.

Trying to focus through the tears, Jeff picked up his mother's purse and emptied the contents of his father's pockets into it. Standing, he whispered, "I'm sorry, Mom." He had stepped back into the aisle when he remembered something. Bending over his parents' clothing, Jeff gently picked up his mother's Bible and stuck it into the purse.

"Jeff?"

Having forgotten about everyone else in the sanctuary, Jeff turned toward the soft voice. "What?"

"I don't know what to do, Jeff. I'm so scared," Amanda cried.

Jeff walked across the front of the church sanctuary and halfway up the opposite aisle to Amanda. Sitting next to her, he felt her body trembling when he put his arm around her shoulders.

She lifted her red, puffy eyes to him. "Daddy just disappeared. His clothes are here, but..." She suddenly bent over as a desperate moan slipped from her lips.

"Amanda!" Jeff commanded. "Amanda, listen to me."

"What?" she whispered. "What are we going to do, Jeff?"

"For right now, I want you to empty your dad's pockets into your purse and let's get out of here. Can you do that?"

Amanda looked down at her father's clothing, shaking her head. "I can't..."

"Yes, you can," Jeff told her. "Come on, I'll help you." He reached over her and picked up a pair of brown dress slacks.

"Oh, Daddy," Amanda cried.

As gently as possible, Jeff said, "Amanda, this is all we can do now. Open your purse, okay?"

With trembling hands, Amanda unzipped her purse as Jeff dropped a wallet, a handful of change and a key ring into her purse. He stood, taking her arm to lead her out of the sanctuary. Just as they stepped into the aisle, Jeff stopped. "Do you want his Bible?"

"Oh, yes," she said. When she picked up the thick, black, leather-bound Bible from the pew, it slipped in her hand and something fell onto the floor. Amanda quickly bent to pick up what looked like a photograph. Looking at it, she sank onto the pew and began to weep again.

"What is it, Amanda?" Jeff asked, sitting next to her.

"It's a picture of my mother," she sobbed. "I didn't know he kept her picture in his Bible."

Jeff took the photo and looked closely at it. "You look like your mom. Where is she?"

"She died in a car wreck three years ago," Amanda said. She took the photo, sliding it back into her dad's Bible.

"I'm really sorry."

"Can we get out of here?" Amanda said, standing quickly.

Jeff jumped up, hurrying through the side door into the foyer where they wasted no time getting outside into the fresh air. Neither young person noticed that the sun was shining. To their traumatized minds, a dark pall covered their world.

"You want to ride with me?" Jeff asked.

Amanda stood still, looking across the parking lot to her father's cream-colored Cadillac. Tears, that seemed to never stop, once more began running down her mascara streaked cheeks. "What about Dad's car?"

"We'll come back and get it."

Amanda nodded her head slowly as she followed Jeff to his pickup truck. When they were seated in the truck, she asked, "Jeff, I *really* don't understand what happened. Dad started going to church after Mom died and said he got saved. But I just started coming with him lately. I don't know much about this stuff. Do you know what in the world happened? How could that many people just disappear like that?"

"Have you ever heard the word 'rapture'?" Jeff asked. His knuckles were white as he gripped the steering wheel.

"No, is it important?"

"It is now," Jeff said. "Every time I heard Pastor Don preach about it, I thought it was a whole lot of hogwash. I thought he was just trying to scare people into getting saved."

"What is 'rapture'?" Amanda asked. "What does it mean?"

"Pastor Don told us that one day the rapture would happen. That meant Jesus was coming back and all Christians would immediately go to Heaven."

"Go to Heaven?" Amanda exclaimed. "You mean to tell me that all those people, including our parents, just went to Heaven? They went without dying?"

Jeff nodded his head.

"But what about us? Why didn't we go?"

Jeff turned to look at her, wondering if she really didn't understand. "Obviously we aren't Christians."

"But...but...you mean, if I become a Christian I can go to Heaven right now too?"

Jeff dropped his head onto the steering wheel.

"Jeff?" Amanda's voice began to take on a shrill edge.

"Amanda," Jeff said, "it's too late for us. We had our chance and we didn't take it."

Violently trembling, Amanda tried to continue her questions through her sobs. "What exactly does this mean, Jeff? What happens to us now?"

"First of all, let's get away from here. You want to go home?" Jeff asked as he backed out of his parking space.

"I...I...I'm too scared to stay by myself."

"I'll go with you and we'll see how things work out. Maybe some of your friends will need a place to stay too. Just tell me how to get there," Jeff said.

After giving him directions, Amanda buried her face in her hands. With her face covered and tears seeping through her fingers, she missed seeing Jeff's knee hit the steering wheel.

The small, secret electronic device the size of a quarter had lain dormant in his pocket for almost four years. Shocked when it buzzed, his knee jerked up colliding with the steering wheel. When he realized what had caused the small electrical shock, he knew he had one hour to make the phone call.

The small electronic buzz not only told him that he had to make a phone call, it also caused four years of W.S.F. training to begin tumbling through his young mind. "This is what they were talking about!" It was suddenly clear to Jeff that this very event is what his training had alluded to.

"What who meant?" Amanda asked. She had managed to gain a fragile control on her emotions.

"Oh, nothing," Jeff said. "I was just thinking out loud."

"That's my house." Amanda pointed to a beige-colored modular home set back from the road. There were baskets of yellow petunias hanging at the corners of the long front porch.

After she climbed down from the truck, Amanda slowly walked onto the porch. When she reached for the doorknob, she began crying. "I…I can't do it."

"Let me help," Jeff said as he gripped the doorknob. "It's locked. Do you have the key?"

Amanda dug through her purse until she found her key. Although she knew her father's key ring was in her purse, she tried not to touch it. When she handed it to Jeff, he unlocked the door, standing back while she slowly stepped inside.

Although Amanda would be seventeen in two weeks, at the moment she stepped into her living room, she felt like a lost three-year-old. She stood in the middle of the living room floor unable to move.

"Where's your room?" Jeff asked, taking her arm forcing her to move.

Moving like a zombie, Amanda allowed Jeff to usher her through the long hallway to her bedroom door. The room was bright as the sun filtered through rose colored mini blinds onto eggshell colored walls. One wall was covered by a large bookcase, a computer desk and her tall dresser.

The focal point in the room was Amanda's full-sized bed which was covered by a deep rose-colored bedspread with princess-pink pillows. On the opposite wall was her vanity with an extra large round mirror.

Amanda walked over to sit on the edge of her bed. Jeff took her purse and her father's Bible from her hand and laid them behind her on the bed.

"It's strange, Jeff. Really strange."

"What's that?" Jeff asked.

"My dad and I got along almost all the time. But for most of this school year, I've thought a hundred times about how much fun it would be to be out on my own. Not have to answer to anybody. Just be my own person."

"Most of us teenagers have those thoughts," Jeff said.

"I know, but now that I've got the opportunity, I don't think I can do it."

"Well, Amanda, it's like this. We don't have a choice. Our parents are gone and we're left here. There's no changing that. So, no matter how scary it is or how hard it's going to be, we've got to deal with it." Jeff stood with his hand in his pocket, fingering the quarter sized object.

After a few moments silence, Amanda said, "You're right. I can't change what's happened, so I've got to get my head together and decide what I'm going to do." After another pause, she asked, "Jeff, I understand that we can't go to Heaven right now, but is it still possible to get saved? I don't want to go to hell."

Jeff sat on the edge of Amanda's bed as he tried to remember some of the things Pastor Don had preached about. Although for years he had tried to turn a deaf ear to the sermons, his ears nonetheless heard and his mind recorded valuable spiritual information that God knew Jeff would need now and in the days to come.

"Yes, Amanda, it's possible to get saved. It's just won't be easy for Christians now. Christians will be killed, there's no doubt about that."

"Oh, no," she moaned.

"Amanda, have you ever heard about the mark of the beast? Do you know what that is?"

"The mark of the beast? No, why? Is it important?" Amanda asked.

"It is now," Jeff said. "Listen to me carefully. At some point, everybody is going to be required to have a mark put on them in order to buy and sell anything. We won't even be able to buy food without it."

"What kind of mark? Will it look like some kind of animal?"

"No, I think it's going to be some kind of number that will have to be put on our foreheads or on our hand. I think it's going to have something to do with the number 666," Jeff said. He turned to look directly into Amanda's face. "Amanda, no matter what, do not take the mark. Do not take it."

"You're scaring me, Jeff. Why shouldn't I take it? I'll need to eat."

"If you take the mark, you'll go to hell for sure," Jeff said. All of his biblical knowledge and all of the W.F.S. training, even though they were totally opposite, began to make sense now.

"I've got to go, Amanda. I've got an important phone call to make. I'll check on you later, okay?" Jeff said as he stood to leave.

"What about getting saved, Jeff. How do I do that?"

Jeff stopped in the doorway, thinking. He turned back into the room as Amanda stood beside her bed. "Do you remember those men who stood at the high school gate giving out little orange New Testaments?" he asked.

"Yeah. I've got one around here somewhere."

"If you can find it, look inside the back cover. It will tell you how to become a Christian," Jeff said. He hurriedly walked through the living room and out the front door as Amanda dug through her desk looking for the small orange New Testament.

SIX

"This is Jeff Howard." Just as he'd been trained to do, Jeff gave only his name.

"Affirmative, Mr. Howard. Tuesday morning at 0800 hours, report to the high school gymnasium. Be in uniform."

"Yes, sir," Jeff said. "Where do I find..." The line went dead. "Wait a minute! Where do I get a uniform?" he shouted.

Intense fear caused him to sink to his knees next to his parents' couch. "One more day and I'll be the one arresting people like Amanda," he moaned. "Will I be able to do it?"

Slowly, Jeff sat on the couch, leaning his head back on a soft cushion. "Why did I tell Amanda that? Why would *I* give anybody information I don't believe myself?" The deafening quietness of the house was terrifying.

Closing his eyes, Jeff tried to remember the events of the morning. His memory of telling his parents that he loved them caused tears to run from the corners of his eyes down to his shirt collar.

He made himself remember the moments just before—just before *it* happened. The song leader had asked everyone to stand and sing hymn number 259. Even though Jeff had a beautiful baritone voice, he rarely sang in church.

He remembered leaning onto the back of the pew, trying to ignore the words of the song.

After the song leader had announced the hymn, Pastor Don had walked up to the podium, putting his arm around the song leader's shoulder, and spoken to the congregation while the organ played softly.

"Church, we need to listen to the words we're singing this morning. We all know the mess our world is in. Jesus Christ could come back any moment. Wouldn't it be wonderful if it is today?"

"Amens" could be heard all over the congregation.

"When that day comes, just like the words of this song says, '*we shall behold Him, then face to face*,'" Pastor Don added.

More "amens!" and just as many "glories!" and "praise the Lords!" filled the sanctuary as the congregation began singing.

The piano and organ music swelled into the chorus the second time around when in a split second, immediate total silence sliced through the sanctuary before falling hymnals began thudding onto the floor.

"I guess they beheld Him," Jeff said. "I didn't believe them. I really didn't believe they knew what they were talking about. Now it's too late. It really doesn't matter if I believed or not."

He stood and walked up the steps and down the hallway to his bedroom. When he opened the door he was shocked to see a large, blue and gold box on his bed. "What?"

Thinking the large box was a graduation gift from his parents, he was reluctant to open it, but when he walked closer he saw a sparkling W.S.F. emblem on top of the box.

Wondering how it had gotten here, he tore the lid off and found four complete, blue uniforms with gold trim. There were boots, a belt, hat, and gloves. A golden eyeglass case revealed a set of mysterious darkened glasses.

Jeff forgot the events of the morning, his parents, and Amanda as he excitedly tore off his clothing and donned one of the uniforms. Admiring himself in the full-length mirror on the back of his bedroom door, Jeff was amazed that everything fit perfectly.

"This is great," he said. "I can't wait for Tuesday." Strangely, having the uniform on caused him to transmute into a World Security Force agent, not only by how he looked in the uniform, but mentally.

When he slipped the darkened glasses over his eyes, his life as Mr. and Mrs. Howard's son, ceased to exist. He was the squad leader. They would bring order to chaos. They would quell rebellions of any kind. They *were* the World Security Force.

SEVEN

After knocking a stack of overdue library books onto the floor in her desperate search, Amanda found her small orange New Testament.

The stiff binding crackled when she pulled the back cover open. Amanda quickly read all the verses along with the instructions. "I still don't understand," she cried. In desperation she looked around, searching for something—she didn't know exactly what.

Frustrated to the point of giving up, Amanda threw herself across her bed, sobbing into her pillow. Rolling over minutes later, she felt something hard under her back. Angrily shoving whatever it was, she discovered her father's Bible.

Gently and reverently she ran her hand over the leather cover. "This book was important to you, Daddy. Why? What did you find in it that gave you so much peace?"

Amanda carefully opened the Bible, thumbing through it. She discovered verse after verse that had been underlined, some in red, some in blue, others in green or yellow.

An hour passed as she read every verse highlighted in bright yellow. Finished, she fell onto her pillow with her face to the wall.

Staring at the wall, it was as if she was watching a panorama of her future. Beginning to tremble, she reached for the multicolored quilt which was folded at the foot of her bed. Even after snuggling under the quilt, her body continued to shake.

Awakened by a violent jerk, Amanda savagely fought her way out of the confines of the quilt to sit trembling on the edge of the bed. "It's dark, I must have dozed off. Oh, Daddy, I'm scared. Help me!"

Unable to remember if she had locked the door after Jeff had left, she jumped up and ran down the hall to check both doors and all the windows. In the darkened house, Amanda went to the kitchen to fix herself a snack and glass of cold milk.

Returning to her bedroom, she shut and locked the door, closed the mini-blinds and pulled the drapes together. Fumbling in her desk drawer for her flashlight, she grabbed it along with her New Testament, crawled under the quilt where she sat cross-legged and began to compare her father's Bible and her New Testament.

"I'm in this thing alone, so I've got to figure it out. All those highlighted verses have to do with Christians dying and going to Heaven. Heaven sounds like a wonderful place and I've got to find out how to get there. I didn't hear a trumpet, but apparently Dad and all those other people did. It looks like Dad had been reading the book of Revelation. I'm going to sit right here and read it all so I'll know what's up."

Having lost all perception of time, Amanda slid from under the quilt and went into the bathroom to finish reading when her flashlight died. The bathroom was the only room in the house without a window, so Amanda placed a rolled up bath towel along the bottom of the door, turned on the light, sat on the floor and leaned against the bathtub.

Screaming sirens dragged Amanda from the world she had become lost in as she devoured the very last book of her father's Bible. Her eyes were bloodshot, the lids puffy from reoccurring episodes of sobbing.

"It's here. Everything in this book has started. How will I survive? Jeff told me to never take the mark of the beast. Now I know why. But, what will happen to me?" Licking her thumb, Amanda pushed the pages back to reread certain verses.

"Where'd I see that? Hm-m-m. There it is. The last verse of chapter twenty. *And whoever was not found written in the book of life was thrown into the lake of fire.* I will not be thrown into hell. I may have to live through hell here, but I won't spend eternity there. Now where's that other verse?"

One of the thin pages ripped as Amanda quickly thumbed until she found what she was looking for. "There! There it is. *Behold I stand at the door and knock. If anyone hears my voice and opens the door, I will come in to him and will have fellowship with him and he with me.*"

Leaving the Bible opened to that page, Amanda jumped up, kicked the towel out of the way, ran to her bedroom, grabbed the New Testament and returned to kneel next to the bathtub.

"Okay, here goes. God, I am so sorry I didn't know you before. But from everything I've read in your Word today, I'm asking you to forgive my sins and save me. Nothing is more important to me than knowing that I am your child. Thank you, Jesus, for what you've done for me. I promise I'll do everything

I can to tell others about you in the time I have left. I realize that I'll probably die a horrible death but I have to trust you to get me through that. From this moment on, I consider myself to be a Christian. Thank you, Jesus."

Amanda Fountain. After she had written her name on the inside of the back cover of her New Testament and included the date, she stood up and looked into the mirror. "I know I belong to Jesus. I can feel it in here," she said, tapping herself on the chest.

Looking at her watch, she was surprised to see that it was seven o'clock in the morning. "I don't know what to do now, but I've got to figure it out soon." She turned around and leaned against the sink. "I think I'll take a shower and clean up. That will help me focus."

After a twenty minute hot shower, Amanda began to feel renewed. Padding her damp feet into her bedroom, she thoughtfully chose a set of comfortable clothes. After her hair was dried and combed just the way she liked it, she made her way to the kitchen to fix something to eat.

While she ate her meal, her eyes watched 8:00 flashing on the stove's digital clock. Constant noises from outside told her that the world she knew had forever changed.

Having finished her meal, Amanda walked into the family room and flipped on the TV. What she saw caused her to sink heavily onto the couch with her mouth opened in shock.

Picture after picture flashed across the screen of airplane crashes, car wrecks, train wrecks, fires of all kinds. When the pictures of looters came onto the screen, Amanda was surprised by the police officers on the scenes. They didn't look like regular police officers.

All of the police were dressed in blue uniforms that were trimmed in gold. "What kind of sunglasses are those?" Amanda asked out loud as she moved closer to the TV screen. "Whose police are those?"

Suddenly a group of odd-looking police officers opened fire on a group of looters as they carried their ill-gotten treasurers from a storefront. Amanda gasped and jumped back. "What kind of guns are those?" The looters seemed to have evaporated.

Terrified, she crawled to the beige-colored couch and buried her face into a maroon and blue checked throw pillow. Her shoulders not only shook from her sobs, but her whole body trembled in terror.

Amanda's red, puffy eyes quickly looked at the TV screen when a special alert sounded, informing the general public that a news conference would be televised at seven o'clock in the evening. The newscasters strongly advised everyone to find a way to watch the news conference.

Lack of sleep added to battered emotions caused Amanda to curl up on the floor with the pillow under her head and a knitted, maroon-colored throw pulled over her. With tears seeping from the corner of her eyes, comforting darkness enveloped her.

EIGHT

It was two o'clock in the afternoon when Jeff drove his Chevy pickup truck into Amanda's driveway. Before leaving his parents' home, Jeff had pulled on a pair of baggie jeans over his uniform. Finding an equally baggy button-up shirt, he put that on also, hoping Amanda wouldn't notice the uniform.

Before exiting the pickup truck, he shoved his special weapon under the seat. Double-checking his door to make certain it was locked, Jeff walked up to Amanda's front door.

Deep in slumber, Amanda was being chased by a horrible creature dressed in blue and gold. Just as the creature with shimmering eyes raised his strange looking gun and his finger touched the trigger, the doorbell rang. Amanda screamed as she bolted from the floor.

"Amanda! Amanda, it's Jeff. Open the door, Amanda," Jeff shouted. Terrified when he heard her earsplitting scream, Jeff grabbed the doorknob.

"Jeff, is it really you?"

"Yes, Amanda. It's really me. Unlock the door, okay?"

Several locks clicked before she was able to let Jeff in. He saw her fear-filled eyes and evidence that she had been doing a lot of crying.

"You okay?" he asked softly.

Amanda quickly slammed the door and double locked it.

"Yes. I'm sorry, Jeff. I was having a nightmare when you rang the doorbell."

"A nightmare, huh? As if life out there isn't enough of a nightmare," he muttered as he bent over and picked up the pillow and throw.

"I haven't been out since we came home yesterday," Amanda said. "Do you want anything to eat or drink?"

"No, but thanks anyway."

"Have you been out much?" she asked as she sat in the softly padded chair close to the couch.

Still concerned about frightening her, he wasn't sure how much to share about his last few hours. "Yeah, I guess. I...I've got a job and so I've been kinda busy."

"Job?! You've actually been able to get out and work?"

"You been watching any television?" Jeff asked, trying to work his way into telling her what he'd been doing. He was thinking, *What's the big deal. We're just friends; it's not like we were dating or anything before yesterday.*

"Yes," Amanda answered quietly. "It looks terrible. And we're all supposed to watch a news conference at seven this evening."

"That's real important. Be sure and watch it," Jeff said.

Amanda looked closely at him, noticing a bright blue patch of something through a hole in his jeans just below his knee. Even though it was springtime, most guys didn't wear long sleeved shirts. And his shoes! What kind of funky looking shoes were those?

"Do you know what it's about?" Amanda stood up and walked toward the kitchen.

Jeff caught her eyes looking at his knee and his shoes. He had forgotten about the hole in his jeans. After all, that was the style so why be concerned about it.

"Amanda?"

"I'm going to get something to drink." She didn't know what to do or where to go. There was no mistaking that particular shade of blue, or those shoes.

"Amanda, come here," Jeff commanded. When Amanda slowly walked back into the living room, Jeff said in a softer voice, "Sit down. I've got something important to tell you."

Envisioning those looters being vaporized, Amanda sat down, her body trembling as she raised fear-filled eyes to Jeff, who was still standing.

"You apparently know about these uniforms," he said as he began to unbutton his shirt. Amanda squeezed her eyes shut as tears ran down her cheeks. "Amanda, please don't be afraid. I need somebody to talk to."

Why does he sound so sad? Amanda opened her eyes as Jeff was removing his shirt. "What does this mean, Jeff?"

"It means more than I bargained for," he said as he removed his jeans. "You want to know when this began?"

Unsure if she wanted to know or not Amanda nodded her head anyway.

"You're a year behind me in school, but did you have to take a special aptitude test when you started high school?" he asked.

"Yes, I think our whole class did."

"That test didn't have anything to do with school. That was a recruitment tool for the World Security Force."

"Recruitment tool? World Security Force?"

"See this emblem?" Jeff asked, pointing to the gold emblem on the left side of his chest. "W.S.F. stands for World Security Force."

"And that's who you work for?"

Jeff nodded his head as he continued. "Apparently I scored the highest on that stupid test and they wanted to recruit me to become part of the security force of the future. I didn't have any idea it would turn into this."

"What do you mean, Jeff?"

"The first two years, all of the students they recruited took a special class where we learned about the security force, how it began, what it does, and what it would become in the future. The next two years we learned all about the weapons we would be using, chain of command, how to make arrests, how to do searches, and things like that."

"Oh, Jeff," Amanda said. Her hands were on her cheeks as she shook her head from side to side.

"Exactly," Jeff said. "Because my grades have always been good, I've basically stayed out of trouble, and I've been pretty much gung ho about this training, I'm now a squad leader."

"That should be good, right?"

"I thought so until—until what happened yesterday morning. Now everything has changed."

Thinking about what she had seen on TV earlier, Amanda quietly asked, "What have you had to do since yesterday?"

"I don't know how they got there, but when I arrived home yesterday my uniforms were in my bedroom."

Her eyebrows went up as she asked, "Do you think your parents bought them for you?"

Shaking his head, Jeff answered, "No, my parents didn't know about me belonging to the World Security Force."

"You're kidding?"

"I wish I was. I had to meet with my superiors last night. After the news conference this evening I have to brief my squad on how we have to bring order to this town."

"I saw some of those 'means' on TV," Amanda whispered.

Jeff leaned back onto the couch looking at the ceiling. Amanda watched him, trying to decide how much she could trust him, especially now.

"Jeff?"

"Yeah," he answered, sitting up where he could look at her.

"I'm a Christian now."

Jumping up, Jeff began pacing through the living room. After several minutes he walked over to stand in front of Amanda. Her fingers dug into the pillow she had pulled from behind her back.

A dark cloud seemed to hang over Jeff as he stared angrily at her. Defiantly staring back at him, Amanda tried not to let him see her tremble.

All at once, it was as if someone had stuck him with a pin, all the air blew out of him. Sinking to his knees in front of her, he said, "Amanda, I'm supposed to kill you."

As she watched the anger dissipate from his face to be replaced by child-like confusion, she tenderly touched his face. "Jeff, if that ever becomes a necessity for you, I want you to know that I forgive you."

"What am I going to do, Amanda?" he asked.

"For now, how about you take me to get my dad's car?" she asked as she gave him a sweet smile.

Somewhat relieved, at least for the time being, Jeff stood. "Sounds like a plan."

Making sure her house was securely locked, Amanda climbed into Jeff's truck for the short ride to the church parking lot. "Do you think you might get into trouble driving me around while you're working?"

"No, I'm actually not on duty yet. Thirty minutes after the news conference I'll have to be with my squad, ready to go to work."

"I see."

"Amanda, I don't understand why all of a sudden I feel like I can talk to you, but I want you to know how important that is to me."

"Thanks, Jeff. Now more than ever, it's important to have friends that we can trust," she said.

"Because you need to know, I have to tell you something about me when I go to work."

"What's that?"

"When I have my full uniform on, something takes over. When I slip on the glasses we have to wear, I literally become a World Security Force warrior." He watched for her reaction.

Amanda's eyes shut as her head bent forward slightly. "What exactly does that mean?"

"It means that if any W.S.F. officer comes to your door, even if it's me, with their full uniform on, including the glasses, be very careful what you say. Never tell them that you're a Christian. In fact, make sure all your Bibles are well hidden."

By the time Jeff's truck pulled up next to Amanda's dad's car, she was trembling again. Reaching into her pocket for her dad's key ring, she said, "Thanks for the ride and thanks for the warning."

Jeff watched Amanda unlock her dad's Cadillac and sit down inside. When he was certain that the car started, he backed out and left the parking lot. He looked at his watch before driving toward his parents' home. "I've got some thinking to do. Maybe if I can get close to Mom, I'll be able to decide what to do."

NINE

Keeping her eye on Jeff's truck, Amanda slowly began to back out of the parking space. Relieved when he was no longer in sight, she parked her car close to the building.

Making certain no one was watching, she jumped out of the car and ran to the east door of the church which was still unlocked. Entering, she found that all the lights were still on.

As silently as possible, Amanda walked into the empty sanctuary. Plans began to form in her mind as she stood looking over the room full of emptiness.

"Okay, if we've only got roughly seven years to try to survive, how can I use this church to save myself and other believers?" Her whisper screamed in the silence.

Spinning around, she ran into the foyer and began locking all the doors. Running to every door and window in the church, she made sure everything was locked.

"I'll have to have keys," she said, running to the pulpit in the sanctuary. Bending to pick up a pair of crumpled, black dress slacks, Amanda began going through the pockets until she found a set of keys.

Before she dropped the slacks, she prayed, "God, please forgive me, but I need money to buy food for the refuge I'm going to make here." Turning around, Amanda picked up the large offering basket from the communion table.

After emptying the pastor's pockets, she began quickly emptying as many pockets and purses as possible. When she had covered half of the sanctuary, it dawned on her that there might be a need for clothing later on.

Realizing how late it was getting, Amanda knew she'd have to return to fold the clothing. For now she had to get all the money just in case anyone should break in. Stuffing the money into a large purse she found on the floor, she locked the door and ran to her car.

As nonchalantly as possible, she stepped from her car, draping the purse strap over her shoulder and sauntered to her front door. Falling back against the inside of the door, her breath caught in her throat. Immediately locking each lock, she ran to her bedroom and stuffed the purse into her dirty clothes hamper.

Scrubbing her hands several times, she still felt dirty. Wiping her hands on a towel as she walked back into her room, Amanda looked at her bedside clock. "Oh, no!" The digital display flashed 6:45. She ran into the living room, grabbed the remote and punched the power button.

TEN

Retrieving his weapon from under the seat, Jeff walked quickly into his house, not stopping until he stood inside his parents' bedroom. His eyes brimming with tears, he walked over to his mother's side of the bed where he had placed her purse after the church episode.

Ever so gently, he sat where his mother had slept just two nights before. Pulling her pillow to his face, he smelled her scent once more. "Mom," he cried, "you never gave up on me."

Desperately sobbing into his mother's pillow, Jeff saw through his blurred vision the numbers on the digital bedside clock. "Oh, no! I've only got an hour." Jumping from the bed, tenderly placing his mother's pillow back in its place, he stepped into his parents' bathroom to wash his face in cold water.

Walking back into the bedroom, his eyes were drawn to the purse. Jeff knelt beside the bed as he carefully dumped the contents of the purse onto the pale blue bedspread.

First to fall out was his mother's small red, well-worn Bible. Lipstick, mints, fingernail file, pens, checkbook, billfold and Kleenex lay in a pile next to his father's fat billfold. Jeff picked up the Bible, tenderly rubbing his hand over its leather cover.

Lifting the front cover, he discovered a lavender-colored envelope with his name on it. "What?"

Turning to sit on the floor, he leaned against the bed as he flipped the envelope over and over before lifting the unsealed flap. Sliding the lavender paper from the inside of the envelope, he unfolded it and began to read.

> *Dear Son,*
>
> *If you are reading this letter, it means that I have either passed away or Jesus has come back to get your dad and me—which also means, that you didn't get to go with us.*

God's Word tells us that there will be no tears in Heaven, but, Jeff, I can't imagine not finding you there without crying.

My precious son, even though you didn't ask Jesus into your heart soon enough, it's not too late. You faithfully attended church with us so you heard His Word. You know that God will give you another chance.

I'll be here asking Jesus face to face, to show mercy on you and lead you to a place where you will give your heart to Him. I have faith in you, son, that you won't say a final "no" and spend eternity in Hell. I won't accept that. I want to see my precious child again. I want us to spend eternity together.

So, until I see you in Heaven, son, know that I'll always love you. On the back of this letter are some verses for you to read to help you find your way to me.

With all my love and many kisses.
Mom

"Oh, Mom, if you only knew," Jeff cried. Carefully replacing the folded letter back in its envelope, he slid it back inside the Bible cover. "I'll read the verses later."

Nauseated, Jeff quickly left the bedroom. Time to meet with his squad had come. He reached for the rest of his uniform, clicked the belt around his waist, shoved his weapon into its holster, and picked up the glasses, knowing what would happen in two seconds.

ELEVEN

Amanda sat staring at the muted TV. After Jeff left, she closed all the blinds and drapes and chose not to turn on any lights. The living room was now dark except from the TV's dancing glow.

Ten minutes passed. Slowly and gently pushing the "off" button, she placed the remote control on the end table before folding her hands between her knees.

"How could things change so drastically in such a short time?" she whispered. "I wonder how many people are going to believe those lies."

The President of the United States had disappeared along with everyone else. The Vice President hadn't been found yet. The Secretary of State announced to the listening audience that invaders from deep space had stolen their leaders and millions of citizens. Their reasoning was that these supposed invaders needed our people to repopulate their planet that had been struck by a devastating cosmic storm.

"How insane do they think we are?" The more Amanda thought about what she had just heard, the angrier she became. "That was the most ignorant garbage I've ever heard."

Too angry to sleep, she made her way into her bathroom and pulled the purse out of the hamper. "Okay, we've got a little while before we'll have to get our money traded in for the new world money. That gives me time to buy as much food, water, and supplies as I can. I'll start first thing in the morning when curfew is lifted."

Sitting in the same spot she'd been in the night before, Amanda began counting; stacking the bills in separate piles. Although her home had three bathrooms, this particular one was built with no windows, therefore she felt safe from prying eyes.

By ten o'clock, she had all the paper money counted and stacked neatly in a shoebox. The pocket change had taken longer, but it was safely secured in an additional shoebox. Altogether she had counted $2,543.98.

"This might look and sound like a lot of money, but it's not going to buy as much as I'd hoped. Our new idiot leader promised that prices for food, water and gas would double, beginning immediately. I'll go to several different stores and hope no one notices what I'm doing. After I get everything stored at church, I'll start riding my bike so I won't have to buy much gas. I sure wish I had somebody to help me. How will I know who to trust?"

Hearing her own voice seemed to calm her. Finally, weariness began to dull Amanda's thinking. After hiding the shoeboxes in the bottom of the clothes hamper, she completed her usual routine, slipped out of her clothes, adding them to the pile already on top of the boxes, pulled on her favorite nightshirt and knelt beside her bed.

"Dear God, I need you so much. What am I going to do?" Tears dripped from her chin onto the edge of her bed. "For any sins I've committed since giving my heart to you, please forgive me. I felt like a thief taking all that money from church, but I know you'd want me to use what's left over to help other believers. I need to know who I can trust. Please lead me to other believers. I promise you that I'll do everything I can for you in whatever time I have left here. And, Father God, show me how to help Jeff come to know you. I'm afraid for him. Please protect me as I go shopping in the morning. Thank you, God. Good night."

Blowing her nose on pink tissues, Amanda wearily slid between pink, flannel sheets and closed her eyes. The terrifying sirens had stopped. In fact, everything was eerily quiet. An occasional vehicle could be heard driving through the neighborhood. Amanda knew that inside the vehicle were two to four police officers in blue and gold uniforms of the World Security Force.

"I can only hope that Jeff is one of them," she whispered as she drifted into a deep, dreamless sleep.

TWELVE

As squad leader, Jeff spent as much time as he could in the high school gymnasium, which doubled as the training center for his men and women. All recruits had been accounted for at their assigned meeting following the televised world news conference.

Jeff had removed his glasses before speaking to his squad members who were all in full gear. He had to admit that they did look impressive.

Although not one of them needed further instructions, Jeff spent several minutes going over their duties for the night. Because the training had been completely thorough, every recruit had anxiously awaited the time when they could put that training into practice. That time had arrived quickly and without warning—just like they'd been told it would.

When the squad members left the building to begin their nightly patrols, Jeff's captain, who had been watching Jeff closely, asked him, "Do you have a problem with your glasses, Mr. Howard?"

Startled, Jeff quickly grabbed his glasses. "No, sir! I wanted a good look at my squad with and without the glasses. I want to see every aspect of those men and women. After all, I am responsible for them and their performance."

Nodding his head, but keeping a wary eye on Jeff, his captain motioned for him to follow. "Come on, you and I are riding together tonight."

"Yes, sir. Very good, sir." Jeff could be good at sucking up when it was necessary.

"What sector do we have?"

Seated in the passenger seat of the jet-black vehicle, Jeff checked his notebook which had each groups' area marked with letters of the alphabet. "We have sector G, which isn't as large as the others. I want to be available if and when any of my squad needs assistance."

"Good thinking."

Jeff had purposefully assigned sector G to himself because each pass took him past Amanda's house. During the first pass, he noted a faint light filtering around the edges of her bedroom window. Thirty minutes later, on their second pass, the light was out. Amanda's house was completely dark.

By two o'clock in the morning, Jeff had dropped off his captain and was now with his partner as they walked into the training center to use the restroom and get something to eat. Knowing the other vehicles would be in soon for the same reasons, Jeff remained in headquarters for an hour and a half.

"Officer needs assistance," a female voice shouted into the radio. The engine roared as he stomped the accelerator, speeding to the scene of the incident.

Agent Bonnie Summers and her partner stood outside the local laundromat in which every available light had been turned on. Even though Jeff could see clothing being tossed back and forth inside the drums of two large dryers, orders had been given to eliminate anyone who broke curfew.

"Inside the building! Everyone, step outside." Agent Summers' voice blasted through her car's outside speaker as spotlights blinded the young couple inside.

Jeff watched as the young mother grabbed her baby, holding it close to her chest. The young father slowly walked toward the door with one arm shielding his eyes and one arm around his wife and baby.

Jeff could see sheer terror in their faces as they inched out the glass door. The baby began wailing. The young mother tried to comfort the child as the father asked, "What's wrong, Officers. We're just doing our laundry."

"You have broken curfew. No one is to be out until 0800."

"Curfew? We didn't know anything about a curfew," the young father exclaimed.

"Everyone heard about the curfew on the televised news conference."

"No, sir, we don't have a television set."

Even though his glasses were securely in place, Jeff closed his eyes as a young innocent family was vaporized against the glass doors."

His jaws clinched, he nodded at Agent Summers, letting her know that she had done her job well. Jeff was well aware that he was being watched.

Seated inside the vehicle, he reached for his electronic notebook and recorded the incident before driving back to G sector for one more patrol before their shift was over. His thoughts troubled him.

When eight o'clock arrived, Jeff was seated at the long table inside headquarters, ready to plug into each groups' notebook. Thirty minutes later, all reports were in. He took several extra minutes reading Agent Summers report before printing out the master copy and sending it on to Captain Mercett.

Agent Bonnie Summers' blond hair was always kept back in a ponytail while she worked. Although she had a figure most young ladies would kill for, she never flaunted it. Jeff considered her to be an exemplary agent.

Twelve curfew breakers had been eliminated. A three page list gave addresses of homes and businesses where lights were on during the night. If anyone was visible through the windows, that was also noted with each address.

Jeff's captain was well pleased with the progress report. "Well done, Mr. Howard."

"Thank you, sir." Jeff saluted smartly. When the other officer left the building, Jeff placed everything into his briefcase and walked outside. Not until he stood inside his own house did he pull the glasses off.

Slowly walking into his parents' bedroom, he peeled off his uniform. Clad only in under shorts, Jeff lifted the bedspread and sheet and slid into his parents' bed, laying his head tenderly onto his mother's pillow.

Mentally, emotionally and physically exhausted, Jeff slipped into the dark arms of slumber as tears soaked into his mother's sweet smelling pillow.

THIRTEEN

Slightly opening one sleepy eye, Amanda smiled when she saw the pink glow on her walls as early morning sun filtered through her rose colored mini blinds. *This will be a good day to get my shopping done,* she thought as she enjoyed a bone-popping stretch.

Snuggled under her rose-colored bedspread, Amanda ears ached to hear her father's voice calling her to breakfast. Tears ran from the corner of her eyes into her long, blond curls spread over her pink pillow. Everything became like a pink prism as she tried to focus through the tears.

Tossing back the bedspread, Amanda sat on the edge of her bed. "Maybe this is what's meant by 'looking through rose-colored glasses.'" She walked into the bathroom to take a shower before beginning her day's activities.

While shampooing her hair, she began thinking about her own supplies. How much shampoo was still in the bottle? How much soap and toothpaste was left? *Before I leave for the store, I need to check the supplies right here in my house.*

With a new directive, she finished getting ready as quickly as possible. Taming her long curls usually took more time, but this morning Amanda pulled them back into a ponytail.

Dressed in her best blue jeans and her blue and gold Mitchell High School sweatshirt, Amanda found a notebook and began to inventory her entire house.

Forty-five minutes later, sitting at the kitchen table with the notebook, she ate a bowl of cereal and a glass of milk—the last drop of milk in the house. "Okay, it looks like there's plenty of stuff here. I mostly just need to get milk, bottled water and food."

While she had been searching the rooms and basement, other thoughts began to take form in Amanda's mind such as where she would be about to hide valuables.

Finished eating, Amanda put the bowl, spoon and glass into the sink. "I don't know how long I'll be safe here, so I need to find secure places to hide my money and valuables. Jeff's a security officer. I don't know how much longer I can trust him."

"Coo-coo." Her great-grandmother's coo-coo clock reminded her that curfew was over and she could now leave for the store.

Afraid to take all the money, Amanda pulled three hundred dollars and stuffed the rest back under her dirty clothes. With her purse's shoulder strap across her body, Amanda stepped outside to shut and lock the door. Clutching her purse close to her side, she unlocked her father's car and slid into the driver's seat.

"God, please help me to be careful. Please don't let me get caught as I do the things I have to do today. Please! Amen."

Scooting a pair of sunglasses onto her ears, Amanda slowly backed out of the driveway and headed toward the local grocery store. "Maybe I should go to Bedford first. There's less chance of being noticed there." She turned north.

FOURTEEN

"Is something wrong with your glasses, Mr. Howard?"

Jeff nearly dropped his darkened glasses at the sound of Captain Mercett's sharp words.

"No, sir. I…I…I don't know, sir, they don't seem to fit just right and I feel like I'm always having to adjust them," Jeff lied.

"Check with supply for a new pair," Captain Mercett ordered.

"It's possible that I'm still trying to adjust to wearing glasses, sir. I would like to try these for a bit longer."

"Agent Howard, you are one of our top leaders. You set the example for your squad. The glasses stay on as long as you are in uniform."

"Yes, sir. Understood, sir." Jeff gave a smart salute, trying to control his trembling body. *That's my second warning. I can't get caught again.*

Jeff's hand visibly shook as he once again placed the glasses onto his face a split second before Captain Mercett spun around and quickly made his way up to his office.

Twenty sets of blue-colored boots clipped across the floor as Jeff's squad members arranged themselves in perfect formation at precisely ten o'clock in the morning.

Jeff spent the next thirty minutes inspecting each member of his squad fastidiously. Each young man and woman knew their leader would accept no slothfulness in dress or in the execution of their duties.

Satisfied that his stringent expectations were all met, he sent them out two by two to patrol their given sectors. At exactly ten o'clock that evening they would reassemble to file their reports.

Jeff appreciated the new schedule he had been given for his squad. This time slot fit his sleep schedule perfectly. Never one to arise early, Jeff was having an even more difficult time waking up since he was unable to fall asleep until the wee hours of the morning.

Allowing his partner to patrol solo, Jeff decided to spend as much time as possible in headquarters checking paperwork and surplus equipment. He knew he'd have to appear completely absorbed in what he was doing so his superiors wouldn't suspect.

Two o'clock arrived and he radioed his partner to swing by for him. Ordering his partner into the passenger side, Jeff slid behind the steering wheel.

At precisely six o'clock, Jeff and half his squad returned to headquarters for a dinner break. Thirty minutes later, to the second, each vehicle was back on the streets. As the bright red ball of the sun began to slowly drop behind the horizon, Jeff's heart began to beat faster.

Curfew was set to begin in a matter of minutes. So far, Jeff had not had to use his weapon on any looters or curfew breakers. *Oh, God, please don't let me find anyone out tonight.*

"What am I doing?" he muttered as he shook his head.

"Excuse me, sir?" his partner asked, looking sideways at Jeff.

So absorbed in his fears, he had totally forgotten his partner who was sitting within inches of him in the front seat of their shiny black vehicle.

"Uh...oh, nothing. I thought I missed a street back there," he lied. His partner had always felt privileged to have been chosen as Jeff Howard's partner therefore he didn't question anything Jeff said.

This shift has got to get over soon. I'm a loose cannon out here this evening. Why would I think I could pray? God isn't going to hear anything I say now. It's far too late for that, Jeff thought as his fear grew by the minute.

At precisely ten o'clock, Jeff was in headquarters receiving and recording the reports handed to him by his squad members. It seemed as if each shift was reporting less and less citizens being eliminated. The public was well informed by now.

His final report having been transmitted to the office high above the gym floor, Jeff was grateful to be in his truck on his way to his parents' home. Entering the front door, he secured the lock before sliding to the floor with his back against the door.

Yanking his glasses from his face, Jeff was tempted to throw them across the room. But he knew if they were damaged and he went to work without them he would not get another chance.

Suddenly, Jeff bounded into the bathroom where he spent several minutes vomiting the contents of his stomach into the stool. Disgusted and weak, he stripped off his uniform and stepped into the shower where he stayed until the steaming water had turned icy cold.

Clad in a large multicolored bath towel, Jeff made his way up to his bedroom to find clean underclothes. Knowing his house would most likely be safe from security patrols, he still had not bothered turning on any lights other than in the bathroom.

After brushing his teeth, Jeff's bare feet padded down the steps to his parents' bedroom, the only place he could find any comfort.

Sliding into his parents' bed, Jeff buried his face into his mother's pillow. Immediately upon smelling her scent, hard sobs racked his body. "Mom! What am I going to do?" he moaned.

Completely spent, Jeff drifted into a strange realm. *Why was he in Woodville's sanctuary again? Pastor Don had just finished his sermon and was giving the invitation. Jeff gripped the wooden edge of the pew until his fingers hurt. Suddenly Pastor Don was standing next to him. Lovingly placing his hands on top of Jeff's, Pastor Don said, "Come, pray with me, Jeff. Jesus wants to enter your heart today." Stubbornly holding in the tears, Jeff squeezed his eyes shut. One tear fought its way free as Jeff released his grip on the pew and followed Pastor Don to the altar. Opening his eyes, Jeff found himself standing at the altar alone. The sanctuary was empty.*

Jeff bolted straight up in bed as a heart rendering groan escaped his throat. Tearing at the bedclothes, he rolled out onto the floor. His fingers clawed the floor until he was leaning against the opposite wall. Deep, painful sobs racked his body as he desperately hugged his knees to his chest.

FIFTEEN

Amanda arrived home two hours before curfew. Quickly showering, she stuffed dirty, cobweb covered clothing into the washing machine. Her chores had to be completed before dark.

Having fixed herself a peanut butter and jelly sandwich and a glass of milk, Amanda spent the next thirty minutes in front of the television set. Local and national news reports were all that was being broadcast since the rapture happened.

Double-checking all the doors and windows, her bare feet padded softly into the sanctuary of her bathroom.

"Okay, let's see what I got accomplished today," Amanda said out loud as she sat on the floor with her purse between her legs. As she counted the money she had left, she thought, *I'm not sure I can do this on my own. Please, God, I need help. It's not safe to ask anybody. What am I going to do?*

Amanda dropped the wad of bills on the floor and covered her face with her hands as her shoulders shook with sobs. *Daddy, I need you. I'm so scared.*

Wiping her face on a damp towel, she took a deep breath. "I can't do this. I have to keep it together. It's just you and me, God."

Slipping the money back into her purse and returning it to its hiding place, she leaned against the bathtub thinking about all she had accomplished in one day.

I'm glad I helped with the last drama at church or else I wouldn't have known about the hiding place under the stage, she thought.

Knowing how much his daughter loved drama class at school, Amanda's father had recommended to Pastor Don's wife that his daughter take part in the Christmas drama. While waiting in the choir room on the east side of the stage for her cue, Amanda and the other teenage actors accidentally kicked the steps that led up to the stage. When the steps moved several inches, the young people discovered an opening underneath the stage.

Presented with an adventure, they pulled the loosened steps away from the wall. All three young people were on their hands and knees deciding which one would be the first to crawl into the dark crevice.

Before any one of them had the opportunity to begin spelunking the dark, man-made cave, the choir room door popped open to reveal an inquisitive pastor's wife. She had assumed that they had just been unable to hear their cue, but was flabbergasted to find her young actors on their knees in front of the dark, gaping hole.

Just about that time, a large, fuzzy, black spider crawled across Amanda's fingers causing her to let out a bloodcurdling scream. Savagely jerking her hand off the floor, she smacked Jimmy Thomas right in the middle of his face, causing blood to pour from his nose.

"What on earth?" the pastor's wife blurted out before bursting into laughter.

When everyone had calmed down, it was discovered that the crawl space was used to check on the baptistery plumbing and the wiring for the sound system.

"I was certainly glad I didn't see any spiders today," Amanda said. "And it sure made a great place to store the water and food in case we should need it later."

Amanda had made several stops in Bedford, buying as much bottled water as she could without attracting attention. She had also purchased canned food, along with a couple manually operated can openers.

Certain that her purchases were safely stored away, Amanda pushed the steps back into place, being careful to leave no telltale signs that anything had been moved. She was relieved that the church doors were all locked when she had arrived just after noon.

"I'll have to remember to buy flashlights and batteries tomorrow, and I'll put food and water in the attic. I just wish I had help. It's going to be hard carrying all that stuff up those steep stairs."

The warm shower caused Amanda to relax. After drying off and donning a nightshirt, she was unable to stifle a large yawn. She rolled up a towel to put under her head. As soon as her head touched the makeshift pillow, she drifted off to sleep.

SIXTEEN

Exhausted from his savage sobbing, Jeff pushed himself up to make his way into the restroom where he splashed cold water into his face.

Sitting on the edge of the bed once more, he pulled the bedspread around him. Never before had he experienced such a deep chill. It was as if his very soul had turned to ice. *Will I ever be warm again? I am so scared, I don't want to be here by myself anymore.*

His eyes darted around the room as he whispered, "Mom, Dad, I'm so scared and you're not here for me. If only you could be here just one more time."

Immediately his tear-distorted vision settled on his mother's Bible. "The letter," Jeff exclaimed as he tossed the bedspread from his shoulders and grabbed the Bible.

Snatching the lavender colored envelope, he pulled out the letter, but when he flipped it over to read the verses, it escaped his fingers and fluttered to the floor like a wounded butterfly.

Jeff's knees quickly hit the floor as he tenderly picked up the paper. He leaned against the bed and pulled the Bible in front of him. As he leafed through the onion skin pages looking up each verse, Jeff had not realized the bodily position he was in.

On his knees searching the Scriptures was not where Jeff would normally have chosen to be. However, at this moment in time he was desperate for answers. He knew the answers he needed would be found right here in his mother's Bible.

At the bottom of the page, under the list of Bible verses, he found one last message of love from his mother.

Have you read them, son? If you do what these verses say, we'll see each other again. Please, my Jeffrey, I can't spend eternity without you. No matter where you go or what happens to you now, know that my love holds you close always.

Mom

Slowly closing the Bible, Jeff placed his forehead on it as the verses kept running through his mind like a runaway freight train. Pushing himself backwards, shaking his head, he moaned, "I can't; they'll kill me."

Standing, Jeff slowly walked toward the door, intent on going to his own room to get dressed. As he reached the door, he stopped and looked back at the bed. *Mom always kept her bed neatly made.* Stepping back to his father's side of the bed, he began smoothing out the bedclothes.

It took a couple extra minutes to straighten his mother's side since that was where the nightmare attacked him. After smoothing each layer, he gently placed her Bible on the nightstand, taking the letter with him to his own room where he slipped it under his pillow.

His digital clock told him it was already nine-fifteen in the morning. Normally, Jeff would have to be at work by ten, but they had been given new orders. He and his squad had been advised to report to headquarters at two in the afternoon.

SEVENTEEN

Knock! Knock! Knock!

Amanda's head jerked up so quickly the back of her head cracked against the side of the bathtub.

Knock! Knock! Knock!

She immediately jumped up, her body trembling with fright as she reached to slam the palm of her hand against the light switch. *They've found out! Somehow they saw my light.*

"Amanda! Amanda, are you home?"

Her bare feet scampered to the front door where she leaned against the wall wiping her tears on the sleeve of her robe. *Please don't let him be here on official business.*

"Jeff, is that you?" Amanda called hoarsely.

"Yes, open the door, Amanda. I need to talk to you."

"Is something wrong? Did I do something wrong?"

"No, it's ten o'clock in the morning and I'm worried about you."

"Ten o'clock?" Amanda whispered. "In the morning? It can't be."

"Come on, Amanda, open the door," Jeff called.

Nervously releasing each lock, Amanda stood back so no one but Jeff could see her. She jumped back, almost fainting with fear, when he pushed inside and slammed the door shut, relocking each lock.

"What is it, Jeff?" Her body was trembling.

Without warning, Jeff grabbed Amanda and pulled her into a tight embrace. Feeling her body trembling, he said, "Oh, Amanda, I didn't mean to scare you. I just needed to talk to you."

Gently pushing away, she cautiously sat in the chair that would leave no room for him.

Seeming not to notice Amanda's hesitancy, Jeff quickly sat on the edge of the couch briskly rubbing his hands together.

"I was scared when you didn't answer your door," Jeff said.

"Why, am I being watched?" Amanda tried to keep the edge of fear out of her voice.

"No, it's not that."

"Then what is it?" Amanda asked.

"I don't know," Jeff muttered as he jumped up and began pacing. "I don't know what to do."

"Do about what?" Amanda almost shouted. Closing her eyes and taking a deep, calming breath, she continued, "Jeff, you are scaring me. Please tell me what's going on."

In two quick steps, Jeff stood in front of Amanda who immediately shrunk back into her chair. *Shoot, I'm scaring her to death.* He dropped to his knees in front of her.

"I'm sorry, Amanda. I know I'm scaring you and I don't want to do that. Please, don't be afraid."

Looking into his eyes, she watched a tear sneak down his cheek. Compassionately, she reached out and wiped it away.

"Okay, Jeff. How about we start over. I'll calm down, you calm down and let's talk about whatever it is that's got you so upset. Deal?"

There was no mistaking the gratitude on Jeff's face as he sank back onto the floor cross-legged. Using the tail of his shirt, he wiped his face and took a deep, ragged breath.

"I may have already told you how I got involved in the W.S.F." Jeff looked at Amanda for affirmation. When she nodded, he continued, "After four years of training I thought I was ready for anything."

The more he talked, the more he relaxed. After a few minutes, he scooted back to lean against the couch. "They told us more or less what to expect, in a generic sort of way. We were ready with our weapons, knowing full well what they'd do."

He shook his head side to side with a mixture of disgust and disbelief.

"From the time I was a little guy, I attended church with my parents almost every Sunday. I went to Sunday school and Children's Church, listened to all of those Bible stories. As I got older and had to sit in the sanctuary listening to sermons, I remember being bored most of the time. But there were a few times when I felt like I wanted to become a Christian, especially after listening to missionaries speak, but I held back.

"When I became a teenager, I started questioning some of the things Pastor Don preached about, especially because of the things we were learning in school. Then I began high school and immediately became involved in the W.S.F. I believed everything they told me."

"And you don't now?" Amanda asked.

"That's just it, I'm not sure of anything anymore." Jeff dropped his head into his hands, nervously sliding his fingers through his short hair.

"Jeff," Amanda began carefully. "Why is it so confusing for you?"

When Jeff slowly dropped his hands and lifted his face toward Amanda, even she could see the fear and confusion in his eyes.

"I was W.S.F.'s top student. I've been a leader since the first month of being in the program. And now I'm a squad leader. My squad is one of the top three squads in a five county area."

"But?"

"But—the rapture happened," Jeff exclaimed as he jumped up and began pacing again.

"They didn't warn you about that?" Amanda asked.

"They told us *something* was going to happen that would take out millions of people. They led us to believe that it would be an invasion from outer space."

"Oh, yeah. That's what they tried to tell us on TV," Amanda said with disgust.

Jeff plopped down on the couch. "Until that Sunday in church, I would have believed that, Amanda. But, being there, seeing everybody disappear, I just don't buy their story anymore."

"But, you said you didn't believe Pastor Don when he preached about the rapture," Amanda commented.

"No, I didn't. I thought they were all nuts. But it happened. It happened just like Pastor Don said it would. And I got left here, just like Pastor Don said we unbelievers would."

"It's not hopeless, Jeff, not yet," Amanda said gently.

Jeff stared hopelessly at Amanda for a few seconds. "Do you have any idea what's going to happen to Christians now?"

"From what I've been reading in my dad's Bible and his books on prophecy, I've got a pretty good idea."

"And that doesn't scare you?"

"To death! I'm terrified. But I won't give up my faith. I refuse to go to hell."

Jamming his hands into his jean pockets, Jeff slumped back into the couch with thoughts that left him unable to speak.

Feeling the letter in his pocket, he was reminded of the main reason he had come to visit Amanda.

Amanda watched silently as her friend tenderly tried to smooth a crumpled envelope. It was obvious to her that there was something very special.

Jeff rose from the couch and knelt in front of Amanda once more, laying the letter on her lap.

"Look at these verses, Amanda, and tell me what you think," Jeff said, looking into her eyes.

Amanda picked up the lavender-colored paper and began to silently read the verses. "I don't believe this. Where'd you get these, Jeff?"

"My mom left them for me to read. On the other side is my last letter from her."

"Oh." Amanda suddenly felt as if she was holding a piece of gold.

"It's okay, you can read it if you want to," Jeff told her.

"No, at least not right now," Amanda said. "But these verses; I have to show you something." She jumped up and ran to her bedroom.

"What is it?" Jeff called after her. He stood up wondering whether or not to follow her.

Soon she was bounding back down the hallway with her long, blond curls swishing back and forth. Jeff smiled, thinking how pretty Amanda looked. With everything that had been happening since *that Sunday,* that thought had never before been an issue.

Clasping his forearm, Amanda led him back to the couch. "Sit here by me and look inside the back cover of this New Testament. You're not going to believe this."

With their elbows touching, Jeff and Amanda read the back page. "You told me that if I looked in the back of this Testament that I'd find something to help me become a Christian," she said.

"I did?" Jeff couldn't for the life of himself remember telling her something so ridiculous.

"Yes, you did. And look at these verses, Jeff. They are the exact same verses your mom left for you."

"You're kidding?" Jeff looked from the New Testament to the letter, comparing each Scripture reference. "This is weird."

"Not really," Amanda smiled. "These verses tell us how to become a Christian, so why wouldn't they be the same?" She pointed to her New Testament. "Look at the first verse. John 3:16."

"I know that verse by heart. Had to learn it in Sunday school," Jeff said without looking at the Bible. "*For God so loved the world that He gave His only begotten Son, that whosoever believes in Him should not perish but have everlasting life.*"

Amanda looked at Jeff in disbelief. “That verse doesn’t mean anything to you?!”

“Well, yeah. It’s just that I’ve heard it all my life and—”

“Jeff, read this. Don’t just say it, look at the words and read them out loud.”

Rolling his eyes, Jeff took the New Testament and began to read. After the first couple words, his reading slowed as the words began to take on new meaning. When he was finished, he stared at the page and bit nervously into his lower lip.

“Well?” Amanda whispered.

Without looking up, Jeff also whispered, “Amanda, I can’t. If they found out, I’d die a horrific death.”

Slowly closing her New Testament, Amanda put her arm around Jeff’s rounded shoulders. “Promise me that you’ll at least think about it, okay?”

Nodding his head, Jeff slowly stood. “I have to go. We’re getting new orders today so I can’t promise when I’ll get to see you again.”

Amanda walked to the door, carefully unlocking each lock. “I have to go to the grocery store today to buy milk and cereal.” She didn’t want Jeff to know what she was really doing.

“You’ll be safe, I promise,” Jeff said as he tenderly put his arms around her.

Uncomfortable, Amanda allowed Jeff’s embrace for only a few seconds. “I slept late so I’ll need to hurry. I hope to see you soon, Jeff. Remember your promise.”

Nodding his head in agreement, Jeff quickly walked to his truck. Just as quickly, Amanda shut her door, making sure each lock was in place before she ran to her bedroom to get ready for her supply trek for the day.

EIGHTEEN

Backing close to the east door of the church and getting out of the car, her eyes caught movement behind the shrubs. Terrified, she turned to grab for her car door, breaking a fingernail in an attempt to escape.

"Please, don't leave," a young woman quietly called after her.

Turning to get a better look, Amanda saw the young woman and a man emerge from behind the bush. "Who are you and what are you doing here?" she demanded.

"We're scared and thought this would be a safe place to hide," the young man said, glancing toward the road and then back at Amanda.

Not knowing whether to believe the couple or not, Amanda remembered her prayer just that morning, asking for help. "I'm going to have to trust You on this one, Lord," she whispered.

Knowing they needed to quickly get inside, Amanda walked to the door with Pastor Don's keys. "Come on inside and we'll talk."

All three quickly stepped inside the stuffy foyer. The frightened young woman clung to the man's arm.

"Who are you?" Amanda asked.

"I'm David Patterson and this is my wife, Gloria."

"I'm Amanda. Why did you choose this church for your hiding place?"

"We used to attend this church years ago. Since *it* happened, we've become Christians," David said. "But, please don't turn us in to the authorities."

"Don't worry, I'm a Christian too." Amanda smiled at the couple, who visibly relaxed.

"Why are you here?" Gloria asked, loosening her death grip on her husband's arm.

"I have to trust you on this," Amanda began. "I've been buying supplies and hiding them in different places in here so we'll have them later when things get much worse."

"What a great idea," David exclaimed. "What can we do to help?"

Amanda noted that David looked young enough to carry heavy supplies up the steep steps into the attic. She didn't see any gray in his short, dark hair.

Gloria didn't look much older than Amanda although she was approximately two inches shorter. Her shoulder length, light brown hair had a healthy shine. She seemed to be unusually sad.

"The trunk of my car is full of water, food and flashlights. Let's get it in here as quickly as possible. We don't want to attract any unwanted attention."

All three hurried out to the car, only having to make two trips to get all the supplies. Amanda showed David where the attic steps were, and in no time at all he lugged everything up the steps.

Gloria stayed in the foyer, keeping watch, while Amanda showed David where to put the supplies so that they'd be completely out of sight. Several flashlights, along with extra batteries, were put where they would be easily available.

Returning to the foyer, Amanda ran to the choir room to place more flashlights in another convenient place. Checking her watch she knew they needed to leave right away. When she advised her new friends, she saw instant panic in their faces.

"You can't stay here. It's not safe."

"We don't have anywhere else to go," David told her.

"Come with me. You can stay at my house." She didn't wait for an answer as she dashed through the door. Turning to lock up, she was surprised that David and Gloria had not followed her.

No! They are enemies. She ran to her car.

"Wait, Amanda!"

Unable to move, Amanda began to tremble.

"Aren't you going to lock the door?" David asked.

"I thought..." Amanda began.

"What?" Gloria asked.

"Never mind," Amanda said.

No one spoke until the car reached Woodville Road where they headed east toward Amanda's housing addition.

"We were shocked when you told us to come with you. We're still not sure if we can trust you."

"Ditto," Amanda said with a smile.

Sitting in the back seat, David reached for Gloria's hand when he noticed tears dripping onto her blouse. She turned her head turned away and wiped her cheeks with her free hand.

Within in minutes, Amanda was maneuvering her Cadillac into her driveway.

"When we get out of the car, walk slowly as if we're old friends," Amanda instructed the Pattersons. "We have no idea who or how we might be watched."

"Sure thing," David said as he squeezed his wife's hand before exiting his side of the vehicle.

Talking and laughing, the trio walked to the front door where David took two sacks of groceries from Amanda while she unlocked the door. Stepping inside, Amanda quickly turned to lock each of the locks securely before leaning her back heavily against the door.

"Oh, my," Gloria breathed, placing her hand over her heart.

David carried the groceries into the kitchen. "You sure you'll be safe with extra company?"

"Yes. I have a friend who told me that families and friends are beginning to live together for safety reasons," Amanda said. "Come on in and sit down. We'll get something to eat later."

"Amanda, you don't know what this means to us." Gloria sat on the couch, patting the cushion next to her for her husband.

"I think I do," Amanda said, sitting in the chair.

"If you don't mind my asking, Amanda, how old are you and how come you're living here alone?" David asked, placing his arm across his wife's shoulders.

"I just turned seventeen," Amanda began.

"Happy birthday." Gloria smiled.

"I can't say it's exactly happy," Amanda said. "My mother died in a car accident some time ago. Dad and I were in church when he just disappeared. One second he was standing beside me singing, and the next he was gone." Her eyes brimmed with tears.

"In church? Wow," David exclaimed.

"I had no idea what happened. I'd never heard about a rapture before," Amanda said.

"How'd you find out what happened?" Gloria asked.

"My friend, Jeff, explained it to me. I came home and read my dad's Bible and a couple other books he had. That's when I became a Christian."

"So, your friend Jeff wasn't a Christian either?" Gloria asked.

"No. Both his parents were taken."

"Is he a Christian now?" David asked.

"No," Amanda said sadly.

"Can you trust him?" David asked.

"I think so. At least for now," Amanda said. "Come on, I'll show you where you can sleep."

Gloria followed Amanda down the hallway to what used to be the guest bedroom. Opening the door, Gloria stepped onto emerald green carpet and surveyed the comfortable room.

The queen sized bed was covered with a dark green comforter with cream and rose-colored flowers. A tall dresser was against the outside wall. The window was covered with emerald green mini-blinds and draperies made with the same material as the comforter. A small, old-fashioned rocking chair sat next to the closet door.

"This room is for you and David as long as you need it," Amanda said. "The door in the corner goes into a small bathroom."

"Thank you, Amanda," Gloria said as she took Amanda's hand in hers. "You are so kind."

Amanda turned to leave as tears threatened to spill from Gloria's eyes. She returned to the living room where David was watching the news on the television. "Anything new?" she asked.

"No, it's still bad," he answered.

Several minutes later Gloria returned to her position next to her husband. Amanda noticed that her nose was red from crying. "You didn't turn on any lights, so neither did I."

"I've gotten kind of used to managing in the dark. I'm terrified of being caught by the World Security Force if they see lights."

"I understand," Gloria said.

"I'll fix us something to eat before it gets too dark." Amanda made her way into the kitchen.

"I'll help, if that's okay," Gloria said as she followed Amanda into the kitchen.

"Sure, I'd love the company," Amanda said. "I've been so lonely, but I've been afraid to make friends. I don't know who I can trust anymore."

David turned off the television and followed the girls into the kitchen. "Amanda, would it be possible for me to look at your dad's books?"

"Yes, I'll get them for you," Amanda said as she hurried to her bathroom.

When she returned, she handed the books to David, who quickly checked the titles and the chapter captions. "This one I've already read. But, if you don't mind, I'd like to get started on this one."

"Help yourself. I've read them both twice." Amanda smiled. She put away the groceries and then began to fix them each a salad and sandwich.

"When have you had a chance to read so much?" Gloria asked as she helped set the meal on the small table.

"I haven't slept very well, so I spend a lot of night time hours in my bathroom reading."

"In your bathroom?" Gloria asked.

"My bathroom doesn't have any outside windows, so I can keep that light on."

"I see," Gloria said.

"David, would you ask the blessing on our food?" Amanda asked.

When David's prayer ended, all eyes were damp. As they began their meal, they were all quiet for several minutes.

David cleared his throat before asking, "Amanda, since you are so young, where did you get the money to buy all of those supplies?"

"I went through all the pockets and purses at church and collected the money. From what I've read, the days ahead are going to be awful and I thought the least I could do was help prepare for them."

"That's smart thinking for a young person," Gloria said. "Is there anything we can do to help?"

"I've prayed that God would send me some help and look how He's answered." Amanda smiled at her new friends. "I had no idea how I was going to get all of that stuff up those steps today."

"Will you be getting any more supplies that we can help with?" David asked.

"To be safe, I'm going to wait a couple days before going back. But when I do I'd love to have help folding and sorting the clothing that's left. I'm sure it will be needed before all of this is over."

"Great, we'll be more than happy to help," Gloria said.

Gloria and Amanda cleared the table and washed the dishes while David turned the television on just as the latest news bulletin began.

While the girls were in finishing up in the kitchen, Amanda asked, "How long have you two been married?"

"We got married as soon as we graduated from high school," Amanda answered.

"Wow." Amanda was surprised, thinking that they were probably newlyweds.

"David had been in Bible college. That is, until *it* happened." Gloria's voice cracked with emotion.

Hanging up the dish towel, Amanda asked, "So you don't have any children yet?"

Gloria's head dropped as she shook it slowly.

Amanda was shocked when Gloria suddenly bent over, falling to the floor with her hands over her stomach, sobbing desperately.

David ran into the kitchen, kneeling next to his wife, enfolding her in his strong arms.

"What's the matter?" Amanda asked. "Do I need to call a doctor?"

"No, no," David said as calmly as he could. "Just give us a minute and I'll explain."

Amanda slowly backed out of the kitchen. Wrapping her arms around herself, she sat on the edge of the couch with her head bowed, praying silently. *Please, God, help her. I don't know what's wrong, but you do.*

Rocking back and fourth, Amanda could hear David's deep voice. It sounded as if he was praying.

Several long, painful minutes later, David and Gloria walked hand in hand into the living room. Gloria was still sniffling, but she seemed to be much better.

Amanda quickly moved to the chair so the couple could sit together on the couch.

As Gloria continuously twisted David's hanky through her fingers, David began, "Do you remember reading in the book of Mark about how in the days we're living in now it was going to be especially bad for pregnant women and women with babies?"

"I think I remember something like that, but I didn't know what it meant," Amanda said.

"Gloria and I found out firsthand what it meant," David said, placing his hand over his wife's. "Gloria was pregnant with our first child when the rapture occurred."

David could see in Amanda's questioning eyes that her youthful mind wasn't comprehending what he was saying.

"Jesus was telling his disciples that when the rapture happened, little babies would be going to Heaven with Him. That meant unborn babies as well as the older ones."

"Oh! Oh, my!" Amanda now understood why Gloria's eyes were so terribly sad.

Placing her hands on her empty stomach, Gloria said, "My baby was moving and kicking and then he was gone. Not dead, just gone."

"Oh, Gloria, I'm so sorry, I didn't know." Amanda felt awful. "Please, forgive me."

"There's nothing to forgive, Amanda," Gloria said as she smiled through her tears. "You had no way of knowing. I'm sorry I scared you."

"Well, yeah, that did scare me," Amanda chuckled.

"I still have a difficult time dealing with it," Gloria said.

"I think that's understandable," Amanda said. "At least, I'll know next time."

"We missed the news tonight," David said. "I hope we didn't miss anything important."

"I think I'll take a shower and go to bed," Amanda said, standing. "Your bathroom has an outside window. It's got a shade and curtains, but you probably shouldn't turn on the light. If you need to take a shower, you are perfectly welcome to use my dad's bathroom."

Looking at his wife, David said, "I think we'll be all right. What do you think, Gloria?"

"We'll be fine, Amanda. You go on to bed. I know you're tired."

"Okay, then. If you need anything, please don't be afraid to wake me up," Amanda said, stifling a yawn.

"Good night, Amanda," David said.

The Pattersons' eyes had adjusted to the darkness when they entered their new bedroom. Gloria had investigated the room and adjoining bathroom earlier, so she navigated through the room fairly well.

David had to stand still for a moment to get his bearings. Carefully making his way across the floor, his toe caught on the edge of the bathroom doorframe, causing him to let out a yelp.

"Sh-h-h-h," Gloria cautioned.

Fifteen minutes later, both David and Gloria were safely snuggled between mint green sheets. David had to stifle another yelp when Gloria accidentally kicked his throbbing toe.

Giggling softly, Gloria scrunched her back against David's hair-covered chest.

"I'm glad you thought that was funny," David said with a contented smile.

"I apologize, honey," Gloria said. "I do love you, you know."

"I love you too, sweetheart," David said. "God has been good to us today, hasn't He?"

"Yes," Gloria whispered just before drifting off to sleep.

"God, thank you for leading us to Amanda. We'll do everything we can for you in the time you've given us. I promise you, Lord," David whispered his prayer before he also dropped into a deep sleep.

NINETEEN

"Good afternoon, sir. I was advised to report early. Is there a problem?" Jeff asked.

"No problem, Mr. Howard," Captain Mercett said. "I have new orders that you will be giving to your squad."

"Very good, sir," Jeff said. "Thank you, sir."

"Familiarize yourself with the orders before your squad arrives so you'll be ready for any questions."

"Yes, sir," Jeff repeated as he reached for the blue and gold folder in Captain Mercett's hand.

Saluting smartly, Jeff spun around and marched out of Captain Mercett's office, knowing that his superior officer was watching his every move. Seated at his desk in the middle of the high school gym's hardwood floor, he quickly flipped open the folder and began to read.

Without looking up, Jeff knew unseen eyes were watching him for any sign of wavering as he read their new orders. Using every ounce of self-control he could muster, he managed to read the entire set of documents without showing any visible signs of distress, hoping the thumping of his heart could not be detected.

With a feigned smirk on his face, Jeff closed the folder and nodded his head in what he hoped showed his complete acceptance. A quick look at his wristwatch told him he had exactly six minutes before his squad would stand at attention before him.

Jeff moved from behind his desk, checked his uniform to make sure everything was perfect, then stood tall and erect as his squad members marched across the hardwood floor, standing at attention in perfect alignment.

A chill ran down Jeff's spine as he proudly inspected his squad of young men and women who looked almost regal in their blue and gold uniforms.

At the completion of his inspection, he took his place in front of his desk, picking up copies of the new orders. Handing a stack to each row, he stepped back to watch the crisp, swiftness of papers being passed along.

"Immediately upon entering your vehicles, you are to familiarize yourselves thoroughly with these new orders. They are to be carried out with the same precision as all previous orders. If you have any questions, you are to return here immediately. Dismissed."

"Yes, sir." In unison his squad responded with respect before they quickly exited the gym, anxious to read their orders and begin their evening duties.

After watching his squad leave the building, Jeff sat behind his desk, awakened his computer, and began the first of his shift's reports.

Will any return with questions? How will I answer them? Jeff's fingers trembled slightly as his troubled thoughts caused his concentration to falter. Feeling an almost overwhelming desire to tear his glasses from his face, Jeff stood and walked quickly toward the restroom door.

TWENTY

The aroma of freshly brewed coffee tickled Amanda's nostrils, bringing a smile to her lips as she slowly awakened. *Daddy! You've got breakfast ready.* Joyfully throwing her bedclothes back, she quickly sat up. Just as her feet touched the carpeted floor, ready to run to the kitchen, she remembered.

Falling back onto her bed, Amanda buried her face into her pillow as she cried desperate tears. "Daddy! Oh, Daddy, I miss you."

The red glowing numbers on the bedside clock indicated that it was past time to get up, but at that moment she didn't care. "How long can I survive anyway? I wish I was dead now," she said as she threw her pillow across the room.

Amanda grabbed clean underclothes from her top dresser drawer and angrily slammed the bathroom door shut before stepping into the shower.

Gloria's head jerked up when Amanda's door slammed. "You think she's okay?" she asked.

"I think so. That sounded like an angry slam. I wonder what's up," David said.

"Maybe we woke her up before she was ready," Gloria said. "I'll apologize as soon as she comes in for breakfast."

Sitting across the small kitchen table from his wife, David shook his head sadly.

"What?" Gloria asked. "What's wrong?"

"Maybe it's just me, but it seems as if every morning is harder to face than the morning before."

Tears stung Gloria's eyes as she nodded her head.

David reached over and covered his wife's hand with his. "I'm sorry, Gloria. I didn't mean to make you cry."

"It's not you, David." She quietly blew her nose into her paper napkin. "It's just that I feel the same way."

"Really?"

Gloria put her hand on her stomach before speaking. "Even though our baby is gone, we still have each other, but what now? What's there to look forward to?"

Neither David nor Gloria had noticed Amanda standing in the doorway until she spoke. "You've got that right. What's there to look forward to?"

"Amanda!" Gloria jumped to her feet, walking quickly to Amanda. "I am so sorry we awakened you so early."

"It's okay, Gloria," Amanda said. "I should have already been up anyway."

"Do you drink coffee?" David asked, reaching for another cup.

"I do now," Amanda said as she took a seat at the end of the table. She carefully sipped the hot, black coffee before pouring herself a bowl of cereal.

"Are you okay?" Gloria asked softly, watching Amanda's face.

Blinking back tears, Amanda said, "I thought my dad was still here when I smelled the coffee." She covered her face with both hands as her shoulders shook.

Gloria handed Amanda a napkin before putting her arm around her shoulders. "Aren't we all just the happiest bunch this morning?"

Amanda snickered as she dried her face. "Aren't we though."

"So, what's the plan today?" David asked.

Amanda shook her head. Not having an answer, she kept on eating until the bowl was empty.

"You know," she finally said, "this is a little strange."

"Strange?" Gloria asked. "What do you mean?"

"All of us feeling the same way."

"Oh," Gloria said.

No one spoke. All three stared into their coffee cups as if an answer might bubble up through the black brew.

"Maybe it's because I'm just tired, but I don't want to do anything," Amanda said. "No, it's more than that. I don't see the point of doing anything."

Gloria nodded her head in agreement.

After several minutes of silence, David spoke up. "Well, we certainly can't give up. Not now, anyway. How about we go back to the church? We can pray awhile then decide if there's anything else we can do. What do you think?"

The girls looked at each other and shrugged their shoulders.

"Whatever," Amanda said.

"Okay," Gloria said. "Wait until I go brush my teeth first." She walked down the hallway to her bedroom.

"Amanda, we can't give up," David said.

Amanda nodded her head, "I know." She walked to her bedroom, shutting the door behind her.

David took his time washing the dishes and rinsing out the coffee pot. Somehow he knew the girls wouldn't be in any hurry to leave the house today.

Twenty minutes later the cheerless trio was in Amanda's Cadillac headed for Woodville Baptist Church.

TWENTY-ONE

Lying on his back in his parents' bed, Jeff stared at the ceiling. "How much longer can I go without sleep? I can't concentrate. I can't work like I used to. What am I going to do?"

Reaching out his arm, he placed his hand on his mother's Bible. "Mom, I never dreamed I'd ever be this scared. I thought I had it all. I didn't need you or dad and certainly not church. Now what am I going to do?"

The stillness of the house was too much for Jeff. He quickly showered, dressed, and drove off in his truck. He knew his food supply was almost gone, so a stop at the grocery store took his mind off things for a matter of fifteen minutes.

Returning home, he quickly stored the food in the refrigerator. Never having to worry about clean clothes before, he now had to learn how to run the washing machine and dryer.

After he had folded the load of towels he'd thrown in the dryer the day before, he tossed in the next load of underclothes and socks. "You'd be proud of me, Mom. I know that I sure do appreciate you more now."

Having stacked the towels back on the bathroom shelves, Jeff wandered into the living room. "I wonder what Amanda is doing today. I wish I could talk to her, but she wants me to get saved and I just can't. They'll kill me, no questions asked."

Sitting on the couch with his head in his hands, he moaned, "What am I going to do? Captain Mercett suspects something, I know he does."

Running his fingers through his hair, Jeff jumped up and once again ran toward his truck. "I've got to find Amanda."

TWENTY-TWO

Amanda, along with her two new friends, was kneeling at the church's altar. "God, we don't know what to do. Please show us what you want. How can we help others when we don't have a clue ourselves?"

She didn't bother saying *amen.* Slowly she pushed herself away from the altar and sat down on the front pew.

David and Gloria raised their heads and watched Amanda before joining her on the pew.

"I don't understand," Amanda whispered. "Up until this morning I was full of ideas and plans. I couldn't find enough time to get it all done. And now, this morning, I can hardly function. What's the matter with me?"

"I think what we're dealing with is an evil spirit that's creeping over everything. God isn't here anymore. His Holy Spirit isn't here anymore, which leaves us wide open for Satan and his evil spirits," David said.

"I'm new at this Christian thing, David," Amanda said. "What can we do?"

"In order to survive we've got to keep busy."

"That's the point; we're not going to survive," Amanda said.

"No, actually we're not," David answered truthfully. "But the time we have left, we should keep busy and try to find other people to help."

Gloria agreed, "We've got to find something to do to keep us busy."

"Yeah, I guess." Amanda gave a weak smile before asking, "How long did you all go to church out here?"

"We actually met here and got married here, didn't we?" Gloria smiled at her husband.

"We sure did. We were part of the youth group a few years ago. We started dating here and finally got married."

"So, why did you stop attending?" Amanda asked. "I haven't attended long, but I don't remember seeing you before."

"We were living in Louisville, Kentucky," David said.

"Louisville?"

"Yes, I was attending Bible college in Louisville," David said with sadness.

"You were in Bible college and you weren't even a Christian?"

"Obviously not," David said with his head bowed.

"He was studying to be a preacher," Gloria said.

"A preacher?" Amanda was astounded. "A preacher? And you weren't even a Christian? How can that happen?"

"I don't know," David said. "I always thought if a person tried to be good enough they'd go to Heaven. There weren't any solid teachings about salvation in the school that I attended."

"And you were going to a Bible college?" Amanda asked again.

"Seminary."

"Unbelievable, huh?" Gloria said.

Amanda sat back and shook her head.

"I had it all planned out. I would get a big church and make a lot of money doing nothing other than preach on Sunday mornings. I'd have a fancy house and a really nice car and a beautiful family."

"And?" Amanda asked.

"And—look at us," David said. "We missed Him. We weren't ready and we missed Him."

"Our baby is with Him, but we weren't ready," Gloria cried.

David wrapped his arms around his wife. "We'll see him soon, honey."

Amanda placed her elbows on her knees and put her face in her hands. "What are we going to do?"

Suddenly Gloria's head jerked up. "Sh-h-h," she cautioned.

"What?" David whispered.

Someone was violently rattling the entry door on the east side of the building. "Anybody in there?"

"That's Jeff," Amanda whispered as she jumped up.

"Who's Jeff?" David asked.

"He's my friend. He was here when the rapture happened," Amanda continued to whisper.

Just then, heavy pounding began on the emergency exit door of the sanctuary. "Amanda? Amanda, are you in there?"

"Can we trust him?" David asked as Gloria clung to his arm.

"I think so," Amanda said as she walked toward the door. "If we don't open the door he will knock it in."

David and Gloria stood, squeezing each other's hand as Amanda opened the emergency door.

"Jeff, is everything all right?" Amanda asked as she shoved open the door.

"Yes, are you all right?" Jeff seemed genuinely concerned as he quickly stepped into the sanctuary and pulled the door closed.

It took several seconds for Jeff's eyes to adjust to the dimness of the sanctuary after being out in the sunlight. Once adjusted, he was startled to see David and Gloria.

"Jeff, these are my friends, David and Gloria," Amanda said. "They used to attend this church a long time ago."

"Really?" Jeff said as he stepped closer to the young couple. "I don't remember you."

"It's been several years since we were here," David said as he reached his hand out to shake Jeff's.

After shaking David's hand, Jeff asked, "What are all of you doing out here?"

"We came out to see if we could find any of our parents' things," Amanda said quickly before the Pattersons could respond.

His trained eyes scanned the dimly lit sanctuary. "What happened to all the clothes?"

"We had some extra time, so we folded them and stacked them on the back pew. Want to see?" Amanda asked.

"Naw, it's too depressing just being in here. I sure don't want to look at that stuff." Jeff turned and placed his hand on the door. "Are you ready to leave?"

David looked at Amanda. "We were going to finish up a couple things first."

"Uh, yes," Amanda said. "We should be finished here in, say about twenty minutes."

Jeff slowly pushed open the door, then turned back towards the trio. "Amanda, I really need to talk to you today. Would that be possible?"

The sadness in his eyes touched her. "We will be at my house in thirty minutes if you want to come over."

"Thanks," Jeff said as he stepped outside and let the door thud shut.

Gloria sank onto one of the deep-rose colored pews. "Amanda, are we still safe? Will he turn us in?" Her eyes were wide with fright.

"I'm not one hundred percent sure about Jeff, but I think we're okay for now. We'd better hurry up and get out of here though."

"I agree," David said. "Come on, honey, let's make sure everything is locked up." He reached for Gloria's hand as they double-checked all the doors to make sure they were locked.

David could feel his wife's hand tremble as they quickly moved through the church building. His own heart was beating faster than usual as he contemplated the coming meeting with Jeff.

Amanda, unable to forget Jeff's eyes, was in a hurry to leave the church building and return home.

With thoughts racing through their heads, not one of the three noticed two sets of shoes under the shrubbery next to the west doors into the foyer.

TWENTY-THREE

"Come on in," Amanda said as she opened the door for Jeff. Once inside, he didn't wait for her to lock up. Without asking, he performed that task himself before turning to lean on the door and take a deep, ragged breath.

David, Gloria, and Amanda silently watched Jeff until he pushed himself off the door and walked into the living room area. "This is getting more insane by the day," he said.

"What do you mean, Jeff?" Amanda asked.

Jeff ran his hand through his short hair, then rubbed his eyes. He looked at David and Gloria as they sat on the couch. "David, I desperately need to talk to Amanda. Do you mind?"

"Not at all, Jeff," David said as he stood and reached for his wife's hand. "Come on, sweetheart, let's go get some rest before lunch." The young couple walked hand in hand to their bedroom.

"They're staying here?" Jeff asked in surprise.

"Yes, they didn't have any place so I invited them to stay here. They've been a big help to me. It's not quite so lonely with them here."

"I understand that," Jeff said as he sat on the couch. "Amanda, I don't know what to do. All I could think about through my last shift was talking to you."

"About what?" Amanda asked, worried.

"I haven't been able to sleep. I keep going over and over Mom's letter and the Bible verses she left for me. I know I need to become a Christian, but I'm scared to death."

"We're all scared, Jeff," Amanda said.

"But you don't understand," Jeff said, getting up to pace behind the couch. "I'm a W.S.F. officer. If they ever found out, I'd die a horrible death."

"And I won't if they find out about me?" Amanda asked.

"But, you're not a..." Jeff started. Quickly looking in Amanda's direction, he hurriedly sat back on the couch. "You're right. Especially now."

"What do you mean, 'especially now'?" Amanda asked with a slight edge to her voice.

Jeff dropped his head into his hands and shook it back in forth. "Oh, Amanda, this is bad—real bad."

Amanda jumped up and grabbed Jeff's shoulder. "What are you talking about, Jeff Howard?"

Jeff took Amanda's hand, drawing her down on the couch beside him. "Amanda, we have been given new orders that take effect Monday morning."

"Which are?" she asked with raised voice.

"If it's ever discovered that I've told you these things, I will be put to death immediately."

"Then why did you come over here?" Amanda had lost all patience.

"I'm going to tell you, I just wanted you to know how serious this is," Jeff said.

"I'm crystal clear," Amanda said as she jerked off the couch and plopped down in the chair.

"If anyone is caught with a Bible, they will immediately be taken to jail. If anyone is caught preaching, they will be annihilated on the spot. You aren't allowed to even talk about God or the Bible to anyone, not even family members."

Amanda's face blanched as she stared at Jeff. "Please tell me that's not true. It can't be." She angrily brushed away tears that slipped from the corners of her eyes.

"It's true," Jeff whispered.

Amanda stood and looked down at Jeff. "So, just what are you telling me? Are you going to arrest me? Are you going to take my Bibles? If that's why you wanted to come in my house, you can just leave." She quickly walked to the door, motioning Jeff out.

"No! No, no, no, Amanda," Jeff cried. He had fallen onto his knees, his red, tear-filled eyes begging.

David and Gloria, on hearing Amanda's raised voice, entered the living room to see Jeff on his knees crying and Amanda pointing to the door.

"Hey, guys, what's going on?" David asked.

"Ask him," Amanda said as she pointed an accusing finger in Jeff's direction. "He's here to spy on us, arrest us, or maybe even to kill us."

In desperation, Jeff fell on his face crying. He was no longer concerned about his position with the World Security Force, his good looks, or anything other than the dark, heavy blanket of hopeless desperation that covered him.

David knelt beside Jeff, placing his arm over his shoulders. "Jeff, is this true?"

The pit of despair was so deep all Jeff could do was shake his head.

Trying to help him, David said, "Come on, Jeff, sit here on the couch and let's talk."

When Amanda saw Jeff's face, she gasped, covering her mouth in alarm.

Once Jeff was seated on the couch, David handed him his own handkerchief. Amanda slowly seated herself in the chair.

"Jeff, I'm so sorry. I thought..." she whispered.

"No, Amanda. Please, it's not you," Jeff said as he tried to compose himself.

Amanda's heart pounded with fear as well as sympathy as she watched Jeff.

"Okay," David said. "Can you talk about what's going on?"

"Amanda has every right to be scared and angry with what I just told her."

Amanda dropped her head as tears spilled from her emerald green eyes.

David looked up to see Gloria standing in the hallway with a look of terror in her eyes as her arms hugged her stomach.

"Okay, Jeff, tell me what you told Amanda and we'll take it from there."

"We were given new orders—" Jeff began.

"Who was given new orders?" David interrupted. "Why would anybody be giving you orders?"

Jeff quickly looked at Amanda. "They don't know?"

Unable to speak, Amanda shook her head.

Taking a deep breath, Jeff continued, "David, I'm a squad leader with the World Security Force."

Gloria gasped loudly. David sat back as if Jeff had slapped him. "You're what?"

"I've been a member of the World Security Force since I began high school four years ago."

"Four years ago?" David exclaimed. "The World Security Force has been active that long?"

"Longer," Jeff said. "Anyway, I've been assigned as a squad leader, but..."

"Wait!" David said as he quickly stood. "If you're a real agent with the World Security Force, why have you kept coming around here?"

"Amanda's right," Gloria's fear-filled voice said. "You've been spying on us and now you're going to kill us."

"No!" Jeff shouted as he too stood. "Tell them, Amanda. I'm not here to hurt anybody."

"Jeff's right, David," Amanda said. "I apologize for getting scared and causing this mess."

David was standing with his arm around his wife. "Okay, I guess we'll have to trust you on this one."

David and Gloria sat on the couch. Amanda remained in her chair.

"Let's hear it, Jeff," David said.

"Like I said, I'm a member of the W.F.S. but it's all falling apart for me. I can't keep on pretending. My commander already suspects me."

"What do you mean?" Amanda asked.

"I can't sleep. Every night I go home and read my mother's Bible and the letter she left me. I have nightmares. I feel like I'm going crazy."

"What verses are you talking about?" David asked.

"My mother left me a letter with the same verses Amanda has in the back of her little orange New Testament."

"The ones in Romans that tells us how to become saved," Amanda told David, who looked to her for an explanation.

"Oh, I see," David said with a smile.

"Anyway, my commander seems to sense that something screwy is going on with me and I'm scared to death. And now we have these new orders and I have to see that they are carried out."

"I see," David repeated.

"Well, I'm glad you see, because I sure don't," Jeff exclaimed.

"Jeff, you need to become a Christian," David said.

"I can't!" Jeff said. "They'll kill me in a second."

"Here's the thing, Jeff," David said. "We're all going to die horrible deaths anyway. We've got to be ready."

"I understand that," Jeff said. "I know I don't want to go to hell, but you just don't understand what they'll do to me if they ever found out."

"Don't let them find out," David said with a smile.

"What are you talking about?" Jeff asked.

"We're all going to die, right?" David asked.

"Yes."

"Then why not ask Jesus to save you now?" David asked. "Then you can be a spy for us instead of against us. Use the W.S.F. instead of them using you."

Jeff became quiet as he stared at David for several seconds. "That's it," he exclaimed. "That's the answer. Why didn't I think of that?"

"That doesn't matter," David said. "Let's just get you saved and we'll decide what we have to do from there."

"Oh, Jeff," Amanda cried as she grabbed his arm.

Jeff immediately knelt beside Amanda's chair. "Amanda, I should have done this years and years ago. Will you kneel beside me?" Tears were running down his face.

Amanda slid out of the chair onto her knees beside Jeff as he bowed his head.

"God, I am so sorry for saying no to you all these years. I'm here now asking you to forgive me and come into my heart and save me. I promise you I'll do anything I can for you with the time I have left. Amen."

Amanda's sobs were muffled against Jeff's chest. David and Gloria joined in, putting their arms around them.

Suddenly, Jeff gently pushed Amanda back while grabbing for his vibrating cell phone. Amanda's tear-filled eyes widened in fear as he answered the call.

"Agent Howard. Yes, sir." Jeff paused as he listened. "I'll be there in thirty minutes, sir." Replacing the phone in its holder, Jeff looked around at the eyes watching him.

"And now it begins," he said.

"Wait, let me pray for you before you leave." David laid his hand on Jeff's head. "God, Jeff now belongs to you. He's on his way to do battle. Please go with him. Give him wisdom. And, please, protect him. Amen."

"Amen," Amanda and Gloria agreed.

All four young people stood as Jeff made his way to the door. "I'll let you know how things go."

Jeff turned to face Amanda, wrapping his arms around her for several seconds. David and Gloria smiled as they watched this exchange.

TWENTY-FOUR

Speeding to his parents' house, Jeff's mind raced with the possibilities of what Captain Mercett might want from him. What surprised him most was the absence of what had been an ever-present fear. Concern was still there, but the suffocating blanket of fear was gone.

Desperately wanting to spend time on his knees beside his mother's bed, Jeff knew he had to double-time it to get into his uniform and report to headquarters.

Calling out, as if his parents were in their room, Jeff said, "Mom, Dad, I'm a Christian. I finally asked Jesus into my heart. I hope you know. I hope you saw. I'll see you again, I promise you. I'll see you again."

Double-checking himself in the full-length mirror, Jeff knew he was ready to face his superior officer. Not until he slid behind the steering wheel of his truck did he place the glasses on his face.

Arriving at the high school gymnasium, Jeff wasted no time in exiting his truck and marching into the World Security Force temporary headquarters. Quickly glancing up, he saw Captain Mercett waiting for him behind the glass partition.

I see a shadow. I wonder who is with him, Jeff wondered as he took the steps two at a time. *Okay, God, here I go. Give me wisdom. Please protect me.*

"Enter," Captain Mercett barked.

"Sir," Jeff said as he saluted smartly.

"At ease, Agent Howard. Please, sit down."

Jeff sat stiffly in one of the folding chairs across from Captain Mercett. *I don't see him, but I know someone else is here.*

"Agent Howard, we have been watching you since we were put on full alert several weeks ago. Your performance record is here." Captain Mercett's hand clutched a shiny blue and gold folder.

"I certainly hope you have been pleased with my performance, sir," Jeff said with as much confidence as he could muster.

Sudden quiet descended upon the small room. Captain Mercett's eyes watched Jeff for what seemed like a lifetime. He suddenly stood and stepped around the desk to stand in front of Jeff, who immediately stood at attention.

"Agent Howard," Captain Mercett said, sticking his hand out to shake Jeff's. "You have an exemplary record. Congratulations."

Shocked, Jeff shook his superior officer's hand. "Thank you, sir. Thank you."

Captain Mercett returned to his position behind his desk. "Your ability to lead your squad has become an example to be followed."

"Thank you, sir."

"Agent Wickes, stand forward," Captain Mercett ordered.

Aw, not this redheaded jerk.

"Yes, sir," Agent Wickes shouted.

"Agent Howard, I am putting Agent Wickes alongside you as you lead your squad. He will be learning from your example as he trains for his own leadership position."

"Yes, sir," Jeff said as he looked at the familiar face of Russell Wickes, one of his own squad members. Russell's mouth twisted into an evil smile that Jeff had grown to hate long before today.

"Four weeks from today, I will expect a complete report from you on my desk in reference to Agent Wickes' performance. Dismissed."

"Yes, sir. Thank you, sir." Jeff saluted before spinning around to exit the room. Catching a glimpse of Russell's evil smirk, Jeff felt nauseated. Closing the door behind him, he hurried down the steps.

Sitting in his truck, he had the distinct feeling that something was different. "Step one," he whispered. He knew that his truck had in all likelihood been bugged.

Slamming into his parents' house, Jeff's face was cherry apple red as he seethed with anger.

Leaning against the door, his words finally burst forth. "Not only have I had to look at that evil sneer on that freckled face every day during inspection, now I have to endure his galling presence during all hours of duty."

Jeff's fists slammed against the door as he marched into his parents' bedroom and sat heavily on the bed.

"I'm not a fool. I've known all along that Russell was a plant to keep an eye on me. Those wicked, green, demon eyes behind those glasses will be watching every move I make."

Without thinking about what he was doing, Jeff automatically reached for his mother's Bible, holding it on his lap while he fumed. "Now what am I going to do?"

Suddenly his mother's Bible slid off his lap, landing on the floor opened to the Old Testament book of Jeremiah. His mother's letter fluttered across the floor.

"Oh, Mom," Jeff cried as he dropped to his knees to grab the lavender paper. As he gently lifted the Bible, he noticed a verse highlighted in bold yellow ink.

"What's this?" Jeff wondered aloud as he laid the Bible on the bed. Still on his knees he began to read verse eleven in chapter twenty-nine. *For I know the thoughts that I think toward you, says the Lord, thoughts of peace, and not of evil, to give you an expected end.*

Awestruck, Jeff read the verse aloud one more time. Slowly he sat on the floor with his back against the bed, his elbows on his knees and his head bowed. Tears gathered in the corners of his eyes as he began to pray.

"God, I'm going to have to learn to trust you. I honestly don't see any peace on the horizon, but you apparently have an expected end for me and I want to be faithful to you until then. I'm asking you to somehow show me what you want me to do now."

Rubbing tears from the side of his face with his shoulder, Jeff lovingly kissed the lavender paper covered in his mother's handwriting. He whispered, "Mom, I'll see you again. I hope you somehow know that."

Checking the time, Jeff walked into the living room and sat on the couch to think. Forty-five minutes later he knew in his heart what he was going to do.

Keeping silent in his truck, Jeff smiled as gratitude replaced the anger and fear. *I don't know how You did it, God, but thank you for showing me what to do. Russell Wickes has no power over me as long as I walk in you. I need to talk to Amanda.*

TWENTY-FIVE

"No! No! No!" cried Amanda as David Patterson parked as closely to the church building as possible.

"What?" Gloria asked as she snapped her head around to look at Amanda in the back seat.

"Look," Amanda whispered hoarsely as she pointed to the church doors.

Great shards of broken glass littered the concrete sidewalk and adjoining grass.

Various items of clothing were strewn over the broken glass.

"No!" Amanda continued to cry as she jumped from the vehicle and darted for the church door.

"Wait," David called out, grabbing her forearm just in time. "We have to be careful. They might still be in there."

Amanda's breaths were coming in deep gulps as she strained to loose David's hold on her.

"David's right, Amanda," Gloria said. "We have to be careful."

Amanda bent over, placing her hands on her knees, trying to catch her breath and stop crying.

Gloria placed her hand on Amanda's back in an effort to comfort her. "When you're ready, we'll all go in together, okay?"

Amanda shook her head, but was unable to gain control for several seconds. David walked through the glass and clothing to survey the destroyed doors.

"It sounds quiet, I think it's probably okay for us to go in," he said, turning to look at his wife and Amanda. "You think you're ready?"

Amanda straightened herself, wiping her eyes and nose on the tail of her shirt. She nodded her head and followed David into the church foyer.

Standing silently in the middle of the foyer, they looked around making sure no one else was in the building. Seeing the opposite set of doors in the same shape as the ones they had just entered, they shook their heads in disbelief.

"Why?" Amanda whispered.

"I don't mean to sound like a know-it-all, Amanda," David said. "But the answer to that question should be clear these days."

"Yes, you're right," Amanda said. "Okay, let's see what else has been destroyed."

All three walked through the middle doors into the sanctuary, stopping immediately inside the doors.

"My word," David exclaimed.

Amanda sank into the pew next to her.

Gloria reached for her husband's hand. "Oh, David."

All windows in the sanctuary had been broken, including the cross-shaped window above the baptistery. The pulpit, along with the piano, had been knocked over.

Whatever had been used to shatter the windows had also been used on the organ. Pews had been torn loose from the floor and shoved over.

All the clothing that Amanda had spent hours folding was now strewn across the floor, throughout the foyer, and some had been tossed out the door.

Suddenly, Amanda ran toward the choir room. "The food!" she cried as she jumped over pews.

Grabbing the doorknob, she was unable to push the door open. "David, help," she yelled.

Already behind her, David said, "Move, Amanda, let me try." He shoved hard until the door inched open. A heavy table had been overturned and was barring entry into the small room.

Amanda ran up on the platform and tried the stage door into the room. "I'm in, David," she called. Surveying the room, it was clear the steps had not been moved.

"They didn't find it," she told David and Gloria. "I wonder about the attic. We better check."

Again, all three hurried to the foyer closet which opened to expose the ladder steps to the attic. David yanked open the door to discover that nothing had been disturbed.

"What are we going to do?" Amanda said as they made their way back into the sanctuary.

Gloria and David sat in the pew directly behind Amanda as they contemplated what their next move would be.

So engrossed in their troubled thoughts, they failed to hear footsteps coming across the foyer floor.

"Hello, anyone in here?"

Amanda swung around so quickly her elbow smashed into Gloria's fingers which had been gripping the back of the pew. As David spun around, he cracked his elbow into the wooden pew end.

David and Gloria simultaneously yelled, "OW."

Jumping to her feet, Amanda's dash for the foyer came to a painful halt as she crashed her knee into the wooden pew end. The next thing she knew, she was looking up from the floor with terrified eyes.

"Who are you? What do you want?" she yelled.

By the time David stumbled into the foyer, the intruders were quickly escaping through the broken doors.

"Wait! Don't go. Stop right there," David called to them.

A somewhat heavyset, middle-aged man slowed his gait, but did not come to a complete halt.

"Wait! Please wait, sir," David begged, reaching the door to observe the man standing on the sidewalk with his arm protectively around his short, grey-headed wife.

"Listen, we don't want any trouble. Just let us alone," the man said.

"Please, sir, let's talk. Why did you come by here today? Did you see anybody leaving or anybody around the outside of the building?" David's questions tumbled over each other as he quickly caught up with the couple.

By now the man and his wife had stopped and half turned toward David. "We don't want any trouble, mister. We just needed help."

"Come on back inside and we'll talk," David said, pointing toward the door. He could see stark terror in the lady's eyes. "We didn't do this, I promise you. We arrived about thirty minutes ago and found this mess."

The man looked at his wife and nodded. Clasping hands, they slowly followed David through the broken doors into the foyer.

Amanda was still sitting on the floor rubbing her knee. Gloria had begun to giggle. Frayed nerves and a wounded knee couldn't stop Amanda from being infected with the same desire.

David and the new couple walked into the sanctuary just as Amanda and Gloria burst into full-blown laughter. Seeming to catch the fever, David's smile exploded into laughter, causing the new couple to wonder just what they had walked into.

Several long minutes later, Amanda and Gloria began to wipe tears from their faces as they slowly regained control. Amanda tried to stand but that action caused pain to shoot through her leg.

"Oh, no," she moaned. "I think it's broken."

"Here, let me see," the female newcomer said. "I'm a nurse."

"Really," Amanda said. "What luck."

"We don't believe in luck anymore," the lady said as she began to gently rub her thumbs around Amanda's knee cap.

"You're right," Amanda said, grimacing. "There's no such thing."

"Well?" David asked, concerned about Amanda's ability to walk, knowing that they'd have to leave soon.

"I don't think it's broken, but it's certainly going to hurt for a few days," the lady said. "Is there any ice we can use?"

"No, the electricity has been turned off," David said.

"I didn't know that," Amanda said. "Are you sure?"

"Yes, I tried all the light switches. None of them work."

"Great!" Amanda said as the nurse and David helped her onto a pew where she could stretch her leg out. "I'm sorry, I didn't hear your name?"

"Sue. Sue Zoller, and this is my husband, George."

"Well, thank you, Sue. I'm very glad to meet you. I'm Amanda Fountain."

"Hello, George. My name is David Patterson and this is my wife, Gloria," David said, shaking George's hand.

"Pleased to meet you," Gloria said, holding out her hand to George and Sue.

"Can you tell me why you are here today?" David asked as he sat next to his wife in the pew directly behind Amanda.

"We've been looking for a safe place and saw this church so we stopped in. Obviously, it's not such a safe place. Why are you here?" George said.

"This had been our home church," David said. "Since *it* happened, we've been kind of using this building to see if we might be able to use it later."

Gloria immediately poked David with her elbow. *Please don't tell them too much.*

He patted her leg before continuing, "I think we can trust the Zollers, don't you, Amanda?"

Amanda nodded her head, her mind more on her pain as she gently rubbed her knee.

"I think the time has come when we have to ban together for safety sake," David said.

"I'm glad you said that, David," Amanda said. "Because I've seriously been considering something that I want to run past you, Gloria, and now the Zollers."

"What's that, Amanda?" Gloria asked, leaning forward.

"I want to okay it with Jeff first, but I've been thinking that we should all move into this church building. It's large enough for lots of people and, like you said, for safety sake we need to be together."

"That sounds like a good idea, but what about the electricity?" George asked.

"Maybe Jeff could help us there," David said.

"Who's Jeff?" Sue asked.

"Jeff's a good friend. We attended the same school and this was his home church, also," Amanda said. *Should I tell them about his job?*

"Am I correct in assuming that the two of you are now Christians?" David asked quickly before Amanda could say any more about Jeff.

George answered, "Yes, David, we are now when it's almost too late. Before all this happened, we were Sunday morning churchgoers."

"We thought we were okay because we were in church almost every Sunday morning," Sue said with sadness dripping from her voice. "Both of us sang in the choir and occasionally helped out in Sunday school."

"We really have no excuse because our pastor preached the truth from the Bible every Sunday morning," George said.

"Somewhere along the line—going to church faithfully; helping out when we could; being there for people in need—somehow covered up the fact that we had never asked Jesus into our hearts," Sue said as tears welled up in her eyes.

"I was in seminary studying to be a preacher," David said.

"You're kidding?" Sue exclaimed.

"Nope. That's what I was doing when the trumpet sounded that I didn't hear," David said as his eyes dampened also.

David wrapped his arm around his sobbing wife, pulling her close. Some of his tears ran into her hair when he laid his head onto hers.

Amanda quickly wiped the back of her hand across a cheek. "My dad was a faithful member of this church. I hadn't been attending very long, so I didn't know."

After several seconds of painful silence, Amanda continued, "That's not completely true. I'd heard enough to know that I needed the Lord. I just hadn't got around to making the decision yet. I was standing right over there." She pointed to the spot where her dad had stood that fateful Sunday morning.

Her words mingled with sobs as she continued, "Dad was singing so beautifully when all of a sudden he was gone—just gone. His clothes piled onto the floor, his Bible was left, but he was gone. No good-bye, no kiss, just gone."

"But, you're a Christian now?" Sue asked, wiping her own face with a tissue.

"Yes. Some men had been at the school and gave us little orange New Testaments. In the back were verses that helped me find the way. I began to read my dad's Bible. He had hundreds of marked verses. By reading those and several of the books on prophesy he had, I've learned all kinds of things about what's happening now."

"There certainly isn't anything good happening, and it's only going to get worse," George said.

"It will always be a good thing when someone gets saved," Gloria said.

"You're right, honey," David said. Suddenly remembering the time, he jerked his wrist up to check his watch. Jumping up, he exclaimed, "We've got to get home before we're caught."

Without a word, everyone got up and quickly walked to the door with Amanda hobbling along behind. Once outside, Jeff realized that there were no new vehicles parked nearby.

"Did you two walk here?"

"Yes, our car was stolen last week," George said.

"Where'd you walk from?" Gloria asked.

"We started out yesterday walking from just this side of the river bridge between here and Bedford," Sue said.

"You've got to be kidding me," Amanda said. "How did you keep from getting caught last night?"

"We've been walking cross country, avoiding the main road," George explained. "We found a barn just before dark. I think it belonged to a doctor."

"God had to be watching out for you for sure. The World Security Force is pretty thorough in their searches," David said, exchanging a knowing look with Amanda.

Sue happened to catch that look. "What?" she asked. "There's something you're not telling us."

"We'll tell you later. Get in the car and go home with us for tonight," Amanda said as she opened the car door.

George and Sue scooted across the back seat, clasping each other's hand. Unseen by anyone else in the car, George's finger gently tapped Sue's knuckle. Sue's knee answered George's unspoken message by pressing against his leg.

TWENTY-SIX

"Agent Wickes, you've done an outstanding job. These reports are in order and are now duly registered." Jeff's finger reluctantly tapped the "send" button.

"Thank you, sir." The corners of Russell Wickes' mouth lifted ever so slightly in a smug smile.

"The best way to teach a man to be a leader is to set the example and then allow him to do the job. Beginning tomorrow, you'll be on your own the first half of the shift and with me the last half."

"Sounds good to me, sir," Wickes said.

"I'll send my remarks to Captain Mercett before leaving and I'll see you tomorrow." Jeff focused on his laptop, immediately ignoring his redheaded enemy.

Agent Wickes' eyes blinked, realizing he had been dismissed. Contemptuous anger caused his freckle-covered face to redden as if sunburned as he spun around and marched out of the gym.

Jeff's fingers flew over the computer keys as his report to his superior officer gave glowing remarks about the man Captain Mercett had put in place to spy on him. It took great resolve to keep his true feelings from showing on his face, which he knew was being watched for any telltale signs of fear or dishonesty.

God, with your help I'll go as far as I can with this plan, Jeff prayed silently as he turned the key in his pickup truck and headed for home.

Walking into his house, he felt it. *Something's different.* Instantly alert, his eyes scanned the room looking for any telltale signs that someone was, or had been, in the house.

Seeing nothing, he moved through each room, silently but thoroughly searching everywhere and everything. After a full hour of searching, Jeff was unable to find anything that proved to him that someone had been here.

Nevertheless, knowing the means the World Security Force had at its disposal, Jeff knew in his heart that his parents' home was no longer safe. Even though he'd been unable to discover them, he was certain there were listening devices and possibly hidden cameras now recording his every move.

As nonchalantly as possible, he took a shower, slipped into a T-shirt and pair of sweatpants, and sat on the edge of his parents' bed. Picking up his mother's Bible, he carefully turned the pages until he found Psalms chapter 23.

Yea, though I walk through the valley of death, I will fear no evil for me thou art with me. He thought, *I now have a clear understanding of what this verse means. I will fear no evil, God, because I know I belong to you, no matter what.*

Jeff lovingly placed the Bible back on the nightstand, turned off the bedside light, slipped between the sheets, laid his head on his beloved mother's pillow and fell into a deep, restful sleep.

TWENTY-SEVEN

Refusing all offers for help, Amanda cleared her father's room from his personal items, storing them in her room. Reluctantly, she offered his room to George and Sue. Since a small bathroom was in the hallway next to that room, she decided not to tell George and Sue about the seclusion of her own bathroom.

Morning arrived with the aroma of fresh coffee and frying bacon. Gloria seemed to enjoy cooking. David had just finished offering the blessing when Jeff's knuckles rapped on the front door.

"Who could that be?" George almost barked.

Amanda held her finger to her lips, signaling everyone to be quiet. After one more knock, Jeff announced himself, "It's me, Amanda."

She began unlocking the row of locks allowing Jeff to step inside. Without words, he immediately gave Amanda a quick, affectionate hug, looking over Amanda's shoulder at the two new guests in her home.

Amanda introduced Jeff to her guests. "Jeff, this is George Zoller and his wife, Sue."

Jeff didn't offer his hand, but nodded his head in their direction. "Glad to meet you, my name is Jeff. Amanda and I are friends from school and church."

"Glad to meet you. Sue and I met Amanda out at church yesterday and she graciously invited us in. This girl's a real lifesaver." George kept his arm around Sue's waist as he spoke, giving her two squeezes that were unnoticed by the others.

"There's plenty eggs and bacon, Jeff. Come join us," Gloria called from the kitchen.

"Morning, Gloria. Breakfast smells good," Jeff smiled.

"Morning, Jeff," David said.

"David," Jeff acknowledged his friend. "Smells as if I timed my visit just right."

"You did at that, my friend," David said.

"Jeff, I need to talk to you before we leave for the day," Amanda said, placing her dirty dishes in the dishwasher.

"Sure thing." Jeff swallowed his last drop of coffee. When his dishes were also placed in the dishwasher, he followed Amanda into her bedroom.

When she turned to close her bedroom door, Jeff knew something was wrong.

"What's going on, Amanda?"

"A couple things. Actually, three things, to be exact," Amanda said as she sat on her bed.

Jeff chose the desk chair instead of sitting on Amanda's bed. "Three things? Wow. We've got lists." Jeff laughter faded when he looked into Amanda's serious eyes.

"First, when we arrived at the church yesterday, someone had been there and broken almost all of the windows."

"What?" Jeff jumped to his feet. "Amanda, it's not safe out there for you anymore."

"Now, wait a minute," Amanda said. "David helped check all the rooms and we couldn't find anyone. The supplies are still hidden, but they made a mess of all the clothing. Some of the pews were knocked over, along with the piano and the pulpit. It's just awful."

"What's number two?" Jeff asked.

"I've been thinking, and David mentioned it also, that we should move into the church so we'd be better protected and have plenty of room for others who might need a place to stay."

"How do you intend to be safe when someone has already broken in?" Jeff asked.

"We think we can make it safe again. And whosoever was in there might not be so brave with someone living there all the time," Amanda said.

"And number three?" Jeff asked, almost afraid to hear any more.

"Actually, there's more to number two," Amanda said with a slight smile.

"Which is?" Jeff said.

"The electricity is turned off at the church. We were wondering if there is anything you could do to get it turned back on." Amanda scrunched up her face as she watched for Jeff's reaction.

"Number three?" was all Jeff said, as he sat with his eyes focused on the floor.

"I can't explain it, but I have a funny feeling around George and Sue," Amanda whispered. "They've been nothing but nice and helpful, so I can't really explain it. I just don't know."

"That's strange, because I felt the same thing when I came in this morning. How much do they know so far?" he asked.

"They don't know about the supplies. They don't know about you and your job. For some unknown reason, I didn't tell them about my bathroom," Amanda continued to whisper.

Jeff's eyebrows arched as he looked at Amanda. "Your bathroom? Am I missing something?"

"Oh, you don't know," Amanda smiled. "My bathroom, right over there," she pointed toward a closed door, "is the only room in the house without a window. David, Gloria and I have Bible studies in there at night. No one can tell when we are in there reading or praying."

"Really?" Jeff said, looking at the door.

Amanda nodded her head as she waited for Jeff to say something as he began pacing the floor.

"Okay. I'll do what I can about the electricity. I don't want you staying out there until I know it's safe. I'll talk to David about the Zollers and we'll all keep our eyes opened."

"Oh, good," Amanda said, breathing a deep sigh of relief. "I knew you'd have the answers.

"I'll go out to the church to see what's needed to make it safe. I'll call you when I'm done inspecting the building, okay?" Jeff said.

"I appreciate that so much," Amanda responded. "Thank you, Jeff."

"Not a problem. I need to talk to you about something, also, but for now we better join the others before they get suspicious."

Amanda and Jeff walked back into the living room where the other three were watching the morning news bulletin. Amanda could hear the dishwasher running and knew the kitchen had been left spotless.

"Thanks, Gloria." She smiled at her friend.

Suddenly getting an idea, Amanda turned to George and Sue. "I need to go get some groceries, would you two like to come with me?"

Looking at each other, Sue said, "Uh, sure, I guess. How about it, George?"

"Fine with me," George said. "We going now?"

"Yes, so we can get our act together for going out to church later."

"Let's go then," George said, reaching for Sue's hand.

"We'll get back here as soon as possible, okay?" Amanda said. "Do any of you need anything from the store?"

"I don't think so," Gloria said.

"Be careful out there," Jeff said. He was sure Amanda had planned this outing to give him the opportunity to speak with David.

"You can count on it," Amanda said. "We won't be long."

"Bye," Sue said as they stepped outside.

As soon as he heard Amanda's car door slam, David turned to Jeff. "What's going on, Jeff?"

"Amanda told me about your idea for using the church building as living quarters. I'll check on the electricity and see what I can do. I need to know that you all will be safe staying there. When I leave here I'm going to check it to see what is needed."

"There's something more, isn't there?" Gloria asked.

"Yes, but neither Amanda nor myself can put our finger on it. Something is just not adding up with George and Sue."

"I knew it," Gloria exclaimed.

"You knew what?" David asked his wife.

"I don't know, honey," Gloria said. "I've just had an uneasy feeling about them."

"Just keep your defenses up, okay?" Jeff asked.

"Yeah, we'll keep our eyes opened," David said. "There's still something else, isn't there, Jeff?"

"Yes, David. My superior officer, Captain Mercett, has put one of my men, Agent Wickes, as my shadow."

"He's actually watching you that closely?" David asked.

"He has made me Agent Wickes' training officer, so Wickes can take over his own squad, supposedly," Jeff said.

"Oh, I see," David said.

"That's right. I've always had a feeling that Agent Wickes was a plant in my squad. Now I'm certain. But, I've decided to use their act against them."

"Gloria and I will be praying for you, Jeff," David said. "If there's anything we can do, let us know."

"I will. There's one more thing."

"What's that?" David asked.

"I'm almost sure my parents' home has been bugged," Jeff said quietly.

"You're kidding," Gloria exclaimed.

Jeff shook his head as he continued to speak. "I was going to ask if I could stay here, but it looks like this house is already full."

"How about staying in the church with us?" David asked.

"I might be able to arrange that. I can use the excuse of keeping an eye on whoever else moves in," Jeff said.

"I'll put George to work today. We'll get the windows boarded up and the mess cleaned up so we can make the move as soon as you give us the go-ahead," David said.

"I think we'll all be safer together," Jeff said. "Gloria, can you keep an eye on Sue?"

"You bet," Gloria said, eager to be of help.

"Keep an eye on Sue for what?" George's voice boomed across the room.

Without missing a beat, Gloria called out sweetly, "I've been concerned about her. You just look awfully tired and worried, Sue, so I've taken it upon myself to make sure you get the rest you need."

Gloria walked over to give Sue a warm hug. *Please forgive me, Lord, for telling a lie.* Guilt induced tears threatened to spill from her eyes, which made Sue think that Gloria truly was concerned for her.

Closing the refrigerator door after storing the new jug of milk, Amanda called out, "Okay, what's the plan?"

"I have three hours before reporting for duty," Jeff said as he walked toward the still unlocked door. "I'm on my way to the church to survey the damage. I'll call and let you know when I'm finished and what you'll need to make it safe."

"Sounds like a plan," David said.

After Jeff backed his pickup truck out of the driveway, Amanda asked if anyone had clothes that needed to be washed.

"David and I have one load," Gloria announced as she walked toward their bedroom. "Sue, you want to throw anything in?"

Sue looked quickly at George, getting a quick nod in return. "We probably have a half load," she called.

"Girls, you better make it snappy," George called. "It's almost time for another news report. We certainly can't afford to miss what our leaders have to say."

Gloria and Sue exited the kitchen area and took their seats by their husbands just as the news cast was beginning. Gloria and David's hands clung together desperately.

As the news reports droned on, David was able to steal a good look at George's face. His skin crawled as he observed George's facial expressions, especially the evil smirk that finally twisted across his face.

God, what have we opened our doors to? How are we going to extricate ourselves from this couple? David's silent, desperate prayer caused him to squeeze Gloria's hand even harder, making her look at him questioningly. David winked at his wife, raising her hand to his lips, tenderly kissing her soft skin.

Sue did not miss the tender, loving exchange between David and Gloria. The ever-present fear inside her welled up to the point that she reached for her husband's hand for comfort.

George had no idea what was going on in Sue's mind or heart. He had his own agenda and he assumed that Sue would be beside him all the way. When he felt Sue's hand touch his, he pulled away, cupping his chin in both his hands.

"I have to use the restroom," Sue whispered to Gloria.

TWENTY-EIGHT

Jeff spent an entire hour checking the damage to the church building and finding supplies for the needed repairs. As he exited the storage shed behind the church building, he stood gazing into the thick woods that lined the edge of the church property.

"I haven't been in the woods since we used to take the little kids on hay rides back there. I wonder if—I'll just have to check it out. I'll do that tomorrow." With that, he turned and walked back to the church building.

Picking up the church phone, Jeff was surprised that it still worked. He quickly punched in Amanda's home number. Amanda answered after two rings.

"It's me, Amanda. I need to speak with David, then I'm going to go into work early and speak to Captain Mercett about the electricity."

"Are you sure this won't backfire on us if they know what we're doing?" Amanda worried.

"I don't think so. I'll come up with a good explanation. Just be praying for me, okay?"

"That's something I can do. Here's David," Amanda said, handing the phone to David.

"David, I've checked the damage and it looks like the windows are going to be our biggest problem. I found plenty of boards, nails and tools in the storage shed that we can use," Jeff told his friend.

"Do you think George and I could begin the work today?" David asked.

"I don't see why not. Just keep your eyes opened," Jeff said.

"Understood."

"Oh, and, David, I'm going in to work early and speak with my superior officer about having the electricity turned back on. I'll give him a good story so there won't be any suspicion at this point."

"Sounds good. We'll load up and head out there. We'll be praying for you."

"Thanks, I'll need it." Jeff hung up the phone and hurried out to his truck.

As Jeff's truck bounced over the railroad tracks, he saw two boys on bicycles peddling in the direction he had just come from.

Grabbing his cell phone, he suddenly realized he had to censure his message to Amanda or David in order to warn them without letting other listening ears know what was going on.

Relieved to hear David's voice answering the phone, he said, "Hello, this is Agent Howard. Just wanted to advise you to postpone your scheduled outing until I get back with you. I'll need to return to the site and do some housecleaning."

He's trying to give me some kind of warning... "Message acknowledged. Thank you, sir." He hung up the phone and immediately offered a silent prayer for Jeff.

"Who was that?" Amanda asked while putting away the clean dishes.

Making sure his back was turned toward the living room, David looked intently at Amanda, willing her to understand. "That was Jeff, he's getting ready for work, then he's going to recheck something at the church."

Amanda squinted her eyes at David, trying to understand the hidden message. Slowly nodding her head, she said, "Good. We'll see him at breakfast, I'm sure."

David mouthed the words, "Pray for him."

"I'll be in my room if anyone needs me," Amanda called out brightly as she hurried to her room. Desperately trying to hold back tears, she quickly stepped into the bathroom and shut the door.

Kneeling next to the bathtub, Amanda quietly prayed for Jeff's protection.

TWENTY-NINE

Jeff parked his truck at the end of the church's driveway. Silently shut the door, he walked resolutely to the side door of the building. Having retrieved his weapon from under his truck seat, he now held it close to his side.

Hearing boyish laughter inside along with the sound of pews falling to the floor, Jeff knew his entrance would not be heard. Nevertheless, he carefully stepped into the foyer watching the two boys gleefully destroy whatever they could get their hands and feet on.

"Having fun, boys?" Jeff shouted.

The taller of the two had just given one of the pews a heavy shove. Hearing Jeff's voice, he fell over with the pew, smashing his face against an exposed support beam.

A loud yell ensued as he tried to stand up but was having difficulty gaining his balance. A deep gash on his forehead gushed blood onto his hands, shirt and the carpeted floor.

"I said, are you having fun, boys?" Jeff shouted.

"Uh, sir, uh, we were just having..." the other boy stammered as he looked from his friend to Jeff.

"I can see how you were just having fun. Follow me," he ordered.

The uninjured boy reached over to help his buddy who was having difficulty seeing through the blood.

"Your names," Jeff asked curtly.

"John Scott," the smaller of the two mumbled.

"Kyle Marcum." His bare hand was unsuccessfully in stopping the flow of blood.

Jeff motioned with his weapon for the boys to exit the sanctuary. Upon entering the foyer, he stopped them. "Step into the restroom and grab some paper towels for your buddy," he ordered John Scott.

John hurried into the rest room and grabbed as many paper towels as he could. Stepping back into the foyer, he helped Kyle hold the towels tightly against his forehead.

"You get some kind of kick out of destroying someone else's property?" Jeff asked.

"It just a church," mumbled Kyle.

"Churches are fair game, from what I hear," John said, wiping his hands down the legs of his jeans.

"I don't know where you're getting your information, but it's wrong—dead wrong," Jeff said.

"You think you're some big shot cop, but you're as phony as they come," sneered Kyle.

"Does this look phony to either of you?" Jeff said, still holding his weapon on the boys.

"That don't scare us none," John said, trying not to look at the weapon. "We know all about you."

Kyle gave a snort as he turned as if to leave.

"Hold it right there," Jeff ordered.

Kyle turned and tossed a handful of bloodied paper towel onto the floor in front of Jeff. "You're as good as dead, Jeff Howard."

"Is that so?" Jeff said. "For two idiots caught red-handed, you're certainly full of it."

"Oh, Wickes told us all about you," John said.

"Shut up, John," Kyle shouted.

"Wickes? You know Agent Wickes?" Jeff was shaken for a few seconds.

"Yeah, he's gonna pay us to trash this place and give him a report on you, you jerk," John sneered.

"So you can put your little squirt gun down before you get all wet." Kyle and John laughed as they headed for the door.

"STOP RIGHT THERE." Jeff's menacing shout caused both young boys to stop dead in their tracks.

Jeff slowly, deliberately stepped around the boys, blocking their escape. "That way," he ordered, pointing toward the steps into the fellowship hall.

"Whatever." Kyle glared at Jeff for a few seconds.

John's eyes began to widen, but he followed his friend, hoping Kyle had a plan.

As the three stepped into the fellowship hall, Jeff motioned them toward the back of the room where the rarely used back stairwell was located.

"Wickes is going to pay us well for our report today," Kyle said.

John nervously snickered as he was shoved forward by Jeff, bumping into Kyle's elbow. The rough paper towel sawed across Kyle's head causing renewed bleeding.

"Sorry," John told his friend.

"Now what?" Kyle asked as they reached the top of the steps. "You gonna take us in or what?"

Oh, man, please don't make us go down there. John's eyes danced with fear.

"Down there," Jeff quietly ordered.

"Why? Ain't nothing down there," Kyle said.

"Move." Jeff kept his weapon trained on the boys.

"Aw, come on, let's get this over with so we can get out of here." John's voice trembled.

"Better make this quick, Jeff," Kyle barked as he and John began to slowly walk down the wooden steps. "If you're going to lock us up in the dark, it better not be for long."

"Stop!" Jeff ordered when the boys were three quarters of the way down the steep steps.

"What?" Kyle said as he turned toward Jeff.

When John turned around, Jeff saw that the front of his jeans was wet down to his knees.

"Come on, Jeff, this ain't funny any more," Kyle said as he brushed spider webs out of his blood soaked hair.

"Who said that it has ever been funny?" Jeff asked. "Let me ask you boys a question."

"What?" John asked in a voice that dripped with fear.

"You two were here in this very church when almost everyone else disappeared, right?"

"Yeah, so what?" Kyle asked.

"Have either one of you thought about that day? Have either one of you thought about becoming a Christian since then?" Jeff asked. His arm lowered slightly.

"Uh...no," John said, blinking his eyes.

"Are you insane?" Kyle exclaimed. "I didn't believe that crap before that preacher disappeared to who knows where, I sure ain't gonna believe it now."

"John?" Jeff asked.

"What's the point. All that stuff's over with now," John said.

"There's still a chance, John. Would you like to become a Christian?" Jeff asked again.

"John, you're an idiot," Kyle said with an evil laugh.

"Am not," John shot back. "No, I don't," he yelled at Jeff.

In two awful seconds, John and Kyle were no longer a threat to Jeff.

Jeff stiffly walked across the fellowship hall floor, down the short stairway, and out of the foyer into the bright sunlight. Tears streamed down his tanned cheeks as he turned on the truck's ignition.

By the time Jeff stepped out of his truck at W.S.F. headquarters, he had managed to gain perfect control—outwardly. Having arrived two hours early, he made his way to Captain Mercett's office door.

"Enter," Captain Mercett said upon hearing three quick knocks.

Jeff stepped smartly to the front of Captain Mercett's desk and saluted his superior officer.

"Is there a problem, Agent Howard?" Captain Mercett asked. "You're two hours early."

"No problem, sir," Jeff said. "I just needed to talk with you about a situation to see if a solution might be found."

"At ease, Howard," Captain Mercett said. "Please, sit."

Jeff sat stiffly in the chair offered by Captain Mercett. "I have a few acquaintances that have been spending time out on Woodville Road at what used to be a church building."

"And?" Captain Mercett asked.

"A young lady who I went to school with has befriended a few more people and they asked if they would be permitted to move into the building since it was no longer used as a church. They thought it would be a way of sharing expenses, such as water, electricity, and so on."

"Uh-huh," Captain Mercett said.

"Since I know three of them, especially the young lady, I would like to volunteer to move in the building also," Jeff asked with a boldness that surprised even himself.

"You? Why would you want to move into a church building?" Captain Mercett asked, moving around to perch on the front of the desk.

"Well, sir, even though the building is no longer a church, I would like to be fully aware, without their knowledge of course, of what is taking place there. They assure me it would make good sense for several people to be living in places such as that building. But I want to make sure they aren't having any meetings or the like," Jeff said.

"I see," Mercett said, rubbing his chin as he kept his eyes glued on Jeff.

Putting what he hoped was a proper sneer on his face, Jeff continued. "Besides, I kind of like the girl and would like to stay in close proximity, if you know what I mean."

"I see," Mercett repeated as he laughed while moving back to his seat behind the desk. "I see no harm in the building being used for housing. And I like the idea of you keeping an eye on things."

"Thank you, sir," Jeff said, standing. "There's one more thing, sir."

"Which is?" Mercett asked.

"Who do I need to contact in reference to having the water and electricity turned back on and kept on?" Jeff asked.

"I'll have it taken care of," Mercett said.

"Thank you, sir, thank you," Jeff said, extending his hand to Captain Mercett.

"Not a problem. Anything else?"

"Not at this time, sir," Jeff said. "I'll keep you posted if anything changes in these living arrangements."

"Yes, you will. Dismissed."

Jeff turned and marched out the door, down the hallway, and gathered his files for the next shift.

Thank you, God, he prayed silently. *I still need to talk to Amanda.*

THIRTY

"It's going to be awfully dark in here with all the windows boarded up," George griped as they all made their way into the church building.

"Jeff is trying to get the electricity turned back on," David commented.

"It's always Jeff this and Jeff that. What makes him so important?" George complained.

"Jeff is my friend," Amanda said defensively.

David gently placed his hand on Amanda's shoulder before speaking. "This is where Jeff and Amanda attended church. Now that it's no longer a church and our world has changed so drastically, we've all decided that we can use this building to live in."

"There's lots of room and we can all share the expenses. Besides, we'll be more protected if we stay together," Gloria added.

"I understand all of that. I asked what Jeff does," George said, turning to look at David, Gloria and Amanda.

After several seconds of strained silence, Amanda said, "Jeff is a World Security Force Agent."

"He's what?" George exclaimed.

"Amanda's right. Jeff is an agent, but we're safe with him. At least for now," David said.

"You mean to tell me that you have asked a W.S.F. agent to live here with us, knowing what their orders are for Christians?" George shouted. Sue's face blanched and she was visibly trembling.

"Calm down, George," Amanda said. "Jeff doesn't know we're Christians and we're going to keep it that way."

Not missing a beat, David added, "He's our friend. We need a place to stay and so does he. Everything else will work out. Being careful about one more thing shouldn't be too difficult."

Realizing that David and Amanda were handling the situation the best way they could, even though they had to lie, Gloria wandered into the sanctuary. What she saw caused her to gasp loudly.

"What?" David asked, hurrying to his wife's side.

"Where did all the blood come from?" Gloria exclaimed.

"Look! There's blood out here too," Amanda said, looking around the foyer floor.

"David, did you talk to Jeff? Do you think he's all right?"

"That's right. Jeff said he was coming out here," George said. "Look at all those pews. There's more of them knocked over since we were here yesterday."

"You're right, George," David said. "Come on, help me get them set back up."

"I'll see if there's something to clean up this blood," Gloria said, heading for the kitchen.

In the excitement no one noticed Sue. When Gloria walked into the foyer she found Sue crumpled to the floor.

"Sue," she yelled. "George! David! Come here. Something's wrong with Sue."

Everyone ran into the foyer as George knelt beside his wife. "Sue, talk to me. Sue."

Amanda ran to the restroom to grab cold, wet towels. When she placed the towels on Sue's forehead, her eyes flutter.

"Sue, can you hear me?" Gloria said gently.

"Can we still call 9-1-1? Is there any help available anymore?" George asked.

"Unless it's absolutely necessary we don't want any of those people to come out here and see what we're doing. We'll have to answer too many questions," David said.

Gloria took one of Sue's hands and gently massaged it. "Sue, can you open your eyes?"

Sue's eyes slowly opened and began to focus on Gloria. Not once did her eyes search for her husband.

"That's a girl. Do you think you can sit up?" Gloria's gentle voice seemed to coax Sue out of her stupor.

George helped his wife sit up while Gloria softly wiped the wet towels over her face, which had begun to turn pink once more.

"Well, that was embarrassing," Sue said in a weak voice.

"Embarrassing?" George exclaimed. "That's all you can think about when you scared all of us half to death?" He stood, allowing Gloria and Amanda to tend to his wife.

"I apologize, girls. I was so frightened anyway and when you said something about seeing a lot of blood; I just don't remember anything after that," Sue said, trying to stand up.

"You think you're ready to stand?" Gloria asked, staying close to Sue's side.

"I think I'll be okay," Sue said. "George, I'm sorry, I never intended…"

"Never mind," George said, turning towards the sanctuary. "Come on, everybody, let's get this work done."

"I think I better use the restroom first," Sue said.

Amanda and Gloria looked at each other sadly.

David put his arms around his wife, giving her a reassuring hug. "I'll go help George. You girls see if you can encourage Sue."

Amanda walked up the steps in the fellowship hall on her way to find cleaning supplies.

Gloria stepped into the restroom to check on her friend. Sue was bent over the sink with a wet towel over her face.

"You going to be all right, Sue?" Gloria asked.

Sue had not heard Gloria enter and visibly jumped when she heard her voice. "Oh, Gloria, I am so sorry. I didn't mean to cause problems for anyone else."

"Don't be silly, Sue," Gloria said. "No one plans to faint, it just happens."

Sue leaned against the cream colored wall, holding the towel on her forehead. "Gloria, I've been so terrified since everybody disappeared. I can't talk to George…"

George's fist banged against the door as he bellowed, "Hurry up in there. We've got work to do."

Both women jumped as if shot.

"Come on, we'll talk later," Gloria said, gently taking Sue's arm.

"We're coming, George," Sue called.

Lunchtime came and went as they labored to put the church building back into livable order. By the time they had to leave, most of the windows had been covered, the pews were righted and most of the blood had been cleaned out of the carpet.

"By this time tomorrow we should have it ready to move into," David said as he looked around the darkened sanctuary. "Hopefully the electricity will be turned on by the end of the week."

Physically exhausted, everyone was exceptionally quiet on the ride to Amanda's. George glared out the side window as a frown creased his forehead. Sue laid her head back against the car seat, closed her eyes and hoped that George wouldn't speak to her.

David's arm was around the back of his wife's seat, her head resting on his shoulder. Amanda's mind was still working overtime as she contemplated where everyone's rooms should be when they moved. *And what about Jeff? God, all that blood. Was it Jeff's? If he doesn't show up at breakfast, what will we do? Please, let him be all right. We're going to need his help to make this happen. Help us know what to do.*

THIRTY-ONE

Having tossed and turned most of the night, Jeff was up, dressed and on his way to Amanda's front door the second curfew was lifted.

Amanda also had been unable to sleep. Unsure of Jeff's fate caused her fear induced imagination to conger up all kinds of images of his demise.

And then there was George. Hearing footsteps in the hallway during the night, Amanda glanced at her bedside clock to see that it was 2:00 a.m. Who was up? Amanda carefully got out of bed, quietly opened her door and padded down the hallway. Peeking around the corner, she saw George standing in the kitchen reaching for the telephone.

Quietly running back to her room, she noisily jerked open the bedroom door and whispered loudly as she hurried toward the kitchen, "I've got to get some water."

Pretending not see George, who quickly moved to stand against the washing machine, Amanda opened the refrigerator and grabbed a bottle of water. She opened the water and turned in George's direction to take a drink.

On the pretense of being startled, Amanda yelped and dropped the bottle of water. "George! I'm sorry, I didn't see anybody in here," she laughed.

George apologized for scaring her and explained that he couldn't sleep so he had come into the kitchen where he could spend some time alone, praying.

After cleaning up the spilled water, Amanda sat down at the table and whispered to George, "I haven't been sleeping well, either. I had to get something to drink then I thought I'd spend some time praying also. Why don't we pray together?"

George stammered, "Well, I've been up for a while now, I think I'll try to get some sleep. See you at breakfast." With that he rushed back down the hallway.

Amanda continued sitting at the table until her trembling was under control.

At three in the morning, she slowly made her way back to her bedroom, softly closing her door. Totally unable to sleep, her ears stayed tuned for any possible movement. Her fear of George, added to her fear for Jeff, kept her wide awake.

When Jeff's knock sounded, much earlier than usual, Amanda was already up, dressed and on the couch. Gloria had just minutes before walked into the kitchen to prepare breakfast.

In her haste to open the locked door, Amanda bent one of her fingernails back into the quick. When Jeff finally stepped into the room, Amanda had tears running down her cheeks.

"What?" Jeff asked, seeing the look in Amanda's eyes.

"I bent my fingernail back," she cried, holding tightly to that particular finger.

"Good morning, Jeff," David called, on his way to help his wife. Seeing the distressed couple at the door, he stopped and turned toward them. "What's going on?"

"Oh, nothing," Amanda said, trying to laugh. "I just broke a fingernail."

By now, George and Sue entered the room as he guided his wife to the couch and sat close beside to her.

"I'm sorry, Amanda," Sue said. "Breaking a fingernail is always bad for us women."

Sue's sweet smile faded as her husband muttered, "Add it to the list."

Jeff and Amanda looked at each other as he lifted her hand. "It's bleeding a little. Got any band aids?"

"In my room," Amanda replied.

"Let's go see what we can do with it," Jeff said.

"Thanks, Sue," Amanda said quietly as she and Jeff walked toward the hallway.

"Breakfast should be ready in about twenty minutes," Gloria called from the kitchen.

"This won't take long," Jeff called back. "Hey, George, want to see if the news is on yet?"

"Sure thing," George said, picking up the remote control and powering on the television.

Safely inside Amanda's room, Jeff whispered, "I don't want him to hear us."

Not stopping until she was in her bathroom, Amanda turned to motion Jeff to follow her.

"Jeff..."

"I..."

Both began talking at the same time.

"Go ahead. I'm sorry," Jeff said.

"Jeff, this morning at about two o'clock, I saw George in the kitchen reaching for the telephone."

"What? What did you do?"

"I pretended that I needed a drink and went into the kitchen to get a bottle of water."

"And?" Jeff said.

"I acted like it scared me to see him there. He told me he couldn't sleep and had come in there to pray."

"Pray? On the telephone?" Jeff said, sitting on the edge of the bathtub.

"Exactly. And he told me he had been there a long time, which I knew was a lie. I heard him walk down the hallway."

"Okay, let me think about how to handle this," Jeff said, dropping his head.

"What were you going to say?" Amanda asked.

"Oh, yeah." Jeff remembered what he had come to share with Amanda. "I am being watched by my superior officer and another of the agents who I'm supposed to be training."

"You're kidding?" Amanda whispered loudly. "Oh, Jeff, what are you going to do?"

"Right now, since I know what's going on, I'm using the situation against them. I don't know how long I can get away with it, but I've been asking God to help me."

"Oh, Jeff." Amanda sat on the tub edge beside him.

"I can't find the bug, but I know my house is no longer safe. They've got some kind of spyware in there. And I think my truck is bugged also. If I should ever call any of you on my cell phone, we have to talk in some type of code."

"So, we really need to get moved into the church soon, don't we?" Amanda asked.

"Yes. Today, if possible."

"Will they have the church bugged too?" Amanda asked, standing to look at Jeff.

"No, at least not yet. I've convinced my captain that I'll be living there to keep and eye on all of you to make sure no meetings or anything like that is taking place."

Amanda sat quietly beside him.

"Don't worry, Amanda," Jeff said, placing his hand over hers. "We know that life is never going to be easy from now on. We just have to outsmart them as long as we can."

"I'm scared, Jeff," Amanda whispered.

"I know. But we all need to be, at least just enough to keep us on our toes. We can't let our defenses down for a minute."

Both sat quietly for a few seconds until Jeff heard Amanda sniff softly. Squeezing her hand, he said, "Amanda, I'll be here for you as much as possible, I promise you that."

"Thanks, Jeff," Amanda said. "I miss my dad so much and wish desperately that I could have gone with him."

"I know," Jeff whispered. "But, you know what? Because of my mom's letter and because of you, I'm ready now. And I plan to help others get ready."

Amanda smiled. "You're right, we can still be used."

Jeff placed his arm around Amanda's shoulders and gently pulled her against him. "Amanda?"

"No, Jeff. I feel the connection between us too, but our time here is so limited, let's just keep things like this, okay?"

"Okay." He kissed the top of her head.

"What are we going to do about George?" Amanda asked.

"Let me think about it this morning. I'll talk to David and we'll keep our eyes on him. I'm afraid something will have to be done before the day is over."

Looking into Jeff's eyes, Amanda saw something she didn't want to deal with. "I don't even want to know, okay?"

"Not a problem." Even though his lips smiled, his eyes had a sad, faraway look in them. "I'll talk to David."

"We better go. Gloria probably has breakfast ready," Amanda said.

At that very moment, Gloria's voice rang out, "Breakfast is served."

"What about Sue?" Amanda asked.

"Do you think she's a threat also?"

"I don't think so," Amanda said. "In fact, I feel sorry for her the way George treats her. And I don't think he trusts her. He won't let her out of his sight for very long."

"Okay, David and I'll discuss that too."

Amanda suddenly turned, bumping into Jeff. "The band aid!"

"Oh, yeah," Jeff laughed, stepping out of Amanda's way as she ran back to the bathroom.

"Here, let me help," Jeff said, taking the band aid, quickly and deftly wrapping it around her finger. When finished, he bent to place a warm kiss on Amanda's lips.

Amanda wrapped her arms around Jeff as they held each other for a brief moment before George's booming voice echoed down the hallway.

"Come on, you two, we've got work to do."

Amanda opened the door, stepped into the hallway and stuck out her tongue at George's back making Jeff guffaw.

"What's so funny?" George asked as they each began to fill their plates.

"Aw, just a joke," Jeff said. "Umm, Gloria, you're a fantastic cook."

"That she is," David said, giving his wife a kiss on the cheek.

When everyone had found a spot to sit and eat their breakfast, Jeff brought up the subject of moving. "I received permission for your move into the church as long as I move in with you. The electricity should be turned on soon, maybe today."

"That's great. Thanks, Jeff," David said.

"Can we get all that work done today?" George asked.

"With all we got accomplished yesterday, I don't see a problem with it," David said.

"Hey, Jeff," George began. "We cleaned up an awfully lot of blood out there yesterday. You know anything about that?"

Sue moaned softly before making her way back to the kitchen with her half eaten meal. Gloria followed.

"As a matter of fact, I do," Jeff said, taking a drink of orange juice. "I was lucky enough yesterday to catch our vandals in the very act. One of them fell onto the pew he had just kicked. You know how head wounds bleed." With effort, Jeff acted as if it were no big deal.

Sue asked, "Were they young kids?"

"Oh, probably sixteen, eighteen, something like that," Jeff answered.

"What's that got to do with anything?" George asked gruffly.

Ignoring her husband, Sue asked, "Is the boy going to be all right?"

"As you saw, he lost a lot of blood but he's going to be okay, physically anyway." Jeff gave David a quick smile.

"So you arrested them?" George asked.

"Let's just say, they learned their lesson. They won't be vandalizing any more buildings for a while." Now it was Jeff's turn to take his plate with uneaten food to the kitchen.

Amanda watched Jeff through this whole exchange. When she saw his eyes, her heart almost stopped.

"Gloria, let me clean up the kitchen this morning, okay?" Amanda asked as she walked into the kitchen with uneaten food on her plate.

"Well, okay, I guess," Gloria said. "I'll straighten up our room so David and I will be ready to go."

"That's a good idea," George said. "Sue, go get our stuff put together."

Sue glared at George's back before she began walking down the hallway.

Looking at his watch, Jeff said, "We should be at the church to begin work in about thirty minutes. Is that good for everybody?"

"I'm almost finished up here," Amanda said.

"Works for me," George said, sitting on the couch.

"I'll see if Gloria needs help," David said, hurrying down the hallway.

"I'll help get all the work done at the church then we'll start moving things. The rest of you might have to finish up without me when I have to go to work."

"I think we can probably manage that," Amanda said, hanging up the kitchen towel. "But what about the stuff from your house?"

"I'll get it tomorrow. I might still spend the night at the church. We'll see," Jeff said.

With his back to George, Jeff mouthed, *Watch George around the phone.*

Amanda nodded just as Sue and the Pattersons walked into the living room.

"Looks like we're all ready. Let's go," Amanda said.

THIRTY-TWO

During one of their trips to the storage shed, Jeff shared with David what Amanda had seen George doing early that morning.

"Who do you think he was going to call?" David asked.

"Since he lied to her about why he was in the kitchen, I'm sure he was up to no good."

"Do you think he's another plant?" David asked.

"I'm sure of it," Jeff answered. "Just be very, very careful tonight. In the morning I want to talk to you about our options with him."

"I'll stay awake tonight and make sure he doesn't do anything else."

"To make this work, we've got to be on our guard constantly," Jeff said.

"On our guard for what?" George's voice startled the other two men. They had failed to see him walk up.

"Even though we're all going to be living out here, we can't just assume we'll be safe," Jeff said.

"Yeah," David added. "We've got to constantly keep up our guard in case anyone comes snooping around. We never know when somebody will try to stop what we're doing."

"Yeah, you're right," George said. "Here let me help with that." George acted as if he wanted to help.

"That's all right, George," Jeff said. "I think we've got it. Grab that can of nails, though. We might need them."

By one o'clock in the afternoon the repairs had been made. Everyone was in the fellowship hall resting and drinking water at one of the tables when the electricity suddenly came on, bringing cheers from everyone.

"I've been thinking all day about who gets which rooms and I believe I have it all figured out," Amanda said.

"This is like going to camp," Gloria said, smiling.

"Boot camp," George muttered. "We gonna be able to use the TV?"

"That won't be a problem," Jeff said, reaching across the table to place his hand warmly over Amanda's. "Amanda, you show everybody their rooms while I'm at work. I'll be back in time for breakfast."

Amanda led the group down the steps into the church basement. Rooms of several different sizes lined both outside walls with three smaller rooms down the middle. Most of the rooms had been Sunday school rooms. The largest room in the middle had been the church nursery.

Several years prior, the church had voted to make two of the connecting rooms into a small apartment for visiting speakers, missionaries and the like. That apartment had its own full bathroom. The other restrooms were located in the far corners of the basement. Each of those restrooms had been equipped with showers.

"Okay, David and Gloria, you take the apartment," Amanda said, opening their door.

"Since Sue and I are the oldest of the group, I think we should have the comforts of the apartment," George griped.

"Age has nothing to do with it, George," Amanda said, bravely. "Follow me."

George gave his wife's back a-none-too gentle shove as they followed Amanda around the corner to the opposite hallway.

Amanda opened the door to the basement's second largest room. The room wasn't very wide, but it was long. The Sunday school class that had met in this room had installed plush, deep-rose colored carpet. The walls were painted a soft rose color and had an elegant looking border running along the top.

Even George couldn't help but exclaim, "Wow."

"Oh, Amanda, this is so pretty," Sue exclaimed as she stepped inside. "And look, George, your bathroom is right down there in the corner."

"There's a shower also, George," Amanda said.

"What about furniture?" George asked.

"We'll bring whatever is at my house. Whatever you need," Amanda assured him.

"Maybe this won't be as bad as I thought," George said, dropping his arm heavily onto Sue's shoulders.

"Where are you going to stay?" Sue asked Amanda.

"I think I'll take the baby nursery. It's not as large as this room, but it's cozy."

"Let's go see," Sue said excitedly as she stepped out the door.

Amanda followed Sue to the door directly across from the steps they had descended into the basement. "This room," she told her friend.

Sue walked into the bright yellow room with powder blue carpet, but stopped halfway in. "Oh."

"What?" Amanda asked, looking to see what the problem was. "Oh."

"Where is everybody?" called Gloria from the end of the hallway.

"Come on. Gloria can't see this," Amanda whispered as she grabbed Sue's arm and quickly turned the light off and closed the door.

"Why?" Sue asked.

"Don't ask," Amanda whispered. "We're right here, Gloria. Like your rooms?"

"Sure do. It's going to be so cozy in there," Gloria said. "Is this your room?"

"Yes, but I want to do some work on it before anybody sees it, okay?" Amanda stood in front of the door.

"Well, okay, I guess." Gloria wasn't sure what was going on with Amanda, but she didn't question her any further.

"Let's go get the first load," George shouted.

"Sounds good," David said. "How about we move the beds and bring some food first. That way if we do run out of time before curfew we'll at least have something to eat and something to sleep on."

"You're so smart." Gloria patted her husband on the chest.

"Here's my keys, David," Amanda said. "Go ahead and start the car, I'll be right out."

"Don't make us late," George grumbled as the four tramped up the steps.

Making sure she was alone, Amanda stepped back into the nursery and quickly began picking up baby clothes, bottles and diapers. After stuffing everything into a cabinet, she looked around to make sure nothing else was lying around in plain sight.

Pulling the door shut, she dashed up the steps and out to the car, tired but excited that they would all be in a safer environment soon.

THIRTY-THREE

Captain Mercett was waiting next to the Jeff's desk when Jeff and Agent Wickes entered the command center near the end of their shift. The men marched across the floor and saluted.

"At ease, men." Captain Mercett sat on the corner of Jeff's desk.

"Is there a problem, sir?" Jeff asked.

"No, Agent Howard, just wanted to touch base with you before calling it a day."

"Everything quiet out there tonight?"

"Exceptionally so, sir," Jeff replied.

Captain Mercett picked up a bright blue and gold folder from Jeff's desk and began to thumb through it. Jeff was almost certain it contained his reports on Agent Wickes.

"I've spent some time going over your reports on Agent Wickes here," Captain Mercett began. "Seems as if you are well pleased with his performance."

"That I am, sir," Jeff said. "It is my opinion that Agent Wickes will be ready for his own squad any time you deem him to be ready, sir."

"Soon, Agent Howard," the captain said "Be in my office at 1430 hours tomorrow, Agent Wickes."

"Yes, sir," Agent Wickes said. Jeff didn't miss his smirky smile.

Both men snapped to attention. "Thank you, sir," they said in unison.

Captain Mercett turned. "Oh, by the way, Agent Howard, the utilities at your new home have been turned back on."

"Thank you, sir," Jeff said.

The squad members began filing in before Agent Wickes had an opportunity to ask questions, if he had any intentions to do so. Jeff suspected that his redheaded enemy knew as much about his life as anyone else.

Jeff finished up his reports in record time so he could escape the presence of squad members coming and going in the command center and the feeling of unseen eyes always watching him.

When Jeff arrived home, he quickly gathered some clothing, his mother's Bible, and his weapon and drove to Amanda's house where he planned to spend the night. Unlocking the door, he was shocked at the emptiness surrounding him.

"How did they move this much stuff so quickly?" he said out loud. After locking the door behind him, Jeff wandered through all the rooms to see what was left to move.

Returning to the living room area, Jeff sank onto the couch, thankful it hadn't moved. Sinking into the cushions, he laid his head on a pillow, pulling the throw over his tired body.

"God, thanks for being here for me today. I don't know how much longer I can do this, but I put my trust in you." A loud, long yawn made him realize how incredibly tired he was. "Please keep my friends safe."

Jeff's body refused to stay awake long enough to finish his prayer as he slipped into a deep, restful sleep.

Hearing the *beep, beep, beep, beep* of his watch's alarm, Jeff's eyes cracked open. *Where am I and why am I here?*

Finally sitting up, he looked around the room. *Oh, yeah.*

After showering and changing clothes, Jeff locked up and headed for the church building. He was apprehensive, almost fearful as he approached the side door of the building. Everything seemed dark and far too quiet.

Just as Jeff's key turned in the lock, the door popped open as George pushed against it. "Whoa!" George shouted.

"Good morning, George," Jeff said. "Going somewhere?"

"Uh, good morning. I was just going to take a security walk around the building."

"Not necessary. I checked as I came in," Jeff said as he stepped inside. "Something sure smells good."

"Gloria just called for breakfast," George said as he reluctantly led the way into the fellowship hall. "You've got good timing."

George had not been able to hide the look of disappointment on his face when his trek outside was halted. Jeff knew he and David would have to take action soon, possibly today.

"Good morning, Jeff," everyone called out.

"Amanda, I slept at your house last night. You people were able to move a lot more than I thought. I almost had to sleep on the floor," Jeff said as he slapped three pancakes onto his plate.

"Amanda's dad had a fairly large trailer behind the garage, so we were able to take large loads," David said.

"We have to clean out the kitchen, move the washer and dryer and the chest of drawers from each bedroom," Amanda said as she poured thick maple syrup over her one lonely pancake.

"Don't forget the TV," George spluttered through his mouthful of food.

"Yeah, don't forget the TV," Sue said, making circles in the air with her finger.

"I think we can get everything from Amanda's in one load," David said. "How much will you be taking from your house, Jeff?"

"No more than one load, probably," Jeff said. Just before putting the last of the pancakes in his mouth, he stopped. "Actually, you all need to look around my house and see if there's anything we can take that will be useful."

Amanda dried the soapy dishwater from her hands as she spoke. "We should get a move on so we can get everything moved today."

"You know what?" George huffed. "I'm really tired, so why don't you all go and load things up and I'll stay and clean up the kitchen. I'll help unload when you get back."

David glanced at Jeff quickly. "No way, George. These girls don't need to be lifting the heavy stuff."

"David's right, George," Jeff added. "It's just two loads at the most. Then we can sit back and rest awhile."

George roughly swiped his napkin across his mouth and slapped it down on the table causing his plate to bounce.

"Could you show me the trailer, David," Jeff asked, scooting his chair back from the table.

"Sure thing." David stood, taking his dirty dishes into the kitchen. After dropping the dishes into the soapy water, he put his arms around his wife and whispered into her ear, "Watch George around the phone." Giving her a kiss, he followed Jeff outside.

When both younger men stood beside the trailer, Jeff looked at David then turned his back.

"What is it, Jeff?" David said.

Taking a deep breath, Jeff turned back around to face his new friend. David saw tears threatening to spill from the younger man's eyes.

"You realize that something has to be done about George, right?" Jeff asked.

David nodded his head. "Yes, but what?"

"I need to tell you something about what happened here the other day," Jeff said, sitting on the edge of the trailer.

"You mean with all the blood?" David asked.

Jeff nodded his head. "I caught two boys in the sanctuary knocking over the pews, just like I said. When I walked in on them, they threatened to report me to Agent Wickes."

"The agent who's watching you?" David asked. "How did they know him?"

"Apparently he had hired them to vandalize this place and to report to him anything that I may or may not be doing."

"I see," David said.

"No, I don't think you do. Not yet anyway," Jeff said. He stood close to David so he wouldn't have to speak very loud.

"David, I had to use my weapon on them." Jeff's voice broke.

David put his arm around Jeff's shoulder. "There was no other way?"

Jeff shook his head. "I gave them every opportunity. I even tried to get the younger of the two to become a Christian. But they were hard, they were determined, they were out to destroy us all."

"Where did you hide the bodies?" David asked.

"You haven't seen one of our weapons work, have you?" Jeff asked as he pulled his handkerchief from his back pocket.

"No, can't say that I have."

"These weapons leave no trace of bodies. The boys were standing there and then they were gone."

David was quiet while his mind tried to comprehend how a weapon could possibly do such a thing. Only in science-fiction movies was anything like that possible.

Jeff straightened his shoulders with determination. He knew what had to be done if they were to survive for any time at all.

David looked up at Jeff's face and knew what was going to have to happen. "When and where?" he asked.

"We've got to get him away from the others long enough to get the job done."

At just that moment, George and the ladies walked through the door, ready to go for the first load of furniture and appliances.

"I'll drive my truck also. That way we can load extras," Jeff said, opening the door and sliding into his vehicle.

"Opportunities will come," David called. A huge smile spread across his face.

"What are you talking about?" Gloria giggled.

David patted her thigh. "Opportunities."

THIRTY-FOUR

"Whew. Am I ever tired," Gloria said as they all sat around a table in the fellowship hall.

"Me too," Sue added. "But isn't it amazing what we've accomplished in such a short time?"

"Short time," George grumbled. "This has taken hours."

"We've not only moved everything, but we've got all of it put away except the food and hooking up the washer and dryer," Amanda said.

"Tell you what," Jeff said. "While you girls put away the food, George, David and I will make one more trip to each house just to take a look around for anything we might have missed that is usable."

"Good idea," David said. He knew full well what this last trip would entail.

"That sounds great," Sue said. "When you get back we'll have food ready. I'll fix everything this time, okay, Gloria?"

"I'd love a break, Sue. Thank you."

"Here's my keys," Amanda said, handing her father's key ring to Jeff.

When the men were loaded into Amanda's car, Jeff kept the gear shift in the "park" position. "Hang on a minute, guys, I need to use the boys' room real quick. Be right back."

George huffed and puffed in the back seat. "Why couldn't he have done that first?"

Jeff ran back into the fellowship hall, startling the ladies.

"Amanda, I need to talk to you real quick," Jeff said, grabbing her hand and leading her into the foyer.

"Anything wrong?" she managed to ask before he led her into the men's restroom.

"Amanda, David and I will not be returning with George," he simply stated.

"Oh." Amanda's eyes blinked. *Oh, no.*

"I don't know if there's any way you can prepare Sue or not, but could you try?"

Amanda was touched by the pain she saw in Jeff's eyes. She had no idea how things were going to happen, but she knew it was going to be difficult for Jeff.

"We'll try," she said, reaching up to touch his cheek.

Jeff grabbed her and hugged her to his chest as if trying to gain some strength from her. Almost as quickly, he released her and reached for the door.

"Gotta go before George suspects something."

"We'll be praying for you," Amanda called softly to Jeff's back as he ran out the door.

Taking a deep breath and rubbing her hands down the sides of her jean clad legs, Amanda reentered the fellowship hall.

"Everything all right?" Sue asked.

"Yeah, he just needed some extra prayer."

Sue walked into the kitchen and began rummaging through boxes and bags of groceries. "I'll find something to cook while you two find places for all of this food."

"Sue, why don't you go ahead and find what you need while Gloria and I go into the sanctuary and pray for a few minutes. Then we'll come back and start putting all the food away."

"Sounds great," Sue said happily.

Gloria followed Amanda into the sanctuary where they sat on the front pew. Gloria's heart was beating faster than usual as fearful thoughts raced through her mind.

"Amanda, what is it?" she whispered.

"Oh, Gloria," Amanda said. "We've got to pray for Jeff and David.

Gloria grabbed Amanda's arm. "Why, what going on?"

Amanda patted Gloria's hand, trying to calm her. Whispering, she told Gloria what Jeff had shared with her.

"What did he mean by not coming back with George?" Gloria said out loud.

"Sh-h-h! Gloria, we haven't shared with you what's been going on," Amanda whispered. "But, George has been trying to sneak and use the phone. We've managed to stop him so far."

"Why would he want to sneak and use the phone?" Gloria asked.

"We believe he is a spy and plans to turn us in to the authorities."

Gloria gasped. "No! Are you sure?"

"As sure as we can be. And we can't afford to take that chance," Amanda said softly.

"So what are Jeff and David going to do?" Gloria's heart continued to race.

"I don't know, nor do I want to know," Amanda said. "We've got to find a way to somehow prepare Sue."

"Oh, Sue." Gloria's hand covered her mouth. "Amanda, how will we ever do that?"

"First of all, we're going to pray," Amanda said. "I don't know if you've noticed how George treats Sue."

"Yes, but..."

"I think Sue is ready for George to be gone. And I think Sue is close to becoming a Christian."

"But I thought they were Christians already." Gloria was shocked to think that the other couple had lied about that.

"They have lied to us from the start, but Sue has come to trust us," Amanda whispered. "So, let's pray for our guys and let's pray for Sue."

Dropping to their knees at the altar, both Amanda and Gloria cried out to God to give David and Jeff the courage and protection they needed. And they prayed for Sue that she would become a Christian and that the news about her husband would be cushioned somehow.

"Hey, girls," Sue called from the sanctuary doors. "I can't find..."

Gloria and Amanda had just finished praying when Sue burst through the door.

"Oh, my, I am so sorry," Sue cried.

"That's okay, Sue," Amanda assured her. "We just finished and were coming back to help you."

Seeing both other women drying their eyes, Sue slowly walked toward them, holding a wooden spoon in one hand. "What's wrong? Something's going on that I need to know about, isn't there?"

"Oh, Sue," Gloria said, walking up and hugging her.

"What? What's going on?" Sue said, pulling back from Gloria.

"Come, sit up here with us for a minute, Sue," Amanda said.

"Okay, I'm scared now. Tell me what's going on," Sue said, sitting between Gloria and Amanda.

"First of all, let me ask you something," Amanda began.

"What?" Sue's voice had taken on an edge.

"Sue, are you a Christian?"

Sue's eyes were large as she looked at Amanda, then at Gloria. So suddenly that it startled both of them, her whole body seemed to wilt. Her head dropped, her arms hung loosely, the wooden spoon fell from her hand.

Taking deep gasps between words, Sue managed to say, "How...did...you...find...out?"

Gloria's arm went around Sue, her other hand clasped her arm. "It's okay, Sue, we're not angry with you. It's okay, really."

"Can you tell us about it?" Amanda asked, patting Sue on the knee and handing her a fist full of tissues.

"I am so ashamed," she finally whispered.

"There's no need to be, Sue," Gloria comforted her. "Just try to tell us what's going on. We're all in this thing together anyway."

With a strangled laugh, Sue said, "I guess we are at that."

"We're your friends, Sue. It would help us tremendously to hear your story," Amanda said.

"It's not a very pretty story," Sue said.

"So," Amanda said.

Sue took a deep breath, wiped her face one more time, stood and began pacing. "No, George and I are not Christians. Well, actually, when I was a little girl, I went forward at vacation Bible school with a bunch of other little kids, but I didn't say anything when they asked us to pray. I got pregnant when I was sixteen. My parents made me give my baby away. I never even had the chance to see it or hold it. I don't even know if it was a boy or a girl."

Gloria's eyes immediately filled with fresh tears. One hand automatically covered her stomach.

"George worked with my father in the foundry. His first wife had died two years before. My dad talked George into marrying me. I tried to be a good wife, but he always treated me like trash. Anyway, after all these years, I finally decided to get out, to get a divorce. We were within days of the divorce being final when all of this happened." Sue's arms flew out.

"George and I had one son. Believe it or not, my son grew up and became a missionary. He and his family were home from South Africa for a month when this happened. I had gone to church with them that Sunday morning. All of a sudden they were gone. My son, my two grandsons, my daughter-in-law. All gone!"

Sue's sobs echoed through the sanctuary as they all cried together. Unseen by any of the ladies, David and Jeff had slipped into the back pew. Both men had their handkerchiefs out dabbing at their eyes.

Contempt, like venom dripping from exposed fangs, dampened each word of Sue's story. "When I finally arrived back home, George was there. He took great pleasure in letting me know that the divorce was now null and void. He could have cared less that our family was gone. He refused to leave, telling me that he was now working for the new government and I either had to do what he said or else."

At this point, Sue looked up and saw David and Jeff. Terrified that George was lurking nearby listening to her confession caused her to crumble onto the floor. Gloria and Amanda, unaware that David and Jeff had returned, fell to their knees beside her.

"Sue! Sue!" Gloria called, patting Sue's cheek.

"I'll get a wet towel," Jeff called, running toward the kitchen.

Amanda's body jerked around in blind fear, unprepared to hear a male voice.

"It's okay, Amanda, we've been back for a while," David said, touching her shoulder and reaching out to Gloria.

"You two scared me to death," Amanda exclaimed.

"I know, and I'm sorry. We didn't want to interrupt her," David said as he felt Sue's wrist for a pulse.

Jeff ran back down the aisle with the cold, wet towel which he handed to Gloria.

"Oh, Jeff," Amanda cried as she grabbed his hand.

Sue's eye lids began to flutter when the cold cloth touched her forehead. Gloria continued to pat her hands.

"Sue, it's Gloria," she said softly. "Everything's okay, Sue. George isn't here."

Sue's eyes opened wide, looking around the group that clustered around her.

"Where is he?" she rasped.

"He's not here right now. You're safe, you don't have to worry," Jeff said gently.

With Gloria and David's help, Sue was able to get up and sit back on the pew. "Guess I'm making a habit of this fainting thing." She softly giggled.

"You keep this up, I'm going to have a heart attack," Gloria laughed.

"Do you feel like finishing your story?" Amanda asked, holding Sue's hand.

"You sure George won't hear me?" Sue asked, looking from Jeff to David.

"Absolutely," Jeff said.

"Oh, my," Sue started. "Where was I?"

"George had returned to your house after the rapture," Amanda refreshed her memory.

"Oh, yeah," Sue continued. "I was terrified of him. I was terrified of what had happened. I was terrified of the government. George was always threatening to turn me in if I didn't go along with what he wanted. He came home one day and told me that we had been given a new assignment. There was this group of people hanging around what used to be a church. These people were involved in suspicious activities. George and I were to infiltrate this group and report everything to the authorities. We had two weeks to collect information and relay it to George's boss, whoever that was."

"So here we are." Jeff sat on the pew behind Sue.

"Yes, here we are," Sue said, covering her face with her hand. "I am so, so very sorry."

Amanda looked back at Jeff, hoping there was some way to give Sue hope, even though Amanda knew George was now out of the picture.

Uncomfortable, tattered moments passed before Jeff and David sat where they could look face to face with Sue.

"Sue, we need to tell you something," Jeff said quietly.

Dropping her hands into her lap, Sue looked at Jeff, noting his sad eyes. "What? Has George finally turned us in?"

"No, Sue, we didn't give him the opportunity," David said.

"What do you mean?" Sue asked.

Taking a deep, ragged breath, Jeff told Sue what had transpired just under an hour before. "David, myself, and Amanda have been keeping our eyes on George because he had been acting suspiciously. Amanda even caught him trying to use the telephone at two o'clock in the morning."

Sue looked at Amanda who dropped her eyes as she toyed with the wet towel.

"We knew that if we didn't take action today, it would be over for all of us," Jeff continued.

"And?" Sue's eyes grew wide.

"Sue, George will no longer be a threat to us, to you or to anyone else."

It took several seconds, but she finally whispered, "You mean…"

"Yes, Sue, George took a nasty fall down the basement steps at my house and broke his neck. I'm sorry."

Silence echoed through the sanctuary. Suddenly a snicker sounded from Sue. "Oh, my," she giggled. "Oh, my. Oh, my. Oh, my." She laughed, jumping up and giving Jeff, David and the ladies big hugs.

"Well, that was easier than I expected," Jeff said.

"Just one more thing," Sue said, plopping down on the pew again.

"What's that?" Jeff asked.

"I want to know how to become a Christian. I want to see my son, my grandchildren, and my daughter-in-law again," she cried. Turning to Gloria, she asked, "Gloria, you show me how, will you?"

Tears ran down Gloria's cheeks as she nodded her head, unable to speak for a few minutes.

"Let's kneel, okay?" Gloria slipped to her knees. When everyone else was lined up on their knees, Gloria began. "Sue, the Bible says that if we believe in our hearts that God raised Jesus from the dead, we will be saved. Do you believe that?"

"Yes, I do," Sue said. "My son explained all of this to me, but I thought I had plenty of time."

"Great." Gloria continued. "Then all you have to do is pray and ask Jesus to forgive your sins and come into your heart to be your Savior, your Redeemer."

Nodding her head, Sue closed her eyes and began the prayer that would change her life for eternity. "Jesus, I am so sorry for my life, for the terrible sinful life I have led. I know you died for me. I know your blood was shed for me. Please come into my heart and save me. Forgive my sins and make me yours. Thank you, Jesus. Thank you. Amen."

Lots of hugging and crying went on before Jeff thought to look at his watch.

Sitting back on his haunches, he said, "I've only got an hour before I have to leave for work."

"I've got some food ready. Will you have time to eat?" Sue said.

"Thanks, Sue, but I really don't think I want to eat right now. I still have to write up a report on George's accident."

"What do you mean?" Amanda asked, thinking the guys had somehow already disposed of George's body.

"Since we suspected that George was a plant to spy on us, we had to think of a way to get rid of him and make it look like an accident," David said.

"And?"

"Like I said, he took a nasty fall down the basement steps."

"And?"

"Okay. Okay. Since I'm certain my house is bugged, I planned it so his accident would be in my house so they'd hear it happen. We called the ambulance and the W.S.F. agents on duty. They took the body away but I told the W.S.F. guys that'd I'd write up a report and personally give it to Captain Mercett."

"Do you think he'll believe you?" Amanda asked.

"That's what I've been praying," Jeff said.

"Let's pray again," Sue said. "And I'll go first." Her excitement seemed to be bubbling over everywhere.

"How can we refuse such an offer?" David smiled.

All ten knees touched the carpeted floor one more time as Sue began entreating God to protect the man who had murdered George. "Please, God, protect Jeff and David, who were protecting the rest of us."

Fifteen minutes later, the group walked out of the sanctuary together, no longer carrying the heavy burden of fear and guilt.

"I'm going to change for work and go in early," Jeff said as everyone else headed for the fellowship hall. "Make sure all the doors are as secure as possible when I leave."

As Jeff showered and pulled on his blue and gold uniform, troubling thoughts kept racing through his mind. "God, your Word says not to kill, that murderers won't go to Heaven. Today made three that I have killed. How will I know I'll be allowed in Heaven? How will I know?"

THIRTY-FIVE

Even though Jeff was certain Captain Mercett knew exactly what had transpired, he went through the motions as if he were still one of the World Security Forces topnotch agents.

Three sharp raps announced his presence at the captain's door; Jeff snapped to attention when Captain Mercett opened the door himself.

"Agent Howard," Mercett said, feigning surprise. "Now, what can I do for you?" He perched on the edge of his desk.

Jeff handed a shiny blue and gold folder to his superior officer. "This is a report, sir, of an incident which took place in my home today."

"An incident?"

"Yes, sir." Jeff continued, "One of the men in the group that has been moving into the church building fell down my basement steps and died."

"You don't say?" Captain Mercett opened the folder as he walked behind his desk. Sitting down, he began to read the report.

"Sit," he ordered Jeff.

His back stiff as a board, Jeff waited patiently for Captain Mercett to finish reading.

"I see," Captain Mercett said, laying the folder to one side. "Too bad, but accidents will happen. Are you and your friends all moved?"

"Yes, sir," Jeff answered. "Tonight will be my first night with them. I will probably sleep in what used to be the sanctuary so I'll know immediately if any of them decide to meet."

"Is your group aware of the 'no funeral' policy?" Captain Mercett asked.

"I don't think so, sir," Jeff said. "I intend to advise them first thing in the morning."

"Good," Captain Mercett said. "And you're clear on the immediate consequences if they try to have any type of service?"

"Absolutely, sir," Jeff said, standing. "That's exactly why I asked permission to move into the facility with them, sir."

"Very good, Agent Howard," Mercett said. "Keep me informed. Dismissed."

Jeff saluted, spinning toward the door. "Thank you, sir."

Jeff walked onto the gymnasium floor to find his squad in the process of lining up for inspection. His redheaded nemesis stood facing the squad, ready to replace him.

"Thank you, Agent Wickes." Jeff nodded slightly toward his enemy. In a quiet voice he added, "Continue with the inspection."

The last half-hour had nearly depleted his reserve of self-control, therefore his entire body burned with rage as he watched Russell Wickes' galling smirk.

To distract himself, he moved to the side of his squad to watch each line of agents as they awaited Wickes inspection. As Wickes walked between the back two rows, he halted in front of a tall, slim, exceptionally pretty, blond female.

Jeff watched Wickes leer at the young lady as if he were going to devour her. Checking his clip board, he eyed her salaciously and said, "Agent Summers, make sure you check your duty schedule at the beginning of the week."

"Yes, sir," the young lady said, swallowing hard.

Jeff walked to the front of his squad and waited for the exact second that Agent Wickes stepped out of the last row.

"Dismissed to your units." The young, blond girl was the first to exit the building.

Agent Wickes placed the clip board onto Jeff's desk and boldly looked directly at him with his wide, ugly smile.

Jeff slammed his hand onto a blue and gold folder, shoving it across his desk. "Agent Wickes, you have performed in an exemplary manner during your training period. Now would be a good time to refresh yourself in the chapter on leadership obligations. When you have reviewed that particular chapter we will discuss it and I will add my findings to your progress report."

"Sir?" Shock removed Wickes' smirk.

"Are you questioning me, Agent Wickes?" Jeff asked, menacingly.

Wickes snapped his heels together and sucked in his breath. "No, sir."

"I didn't think so," Jeff continued. "It is my responsibility to be one hundred percent certain that you are going to be one of our topnotch agents. Each of us has at least one weak area, and I don't want any little mistakes to ruin your career."

"Yes, sir," Wickes barked.

"Let's go to work," Jeff said, snapping his briefcase shut and walking quickly to the door.

Agent Wickes gave a long look upward toward the dark window of Captain Mercett's office. Jeff knew that would occur, but at this point he didn't care. In fact, it was becoming clear to him that at some point Agent Wickes might have to have an accident.

God, please help me.

THIRTY-SIX

After breakfast the next morning, the residents of what used to be Woodville Baptist Church, gathered in the front of the sanctuary to discuss their futures and to pray. Even though Jeff considered them to be safe from unseen ears or eyes for now, he knew he would have to be constantly on guard.

"Right now we have a good supply of food and cleaning supplies, but we will need to consider our options for the weeks and months to come. We probably need to consider finding jobs," David told the group.

"You're right, David," Jeff said. "We have to be able to provide for ourselves and those others who will find their way here for safety."

"How will we know whom we can trust?" Gloria asked.

"So far we've been able to sort of just know," Amanda said.

"If any one of us suspects anything at all, we need to share that with each other right away," David said.

"I really am a nurse, so I can try to get a job at a doctor's office or at one of the hospitals," Sue said.

"That's great, Sue," Amanda said. "Do you think I could do something there too, even though I didn't get the chance to graduate?"

"As soon as I find a job, I'll ask," Sue said.

"We won't lack transportation for a while," David said with a smile. "We've got our pick of cars and trucks in the parking lot."

"The money situation will change sometime soon, remember?" Amanda said.

"For now we're okay with that," Jeff said. "But when the time comes when we're ordered to take the mark, everything will change."

"The mark?" Sue asked.

"The Bible calls it the *mark of the beast,*" David said.

"You'll have to tell me what that is," Sue said with fear in her eyes. "I've never heard about it."

"It's a mark of some kind that we'll be asked to take on our hand or our foreheads. We will not be able to buy or sell anything without it," Amanda said.

"Why shouldn't we take it?"

"If we take the mark, we won't belong to God any longer," David said.

"Even if we're already Christians?" Sue couldn't believe what she was hearing.

"Even if we're Christians," Amanda said.

"But how will we survive?" Her voice took on an edge of fear.

"We won't. Not for long anyway," Jeff said.

All five sat quietly as the ramifications of not taking the mark became clear to them.

"So," Sue began, "in the meantime we'll need to save all our money so we'll have plenty when that time comes, right?"

When all eyes turned to look at her, she knew the answer would not be good.

"That won't work, Sue," David said.

"Our money will no longer be any good at that point," Amanda added.

"Well, I know what we can do then," Gloria said.

"What's that, honey?" David asked his wife.

"Instead of saving the money, we'll use what we make now to buy food and supplies that we can store for our needs at that time."

"That's a wonderful idea, Gloria," Sue said. "That makes a lot more sense."

"Yes, it does," Jeff said. "But, we have to always be aware that life is not going to be easy. We can never let our guard down, not for a second. At any time, any one of us can be arrested. Any one of us can disappear. And if that happens, those of us that are left have to be even more careful."

Again, everything became quiet.

"Okay, here's the plan," Amanda said. "Tomorrow morning, those of us who want to look for jobs will leave following breakfast and try to be back here before Jeff leaves for work. Agreed?"

"Agreed," Sue said.

"Would anyone be disappointed if I stay here as chief cook and bottle washer, so to speak?" Gloria tried to smile.

"I don't have a problem with that," David said.

"Me either," Sue added.

"Besides, we need someone here to keep watch for any others who may come by looking for a place to stay," Amanda said.

"Sounds like a plan," Jeff said. "I think today we might as well settle into our rooms and just kick back for a while.

"Could I ask one thing of you guys?" Gloria asked, looking at Jeff and David.

"Just one?" David laughed.

"For now." Gloria smiled. "Do you think we could get the washer and dryer hooked up today?"

"Guess what I found last night?" David said.

"What?"

"I was looking around the basement and found where a hookup for a washer and dryer had been installed not too long ago," David said, standing.

"You're kidding?" Gloria cried. "Thank you, Jesus."

"They must have done that when they built the apartment you two are in," Jeff said.

"So, Gloria, yes we'll get the washer and dryer hooked up today," David said, taking his wife's hand and leading her out of the sanctuary.

Gloria turned back and called to Amanda, "Amanda, I'll be glad to help you in your room."

"Uh...how about giving me about an hour first," Amanda said. "Then if I still need help, I'll yell."

When David and Gloria made their way down the steps into the basement, Jeff looked at Amanda. "What was that all about?"

"I chose the church nursery for my room," Amanda said.

"I was going to ask you about that," Sue said. "Why didn't you want Gloria to see your room earlier?"

"Oh," Jeff said, suddenly remembering.

"Sue, Gloria was pregnant when the rapture happened," Amanda whispered.

"What happened to her baby?" Sue exclaimed.

"Sh-h-h!" Amanda placed her finger across her lips. "When the rapture happened, all babies everywhere, even those not yet born were taken to Heaven with Jesus."

Sue sat in stunned silence, looking into Amanda's eyes as if her mind was trying to comprehend what she'd just heard.

"How could that be?" she finally asked.

Amanda shook her head. "I don't understand it either. But Gloria told us that the baby was gone, just gone."

"Oh, how awful," Sue said. "I know how I felt when my baby was given to someone else and when the rest of my family was taken in the rapture, but how awful to have a baby disappear from your stomach." Her hand covered her own stomach.

"I'm going to help David with the washer and dryer," Jeff said, walking toward the sanctuary doors.

"And I'm going to clear George's things from my room," Sue said.

"Are you really okay with George being gone, Sue?" Amanda asked, truly concerned for her new friend.

"Yes," Sue said. "Amanda, living with him was pure hell. I feel like a brand-new person since I've asked Jesus to come into my heart. And knowing that I don't have to face George any longer gives me peace."

"Okay, let's get busy," Amanda said as they walked out of the sanctuary together.

Forty-five minutes later, Amanda had stuffed all the baby items into trash bags and set them in the hallway for the men to carry outside. She managed to push her bed and chest of drawers into the spots she thought looked the most comfortable. Jeff had also brought an easy chair, floor lamp and a set of bookshelves down to her room.

After placing the black trash bags into the hallway, Amanda left her door open. Looking around with satisfaction at her finished work, she plopped down into the easy chair. Looking up she saw Gloria smiling at her from the doorway.

"Come in, Gloria," she said.

"Wow. It looks really pretty in here," Gloria said. "Who's class was this? It's so bright and cherry."

Pursing her lips, Amanda decided to tell her the truth and get it out in the open. "This was the church nursery," she said gently, watching Gloria carefully.

Gloria's hand automatically went to her stomach. "Oh."

Amanda was pleasantly surprised when no tears spilled from Gloria's eyes. Her friend slowly sat on a padded stool which was shoved against the opposite wall.

"Someone certainly chose good colors for a nursery," Gloria said, looking around. "Who would ever have thought that powder blue carpet would look so good with daffodil-yellow walls? It must have been comforting for little ones in here."

"Are you doing okay, Gloria?" Amanda asked.

"Yes, I think I'm doing better. I just keep telling myself that my baby is safe and I'm going to be with him soon."

"Obviously, I don't have a clue what you've gone through, but I certainly do admire you," Amanda said.

"I try not to think too far ahead. I just wish we could all go without having to face what we're going to have to," Gloria said sadly.

"Me too," David said, walking into Amanda's room and sitting on the floor next to his wife.

"It's going to be really bad, isn't it?" Sue asked, entering the room right behind David.

"According to those books," Amanda said, pointing to her father's books which were stacked neatly on her bookshelves, "we can't even imagine how bad."

Sue sat on Amanda's bed as she talked. "When I think about it, I get so scared I almost get sick."

"What scares me the most is the realization that we can't go anywhere to escape what's happening," Amanda said.

"I'm afraid you're right about that," David said. "We've now got less than seven years to try to survive."

"Do you think we'll be able to?" Gloria asked, looking down at her husband.

David shook his head slowly. "I don't see how, but knowing what we're facing gives us an edge even though being Christians certainly puts us in greater danger."

Jeff, dressed in his beautiful uniform, stood in the doorway of Amanda's room. "I'm leaving. David, will you lock up behind me?"

David followed Jeff to the door. "We'll be praying for your safety, Jeff."

"That's good to know because every day it gets more and more difficult to play the part of a good, committed World Security Force agent. I know I'm being watched closely."

"Jeff, what do we do if someone knocks on the door while you're gone?" Amanda asked.

"Let David answer the door," Jeff advised. "If David thinks it's okay, all of you meet with the person and try to get a good feel for their sincerity."

Amanda followed Jeff up the steps, with David right behind. When they reached the door, Jeff turned to speak to his friends, looking mainly into Amanda's eyes. "Every time I leave here in this uniform, it could be my last. I can no longer promise that I'll return. You understand that, right?"

Amanda's eyes became moist as she nodded her head. "What will we do if you should not come back?"

"We'll talk about that tomorrow, okay?" Jeff said, reaching out to touch Amanda's face.

"Which means you'll be coming back tonight," Amanda said with hope shining in her eyes.

"I'll certainly do my best." Jeff leaned over and kissed Amanda's lips before turning to walk out the door.

David immediately locked the door behind Jeff. "Too bad we don't have a peephole in this plywood."

Amanda leaned her forehead against the door. "You know, it'd be real easy to get depressed."

"Come on, let's go back and join the girls," David said, putting his arm around Amanda's shoulder. "We need each other to keep from sinking too deep in despair. Too much is at stake."

"Yeah, you're right," Amanda said, bouncing down the steps.

THIRTY-SEVEN

Jeff arrived at his desk fifteen minutes early to make certain everything was in order before his squad arrived. Glancing up from his records, he saw Agent Wickes walking toward him from the direction of the captain's office.

"Agent Wickes," Jeff acknowledged his enemy's presence.

"Agent Howard, I've been asked to inform you that Captain Mercett would like a word with you before we leave on patrol," Wickes said with his usual wicked smile.

"Thank you," Jeff said, keeping his face blank. "I want you to be in charge of inspection again today."

"Yes, sir," Agent Wickes said, obviously disappointed that Jeff didn't seem to be worried about meeting with their superior officer.

Jeff was pleased that his enemy had not yet mastered the art of hiding his thoughts and feelings behind an expressionless composure. During his years of high school training, Jeff had become proficient at that very thing.

Jeff stood to one side again, watching Agent Wickes as he went through the inspection process. Jeff watched closely as he inspected the back row where the young, blond female agent stood.

Agent Wickes ended his inspection without as much as a nod in the female's direction. Jeff knew she was frightened when he saw the legs of her uniform tremble as Wickes walked past her.

After the squad had been dismissed, Agent Wickes stood facing Jeff's desk, awaiting his own instructions.

Purposely, Jeff took his time getting his records in order before standing. "I don't know how long my interview will be with Captain Mercett, so why don't you go ahead and start patrolling. I'll radio you when I'm ready."

"Yes, sir," Agent Wickes said, spinning around and quickly walking from the building.

Picking up his notebook, Jeff made his way to Captain Mercett's door.

"Enter," he heard from behind the door.

Jeff stepped into the office and saluted. "Sir."

"Have a seat, Agent Howard," his superior officer said, not rising from his own chair.

"Thank you, sir," Jeff said, sitting on the edge of the offered chair.

"I won't keep you long, Agent Howard," Mercett began. "Just a couple things I want to go over with you."

"Is there a problem, sir?" Jeff asked.

"Let's hope not," Captain Mercett said, picking up a blue and gold folder. "It has come to my attention that two teenage boys were seen hanging around your present living quarters. Do you know anything about them?"

"Two teenage boys?" Jeff said, acting as if he were trying to remember. "Yes, sir. If they are the same ones you're asking about, I had an incident at the former church building one morning last week involving two boys."

"Is there some reason I haven't received a report from you in reference to that incident?"

At this point, it was taking every ounce of control Jeff could muster. "Sir, I ran into the boys before I was on duty, fairly early in the day. And the incident wasn't serious enough to warrant a report."

"Give me the details and I will make that determination." Captain Mercett's voice no longer held any hint of kindness.

"I had discovered vandalism at the former church building two days earlier. On that particular morning, I stopped at the building to see what supplies would be necessary to make the needed repairs."

"I've seen no vandalism reports either."

"No, sir. Up to that point, it was just an unused church building. It wasn't until this group of people began to inquire about living there, that I thought I'd check on supplies for the clean up process," Jeff said, standing.

"Continue," Captain Mercett said.

"I walked into the building and found two young men pushing over pews and generally making a mess. I advised them to leave. One of the young men tripped and fell, hitting his head on one of the pews. I assisted him in cleaning himself up. I found a first aid kit, patched a cut on his forehead and sent them on their way."

"That's it?" Captain Mercett asked, not sure whether to believe Jeff or not.

"Yes, sir. In no way did I consider the incident worthy of a report. They were just boys having fun, sir. May I ask why this is a problem now, sir?"

"Apparently, two teenage boys last seen in the vicinity of the old church building have not been seen for several days."

"I can assure you, sir, when I sent them on their way they were fine. I suppose it's possible that they may have gotten into some kind of difficulty later at another place, but I can't really say, sir." Jeff tried to sound truly concerned for the welfare of the boys.

"Give me your weapon, Agent Howard," Mercett ordered.

Without hesitation, Jeff handed his weapon to his superior officer with great care.

Jeff knew the weapon would show that it had been used exactly two times.

When Captain Mercett turned the weapon over to inspect the digital gauge, he looked across the desk at Jeff. "Can you explain this?"

"Yes, sir," Jeff said with confidence. Jeff dropped his head, trying to look embarrassed. "I suppose you only want the truth, sir."

Captain Mercett, certain that he had finally entrapped Jeff, walked around his desk and sat on the edge of it. "Agent Howard, I will only hear the truth," he barked.

Taking a deep breath, Jeff began, "Sir, during my years in training, I became an expert marksman, the top in my class."

"That's a matter of record, it has nothing to do with today," Mercett said.

"When the World Security Force became active, sir, I took great pride in patrolling alongside my squad. During the first week, we had to use lethal force almost every shift, unlike now when everyone pretty much knows the rules. As I watched my squad members perform their duties in eradicating curfew violators, I was a bit envious but I found that I was also embarrassed to realize that I didn't know how I would react if I had to actually use my weapon on a real person."

"So?" Captain Mercett asked roughly.

"Sir...oh, man, this is so embarrassing, but you want the truth," Jeff said, pleased by his acting abilities. "I used my weapon the first time on a stupid cat. The second time, when no one was around, I used it on a cow."

"You expect me to believe this crap?" Mercett's face turned red with anger.

"No, sir, I suppose I don't expect you to believe something so juvenile. I've never been so embarrassed in my whole life. But, sir, it is the truth."

Captain Mercett walked around the desk and sat down without saying anything. Finally looking up at Jeff, he said in a calmer voice, obviously trying to control himself, "Did it work?"

"Yes, sir, I believe it did," Jeff said, looking directly at Captain Mercett. "Sir, I have no doubt now that I would use my weapon on a person should it become necessary, sir."

"So you're telling me that you didn't see these boys again, nor did you annihilate them?"

"No, sir," Jeff stated emphatically. "I would definitely have written a report if that had occurred, sir. In fact, I would have also given you a verbal report on an incident such as that."

Using the tips of his fingers, Captain Mercett rubbed circles across his forehead as he contemplated whether to believe Jeff's story. Other than suspicions, negative reports from Agent Wickes, Captain Mercett still had no hard facts that Jeff was anything other than a topnotch agent.

"Canvas the neighborhood. See if you can find out if anyone has seen the boys." Captain Mercett tossed two pictures across the desk at Jeff.

Jeff picked up the pictures, studying them intently, hoping to give his superior officer confidence that he had told him the truth. Turning the pictures over, he read their names on the backs.

"That's them," Jeff said. "I think they used to go to church out there, sir."

Tired of the way this meeting had gone, Captain Mercett moved on to the next issue at hand. "I also want you to take Agent Wickes with you to Bedford and watch the construction on the courthouse square. After inspection tomorrow, return to my office with Agent Wickes and we'll discuss it."

"Yes, sir," Jeff said.

"Dismissed," Captain Mercett rasped.

Jeff saluted and quickly stepped from the office. On his way down the steps and across the wooden floor, Jeff radioed for Agent Wickes to pick him up.

While he waited, Jeff brushed his uniform legs with his hands, trying to hide any hint of his racing heart and his trembling legs.

Who in their right mind would ever believe such an incredibly stupid lie? God, you're the only One who can make Captain Mercett believe what he just heard.

Watching his shiny black SUV pulling up to the curb, Jeff purposely walked around to the driver's door and ordered Wickes to the passenger side.

Thirty minutes of patrolling passed without a single word being exchanged between Jeff and his enemy. Although Agent Wickes had been angry for being ordered out of the driver's seat, his annoying smirk soon settled onto his face as he assumed that things had gone badly in Jeff's interview.

"Agent Wickes," Jeff said sharply, startling Wickes.

"Sir?" he replied.

"We'll be finished with our first round of patrols in approximately thirty minutes. You and I will be taking a little trip to Bedford to observe a construction site on the courthouse lawn. Following tomorrow morning's inspection, we are to report to Captain Mercett's office for a debriefing on that construction." Jeff spoke crisply and quickly, not giving Wickes an opportunity to ask any questions or make any comments.

Wickes remained quiet.

"Did you understand me, Agent Wickes?" Jeff demanded.

"Yes, sir. I did, sir," Wickes replied.

Later, as they crossed the White River bridge, Agent Wickes asked Jeff, "Sir, could we stop and get some bottled water?"

"No," Jeff said. "We have to return in time for our last patrol."

A string of dark expletives sped through Wickes' mind. Venomous hate cursed through his body.

Although Jeff couldn't see his face, he could almost smell the hate radiating from Wickes. From the corner of his eye, he saw Wickes' hand move to his right side where his weapon sat snuggly in its holster.

Suddenly, without any warning, Jeff whipped the SUV around the corner onto 16th Street. The left tires of the SUV squalled as the right tires barely touched pavement. Wickes' seatbelt immediately jerked tightly, slapping him back into his seat.

"What the..." Wickes shouted a split second before the SUV bounced back on all four tires causing his head to smash into the passenger window.

"Sorry about that, Agent Wickes," Jeff shouted. "We're late so I have to hurry."

Rubbing the right side of his head, Wickes didn't notice the railroad tracks coming up quickly—too quickly. The SUV bounced violently across the tracks. One more time, Wickes' head hit the window.

Jeff jerked the SUV into a diagonal parking spot on the south side of the courthouse square, released his seatbelt and quickly stepped out of the vehicle, making his way to the front of the courthouse without looking back for Agent Wickes.

Stunned by the double head bashing, Agent Wickes' fingers had trouble finding the belt release button. Since the belt was taut, when his thumb did push down on the release, the belt flew across his body clanging into the window.

Wickes stumbled out of the vehicle, his vision blurred as he watched his mortal enemy move swiftly and smartly to stand with a small crowd of blue and gold clad men and women watching the construction proceeding.

"You will die for this." Wickes muttered under his breath as he managed to straighten his body and, with great effort, walk without staggering. In the last ten minutes, his hatred for Jeff Howard had multiplied one hundred fold.

NO! NO! No! Jeff's mind screamed when he was close enough to see what was being constructed. *It's too early for this. This can't begin so soon. Oh, please, God, NO!*

Agent Wickes was careful not to stand too close to Jeff. When his hate filled eyes looked up to see what the group of fellow agents were watching, he barely contained a *whoop!* Immediately his vision cleared.

"It's about time," he exclaimed.

"You think so?" asked another young man standing next to him.

"I was of the understanding that this would not be used for some time yet."

"Do you have a problem with it?" Agent Wickes asked with a superior attitude.

"No, sir," the young man quickly answered. "No, sir. It's obvious that we're going to need to use it much sooner than anticipated."

"I'm anxious to see this baby in action," another young agent said with a wide grin.

"Too bad we can't try it out today," Agent Wickes said, giving Jeff a sideways glance.

Jeff ignored him, his heart pounding as he watched the work progress on a double guillotine. Vigilantly keeping his fear buried, he reached into his pocket for a small notebook and pen.

Agent Wickes watched as Jeff drew several pictures of the structure. With bravado, bolstered by burning hatred, he stepped closer to watch the drawings unfold on the pages of Jeff's notebook.

"You going to build one at home, sir?" he asked with a laugh.

With utter control and without looking up from his drawings, Jeff replied, "This is amazing, Agent Wickes." He was rewarded by seeing his enemy actually jerk away. "This is truly amazing." With that he snapped his notebook shut and shoved it and the pen back into his pocket.

Looking at his watch, he announced, "We've just got time to make it back to Mitchell and complete our last patrol. Ready?" He didn't wait for an answer as he spun around and walked quickly to the SUV.

Wickes turned to follow but stopped for one last, long look at what he thought was the most beautiful structure he'd ever seen. Visions of Jeff Howard's head rolling down the chute caused his freckled face to break into an ear-to-ear smile which shot a sharp pain up the right side of his head.

At the end of their shift, Jeff dismissed Wickes, allowing him to go home to put ice on the large bump that protruded from the side of his head.

"Be ready for our debriefing after inspection in the morning," he called to his enemy as he walked toward the door.

When he finally finished compiling his squad's reports and sent them on to Captain Mercett's office computer with a touch of the SEND button, Jeff cautiously left the building and climbed into his truck.

My head may be the first to roll, but today was worth it. The pop of that redhead against the window was worth the whole day. Emotional fatigue caused his eyes to burn as he made his way to the parking lot of his new home.

Carefully locking the door behind him, Jeff went to his room, pulled out a blanket and pillow and returned to the foyer where he lay down in the floor in front of the door and immediately fell into an exhausted sleep.

Amanda, hearing the quiet click of the door followed by footsteps across the floor, quietly left her room and climbed the stairs to the foyer where she found Jeff already fast asleep even though he was still dressed in his uniform.

Using her small flashlight, she looked at Jeff's face, not missing the darkness under his eyes. Lovingly laying her hand against his cheek and kissing his forehead, she whispered, "What terrible thing happened to you today?"

Fearful of leaving Jeff alone in the dark, empty foyer, she sat next to him, praying.

"God, seeing Jeff like this scares me. Please help us."

Long after Jeff had fallen asleep, Amanda's eyelids could no longer win the battle with fatigue. Without blanket or pillow, she scooted down next to Jeff and fell asleep.

Many hours later, just before dawn, Jeff's eyes fluttered open. Although darkness permeated the foyer, Jeff's eyes could see a dark form lying next to him. Rising on an elbow, he could smell Amanda's freshly washed hair.

"Oh, Amanda, you shouldn't be here," he whispered. He softly touched her hair. "But I'm glad you are."

Not wanting the others to find them sleeping next to each other, Jeff placed a kiss on her head before draping the blanket over her and shoving his pillow close to her head.

Returning to his room, he removed the uniform he had grown to detest. "I used to be so proud of this, but now—" he said quietly as he tossed it into a corner. Lying on the bed, images of the horrible object he had seen a few hours earlier continued to trouble him.

"How can I tell the others? They'll be terrified," he said as he rolled over onto his side. Tears escaped his tightly squeezed eyes, dampening his bed as he cried, "Just like I'm terrified."

THIRTY-EIGHT

Although their apartment had a kitchenette, Gloria used the church's kitchen to cook for the group. On her way to the kitchen, her heart skipped a beat when she saw Amanda lying on the foyer floor covered with a blanket.

"Amanda," she cried, rushing over to her friend.

George's slime-covered bony hand had just closed around her throat. Hearing Gloria's cry, she immediately began gagging and coughing as she tossed off the blanket. "Aaugh."

"Amanda, what's wrong?" Gloria's voice echoed in the large room.

Amanda's hands grabbed at her own throat, trying to pull away bony, slimy fingers. Gloria's voice brought the light of reality into Amanda's eyes.

"Oh, Gloria," she cried, wrapping her trembling arms around her friend.

"What on earth is wrong, honey?" Gloria asked.

Hearing Gloria's cries, David and Jeff ran into the foyer.

"What's going on?" David demanded.

Amanda released her grip on Gloria and sat back on the floor, clasping her knees to her chest, lowering her head.

"Amanda?" Jeff asked, kneeling next to her.

Amanda's shoulders began to shake. Gloria placed her hand on Amanda's arm, thinking she was crying.

When Amanda lifted her head, everyone was surprised that she was laughing. "Oh, you guys, this is so silly."

"Are you okay?" Jeff asked.

"It's nothing, really," Amanda giggled. "Old George was choking me with his slimy, bony fingers, is all."

"George is back?" Sue gasped. No one had noticed Sue enter the room. Her hand automatically reached for her own throat.

Amanda immediately stopped giggling when she saw the terror in Sue's eyes. "No, Sue. It was a dream. Actually it was a nightmare."

"Well, you sure gave me a fright," Gloria said with a slight smile. "First I find you lying in the middle of the floor, then you start choking. Don't do that to me again, girl."

"I promise," Amanda said. "Sue, I'm so sorry. I was just having this awful nightmare about George."

"At least the *real* nightmare is over," Sue said. "I think you gave me a few more gray hairs, though."

Gloria laughed as she, Amanda and Jeff stood. "Come on, Sue. Help me with breakfast."

Jeff reached for Amanda's hand, pulling her close to his side. "You sure you're all right?"

"As well as can be expected," Amanda said with a smile on her lips, but with very sad eyes. Making sure everyone else had left the room, she asked, "What happened yesterday, Jeff? I've never seen you look like you did when I found you sleeping out here last night."

Jeff slumped onto the short pew that was pushed up against the foyer wall. Gripping her hand tightly, he pulled her down beside him. "Things out there are happening far too fast. After breakfast, I need to talk to all of you."

"You're scaring me, Jeff," Amanda's voice trembled.

"Good," Jeff said. "We need to be scared."

Amanda's fingers ached from the tight hold Jeff unknowingly had on them. "You're hurting me," she whispered.

"Oh, Amanda, I'm so sorry," Jeff immediately released his grip. Amanda saw tears glistening in his eyelashes and lovingly placed her other hand against his cheek. His head fell against her shoulder. "How I wish this was all over," he whispered.

Gloria's voice called out, "Breakfast is ready."

Jeff raised his head and looked into Amanda's eyes. "I realize that life is nowhere close to normal, but I think that I'm growing to love you more each day."

"Come on, I'm hungry," she said, jumping up and pulling on his hand to follow.

Sue and Gloria cooked a breakfast of pancakes, bacon, coffee, and orange juice. David pushed back from the table and announced, "That was marvelous, girls. How about I do the dishes before we all take off for job hunting?"

"Please, sit down, David," Jeff said, pushing his plate back. "We need to talk."

"You make it sound so serious," David said as he sat down and placed his hand over Gloria's.

"It is," Jeff stated simply. "I…I…" Jeff's shoulders sagged.

"Jeff, what is it?" Sue asked.

"I don't even know how to tell you without scaring you half to death."

"Just say it, my friend," David said. "It's obviously something we need to know."

Jeff automatically reached for Amanda's hand as he looked around the group. "Okay, the time has come to be open and honest about everything so that we all are prepared for whatever happens." He felt Amanda's hand tighten.

"David already knows part of this, but you girls need to know too. The boys that I found in here, the ones who left all the blood?" The women nodded their heads.

"One of them injured himself, just like I said. But they also bragged about how they were going to get paid for turning me in for what we are doing here."

"Oh, no," Sue said, covering her mouth with her hand.

"It's okay, they won't be turning anyone in. I gave them every chance, but finally had to use my weapon on them."

"You killed them?" Amanda exclaimed, slowly pulling her hand from Jeff's.

"I had to, Amanda," Jeff said. "David knows how our weapons work. When they're used, the target is annihilated. There's no body, no anything. Agent Wickes had hired the boys, so he apparently advised the captain that two boys had disappeared. Captain Mercett questioned me about them and checked my weapon."

"Why did he check your weapon?" David asked.

"There is a tiny readout located on the underside that records how many times the gun has been used. Mine recorded two."

"So, now what?" Amanda asked.

"I told him a really stupidly ignorant lie. But I believe it was so incredibly stupid that he believed it."

"You're kidding?" David said.

"I told him that after I watched some of my squad members use their weapons on curfew violators, I began to wonder whether I could actually use mine on a real person, even with all my training. So I had used it on a cat and later on a cow."

"And he believed that?" Amanda asked.

"Apparently," Jeff said. "Anyway, he finally told me to take Wickes and go to Bedford to observe a construction project taking place on the courthouse square."

"And?" Amanda asked.

Jeff dropped his head into his hands.

"Jeff, you have to tell us," Gloria said.

Again, Jeff looked around the group before he spoke. "They are in the process of building a huge, double guillotine."

No one was able to speak for several long seconds.

"No, that just can't be. It's too soon," Amanda whispered, shaking her head.

"That's what I thought; but that's exactly what they are doing," Jeff said.

"Please, explain to me why a guillotine is being built," Sue said, desperation inching into her voice.

Amanda reached across the table for Sue's hand. Sue yanked away. "Just tell me."

"According to the prophecy books my dad left, the guillotine will be the instrument used for capitol punishment sometime during the latter part of the time we have left."

"So, it's for murderers and such?" Sue asked, her voice continuing to rise.

David shook his head. "No. It's going to be used to kill Christians."

Sue sprang to her feet, shoving her metal folding chair back so suddenly it clanged to the floor. "No. This is too horrible. I can't...I can't die like that."

David jumped up to wrap his arms around Sue, but her flailing arms struck him several times until she slid to the floor weeping uncontrollably. "No," she wailed.

Gloria gently moved David aside and knelt beside Sue, taking her in her arms and rocking back and forth until her sobs subsided. "Sue, we're all in this together. We need each other."

Sue's head slowly nodded as she took the wad of tissues Amanda offered her. "Here, let me have one of those back." Amanda laughed slightly as she pulled one of the tissues from the wad and dried her own eyes.

"Me too," Gloria said, pulling gently on the delicate tissues.

"Aren't we a sorry mess?" Sue sniffed.

"Gloria's right, Sue," Jeff said as he squatted next to Amanda. "We are all in this together."

"For the duration," David added, sitting on the floor next to his wife, putting his arm around her waist.

Tired of squatting, Jeff joined the rest of the group by sitting on the floor. "I know you had plans to go job hunting today, but I think we need to spend one more day together. What do you think?"

"There's no way I want to leave this building today," Sue said.

"I agree," David said. "How about we get your prophecy books and study them together, Amanda?"

"Fine with me," she said.

"I'll help Gloria clean up the kitchen, then we can sit together and put this all in perspective," Sue said as she was helped up by David's strong hands.

"I'll help you carry the books," Jeff said. "I still have a few hours before I have to report for duty."

David helped Gloria and Sue clean off the table and right the fallen chair. After the table was washed and everything was carried into the kitchen, Jeff and Amanda entered with four books and two Bibles.

"Even though I attended church almost every Sunday, I tried not to pay too much attention to what was being preached," Jeff admitted. "But one thing I do remember was my dad saying to check everything by the Bible. So that's what we need to do with these books if we want to find out what we're facing in the days to come."

During the next hour, very little was said as everyone delved into the subject of prophecy. Gloria paced as she read, expelling nervous energy. Sue eagerly devoured the book she had reached for. David and Jeff kept reaching for the Bible, checking particular points. Amanda had brought a notebook to record her findings.

Finally, Jeff dog-eared the page he was reading before slowly closing his book. "I need to ask a favor before I get ready for work." His fingers drummed the book cover.

All eyes focused on his troubled face. "What is it, Jeff?" Gloria asked.

"Yesterday was absolutely the worst at work. First, Mercett questioned me about my weapon. Then the whole Bedford trip was a nightmare." He chuckled before continuing. "I did some terrible things to Wickes, for which I may very well lose my life."

"And it's funny?" Amanda asked.

"It wasn't yesterday, but now it is," Jeff said. "Right at this moment, I feel like it was worth whatever happens to me. I'm just worried about the rest of you."

"Are we in more danger because of what you did?" David asked.

"No, not because of what I did," Jeff said. "It's just that if anything happens to me, the rest of you are fair game."

"Just what did you do?" Sue asked.

"After my meeting with Mercett, I was in a dark mood. So when Wickes asked to stop for something to drink, I told him no. I proceeded to made two quick, rather violent moves in the vehicle which caused him to smash his head against the window—twice. By the time we finished our shift, he had a big goose egg on the side of his head. Man, was he angry."

Amanda started to giggle as the other three looked at Jeff as if they were seeing him for the first time.

"And here I thought you were this W.S.F. agent who always had it all together," David said.

"I'm telling you, guys, I'm truly losing it," Jeff said.

"Okay, let's do this right," Amanda said, pulling her chair out into the floor. "Come sit here, Jeff."

"Why?"

"We want to pray for you," she said simply. "You sit here and we'll all put our hands on you and cover you with our prayers. Come on, everybody, gather around."

Embarrassed at first, Jeff slid onto the metal chair as eight hands rested on his head, back and shoulders. One by one, his friends prayed for God's protection to be upon Jeff as he went to work, with added prayers for God's wisdom to be in his mind and heart as he faced more meetings with his boss and vile Agent Wickes.

THIRTY-NINE

"I see," mused Captain Mercett as he looked over Jeff's detailed report. He laid the blue and gold folder aside. "I haven't seen it yet, but I can tell by your drawings that you were impressed."

Jeff could tell by the squint in the corners of Captain Mercett's eyes that he still didn't trust him.

"I have to admit that I was surprised, but, Captain, I was also duly impressed," Jeff lied.

"Kind of gives a whole new meaning to the phrase, 'heads are going to roll,' doesn't it?" Captain Mercett said with an evil laugh.

"Yes, sir," Jeff answered. "It does at that."

"I haven't seen Agent Wickes' report. Is he aware that I'm expecting one?"

"Yes, sir," Jeff said. "I'll remind him, sir."

"Is everything copasetic between the two of you?" Captain Mercett asked. The squint was more pronounced.

"Yes, sir," Jeff answered. "We had a little accident yesterday, but he should be fine today. He didn't mention any problems during inspection."

"What sort of accident?" Mercett asked.

"Knowing we had to be back for final inspection, I drove a little fast. In making a sharp turn, his head bumped on the side window. I gave him permission to leave work early so he could keep an ice pack on it."

"I see," Mercett said, squinting at Jeff. "And he didn't seem to have any problems this morning?"

"No, sir," Jeff said. "He sailed right through inspection without any difficulty."

"Dismissed."

"Thank you, sir," Jeff said. Just as he reached for the doorknob, Mercett stopped him.

"Agent Howard."

"Yes, sir." Jeff spun around, expecting the worst.

"It will be put into service within thirty days."

"Excuse me, sir?" Jeff asked.

"The capital punishment device."

"Oh. Very good news, sir." His damp palm turned the doorknob, letting himself out of his enemy's lair. Knowing full well that somewhere a camera was watching him, Jeff smiled broadly as he squared his shoulders and bounded down the steps.

"Agent Wickes," Jeff called on his radio.

Several seconds passed before Wickes answered. "Sir."

"What's your location?"

"I can be there is ten minutes, sir," Wickes said. Jeff didn't miss the fact that Agent Wickes had avoided telling him where he was.

While waiting to be picked up, Jeff noted that his vehicle was parked where he had left it. As he looked around, thinking Wickes might possibly be lurking nearby, he saw another SUV approach. Although the windows were darkly tinted, he was almost certain he saw Agent Summers' blond hair through the windshield.

Wickes stepped from the passenger's side of the vehicle, walked around to the front and slapped the hood before waving to Agent Summers. Watching Agent Wickes swagger toward him with a wicked smirk on his face, Jeff used every ounce of self-control to keep from thumping his redheaded adversary.

"Is there a problem with Agent Summers?" he asked, looking Wickes squarely in the eyes.

"No, sir," Wickes answered. "No problem whatsoever."

"Do you remember the conversation we had regarding unprofessional performance of your duties?" Jeff asked sternly.

"Yes, sir," Wickes answered. He tried to stare Jeff down, but Jeff determination won out.

"Agent Wickes, up to this point I have had no reason for any negative remarks on my daily reports regarding your performance. Let's keep it that way."

"Yes, sir," Wickes answered.

"Captain Mercett needs your report on the construction project ASAP."

"Yes, sir," Wickes said. "It's in your vehicle, sir. With your permission, sir, I'll take it to him now."

"That would be a wise decision," Jeff said, walking to the driver's door of his SUV. "I'll return for you in thirty minutes."

Agent Wickes slammed the door in the same instant that Jeff backed the vehicle. The passenger side mirror brushed Wickes arm causing the blue and gold folder to fall to the ground.

Jeff smiled as he watched his enemy stoop to pick up his folder, watching his mouth as explicitly ugly words twisted his lips.

As Jeff began his patrol, his thoughts turned to Agent Summers, wondering what had transpired between them.

I'll find a way to visit with her later tonight or tomorrow. If he has touched her or threatened her in any way, he will pay.

At the appointed time, Jeff whipped his vehicle into the parking lot. Until now, Jeff didn't know that Wickes smoked. He smiled as he watched his enemy savagely puffing on a cigarette.

FORTY

Jeff decided to wait until morning to visit Agent Summers, not wanting to arouse any suspicions. Instead he drove straight to his new address.

Furtive movement next to the building caught his eye. Jeff slid into his parking place, leaving his lights on to illuminate the area around the double doors. Jumping out of his truck, he quickly ran toward the dark form he had seen dive behind one of the shrubs.

“Come out of there,” he shouted.

Shaking all over, a young, black man stood, slowly walking from behind the shrub, followed by a young, very pretty, black woman.

“Please, sir, we weren’t doing anything wrong,” the young man said, gripping the woman’s hand.

“What are you doing here?” Jeff ordered.

“We didn’t know where else to go, sir,” the young man said.

“It’s after curfew,” Jeff said sternly. “You are aware of the penalty for breaking curfew?”

“Yes, sir.” The young woman had tears streaming down her face as she clung to the man’s arm.

“We just need a place to stay, sir,” the man said. “We couldn’t find anything else.”

Pulling his keys from his pocket and unlocking the door, he motioned to them. “Step inside.”

The young man put his arm protectively around the woman’s waist and led her inside to wait for Jeff.

Hearing the commotion outside, David and the women were waiting in the foyer.

“What’s going on?” David asked.

“That’s what we’re about to find out,” Jeff said, winking at his friends before turning to glare at the newcomers.

"Your names?" he asked.

"I'm Bill Short and this is my wife, Alice." Alice's eyes were wide with fright and tears continued to dribble down her cheeks.

"And what made you show up here at this hour?" Jeff asked.

"We were evicted from our apartment today and we've been looking for somewhere to stay ever since. When we saw this church building, we thought we might be able to stay here. We didn't know anyone else was here."

"Why were you evicted?" Jeff's questions didn't let up.

"We didn't have any money to pay the rent."

"You can't work?" Jeff asked.

"We were both teachers but were told not to bother trying to come back to school."

In a much gentler voice, Jeff asked. "Are you Christians?"

Because Jeff was in full uniform, Bill and Alice clung to each other in terror. After several seconds, they both slowly nodded.

Turning to his friends, he nodded slightly, giving them the go ahead to help the new couple.

"Come with us, everything's going to be all right," Gloria said, gently taking Alice's hand.

Alice looked at Gloria then back at her husband before allowing herself to be drawn toward the dark stairway into the basement.

David stuck out his hand to shake Bill's. "We can't turn on the lights up here, but we'll be safe in the basement. I'm David and that's my wife, Gloria."

Sue followed behind and Amanda waited for Jeff as he hurried to his room to change out of his uniform. When he returned, he whispered, "What do you think?"

"It's hard to tell without much light," Amanda said. "Let's go down and I'll know more as we get acquainted."

Jeff took Amanda's hand as they stepped close to the stairs. Making sure the door at the bottom of the steps was closed, they followed the light that shown from David and Gloria's apartment. Once inside, they shut that door also, taking no chance of light showing on the outside.

Sue and Gloria were handing the newcomers cups of hot coffee as everyone found a seat.

"You actually live here?" Bill asked.

"Yes, and we've got plenty room for others," Gloria said, smiling at Alice who had began to relax.

"How is it that you wear a uniform but are still a Christian?" Bill asked Jeff.

"I'll explain that later. First you tell us how and why you became Christians after the rapture happened," Jeff said.

Bill and Alice looked at each other before Bill began their story. "We already told you that we were both teachers. We attended another church in town that believed that if we were baptized we would be saved. Since we're still here, obviously they were wrong."

"How did you know what to do later?" David asked.

"Actually we visited this church several years ago when a visiting preacher spoke on prophecy, which we were both interested in," Alice said.

"I think his name was Hollis, or something like that," Bill added. "He ended every session with a gospel invitation to accept Jesus as our Savior. Of course, we thought we were all right so we didn't respond."

"And now?" Jeff asked.

"Finding ourselves left here, we knew immediately what we had to do," Alice said.

"No matter what," Bill added.

"Then you realize what we're facing?" David asked.

"I'm afraid so," Bill said softly. Raising his head and looking around the group, he asked, "What's the story on the rest of you?"

"I'd been attending church here for a little while with my dad," Amanda began. "After he disappeared I searched for the way to become a Christian because I don't want to go to hell."

"I was in seminary, believe it or not," David began.

Bill's eyes opened wide. "Seminary? You've got to be kidding me."

"I wish I was," David continued. "After the rapture, Gloria and I became Christians and made our way back to this building."

"I guess I'm the newest Christian," Sue said. "My husband was working for the W.S.F. as a spy. But he had an unfortunate accident a few days ago." She smiled a bit before continuing. "It didn't take me long to become a Christian."

Looking at Jeff, Bill prompted, "And that leaves you."

"This was my home church. Been here all my life, just didn't see the need to get saved, until it was too late, that is."

"You became a Christian even though you're with the W.S.F.? And you get away with it?" Bill asked.

"Yes, on all counts," Jeff answered. "It took awhile, but I finally decided I didn't want to go to hell either. So I got saved and have been walking a very scary, thin line ever since."

"Tell them about the courthouse, Jeff," David said.

"Good idea." Jeff nodded at David. "You need to know this information. A guillotine is being constructed on the courthouse square as we speak."

Bill's mouth fell open. Alice grabbed his arm in sheer terror. "A guillotine? But that means..."

"That's right," Jeff said. "They intend to begin using it within thirty days."

Bill put his arm around his wife's trembling shoulders. "I didn't think it was supposed to be this soon."

"None of us did," David said.

"So now what?" Bill asked.

"We take a day at a time and try to survive," Jeff said.

"As cautiously as we possibly can, we have to try to help others find their way to God," David added.

"Listen, everybody," Gloria said. "It's very late and we've all got things to do tomorrow, so how about we get some sleep?"

"Sounds great to me," Amanda said.

"Sue, why don't you show Bill and Alice the room at the other end of this hall," Gloria directed.

"Sure thing," Sue said, standing and motioning for the new couple to follow. As they made their way to their doorway, Sue pointed back down the hallway. "Down there are the restrooms. Each has a shower, so make yourselves at home. We usually eat breakfast together upstairs."

"Thank you so much," Alice said, still holding tightly to her husband's hand.

"Good night," Bill said, softly closing the door.

Sue could hear Alice crying soon after the door was closed. In a whispered voice she shared that information with the group.

"What do you think?" Jeff asked the group, but looked directly at Amanda.

"I think they are being honest," Amanda said.

"Me too," David agreed.

Gloria and Sue both nodded their heads in agreement.

"Okay, let's sleep on it," Jeff said. "Everybody stay alert. If anything funny goes on, report it immediately."

"Good night," Amanda said as she left the Pattersons' apartment.

"Good night, Amanda." Sue entered her own room. Amanda and Jeff both waved to Sue.

"After breakfast I have to visit one of my agents," Jeff said as he held on to Amanda's hand.

"Another enemy?" she asked him, watching his worried face.

"I don't think so," Jeff said. "Can we talk in your room, just for a minute?"

After the couple stepped into Amanda's room, Jeff quietly closed the door. "Wickes was on patrol with one of my female agents, Bonnie Summers, today."

"And?" Amanda asked.

"Several days after I began letting Wickes take over inspections as part of his training, he began making non-verbal moves on this young lady."

"Is she pretty?" Amanda asked.

"Very," Jeff said. "She's built well and has long blond hair. But, I've had a sneaking suspicion that she might not have her heart in the job."

"She's not a good agent?" Amanda asked.

"No, she's an excellent agent, one of my best," Jeff tried to explain.

"I'm sorry, Jeff, I'm not understanding." Amanda walked over to her chair and plopped down.

"I have nothing concrete to go on here, but I think she might be a Christian, or wants to be one," Jeff blurted out.

"And how does Wickes enter into this picture?"

Jeff continued, "Today, while I was with Captain Mercett, he was in her vehicle. I've got to find out what he said, or did."

"Is there any way you can make Wickes disappear," Amanda asked.

"I'm working on it," Jeff replied. "Now that that guillotine is going up, it's just...I don't know, Amanda."

"I know," she said. "We're all more frightened now."

"I know we're going to go to Heaven, it's just that now I'm responsible for you and the rest of our group."

"Go get some sleep," Amanda said, giving him a hug. "I'll be praying for your meeting in the morning."

"Thanks," Jeff murmured into her hair. "I wish we could have known each other better before all of this."

Amanda nodded her head against Jeff's shoulder. When she released her hug, Jeff looked into her tear-filled eyes.

"We'll take this one day at a time," Jeff whispered. "Until one of us is taken out, we'll be here for each other. Deal?"

Amanda nodded her head as she tried to smile. Jeff placed a quick kiss on her lips before slipping out of her room.

Amanda sank to the floor as her shoulders shook with quiet sobs. *Oh, God, how I wish I could have gone with Daddy. This is all going to end so badly. Please help us.*

FORTY-ONE

The smell of frying bacon and brewing coffee wafted down the stairwells and through the air vents to awaken any of the group who might still be sleeping.

"Thank you so much for helping, Alice," Gloria said.

"I love to cook," Alice replied. "And it's the least I can do to show our gratitude. I have to tell you, I had almost given up hope of finding any kind of safety."

"I understand," Gloria said as she began to gently stir the scrambled eggs. "Who would ever have thought that we'd actually live in a church building?"

"Gloria, can I tell you something in private?" Alice whispered as she stood close to her new friend.

"Sure, honey, anything," Gloria said. *What is it about the pain in her eyes?*

"I was pregnant," Alice whispered with a catch in her voice.

Gloria dropped the wooden spoon on the floor, scattering eggs around their feet.

"Oh, no! I'm sorry." Alice grabbed for a dishtowel.

"No, no, Alice." Gloria's arms grabbing Alice in a bear hug.

"What?" Alice cried.

Gloria pulled back. With tears in her eyes, she said, "I was pregnant, too."

Alice gasped, "No, you're kidding."

"I wish I was." Gloria snatched the skillet from the hot burner. "Oh, dear, I hope they didn't burn."

Alice cleaned up the eggs while Gloria hurriedly checked to make sure the rest of them weren't burnt.

When she was certain everything was as it should be, Gloria wiped her cheek on her shoulder. "Finally, someone I can talk to who truly knows how I feel."

"Do you think after breakfast we could find a quiet place to talk?" Alice asked.

"You bet."

"Anything we can do to help?" David asked, bounding up the steps into the fellowship hall. It didn't take him long to notice that something else was going on between his wife and Alice.

Sue entered the kitchen next, getting the milk and orange juice from the refrigerator. "We're getting kind of low on supplies; someone will have to make a run to the store."

"I'll do that," Amanda offered as she poured herself a large glass of cold milk. "Want to come along, Sue?"

Hesitating, Sue finally answered, "Sure, I guess so."

"I'm scared, too," Amanda assured her. "Every time I leave this building, I'm scared. If we're going to look for jobs later, we might as well venture out for the short trips."

"You're right," Sue said. "I've got to pull myself together if I plan on looking for a job at the hospital."

"I don't have to work today or tomorrow," Jeff said. "So after my meeting this morning, I'll need you guys to help me check around the grounds to see if there's anything out there that will be useful to us."

"Not a problem." Bill was sitting at one of the long tables drinking coffee.

David offered to say the blessing when everyone was seated. Gloria and Alice chose to sit next to each other. A black hand clasped a white hand under the table.

"Ladies, you have outdone yourselves this morning," David said after he finished his prayer and everyone began passing plates of food around.

"Thank you," both ladies said.

Conversation was light during the meal; everyone seemed to be lost in their own thoughts. Pushing his plate back when he finished, Jeff looked around the group.

"Before I leave, can we pray together?"

"Great idea," David said.

Everyone clasped the hand of the person next to them as they all bowed their heads. Afterwards everyone was smiling through their tears.

"I'll be back as soon as I can." Jeff pushed his chair up to the table.

"Us too," Amanda said. "Sue and I will grab our purses and head to the store. Do any of you need anything in particular besides food?"

"I don't think so," Gloria said. "Alice and I will clean up from breakfast then we're going to spend some time getting better acquainted."

"If you don't mind, I think I'll go lie down until Jeff returns," Bill said. "I've got a very bad headache."

"Why didn't you say something, honey?" Alice slid her arms around her husband's waist.

"Didn't have it earlier," Bill said, blinking his eyes.

"I've got migraine medicine if you think you need it," Sue said, watching Bill closely.

"That might be good," Bill replied, rubbing the back of his neck.

Sue dashed down the steps to get the medication. Just as she bounced back into the fellowship hall, Bill collapsed onto the floor.

"Bill," cried Alice. "Somebody, do something."

Grateful that she had grabbed her blood pressure cuff, she immediately wrapped it around Bill's arm, pumping the bulb. The results frightened her.

"His blood pressure is sky high," she announced.

"What can we do?" Alice asked.

"Has he been on any medication?" Sue asked.

"I think he was, before—"Alice cried.

"I understand," Sue said. "Let me run down and see what I have left in my bag." She again ran down the steps, stumbling on the last two. Her ankle twisted in pain but she kept going, searching her bag for just the right medication. Hobbling back up the steps, she yelled for a glass of water.

Water ran from the corner of Bill's mouth when Sue pressed in the medication followed by cold water.

"Oh, Bill, please be all right," Alice cried softly.

"I'm okay, honey," he whispered.

"Sure you are." She tried to smile.

"Thanks, Sue," he said gratefully.

"You're lucky I was able to find a couple of these pills." Sue began to check his blood pressure, pleased to see that it had lowered a bit.

"Luck didn't have anything to do with it," David said.

"You're right," Sue acknowledged. "God still supplies all our needs. I have exactly three pills left. Somehow, we're going to have to find a way to get more."

"Actually, I think I still have a prescription my doctor gave me. We didn't have the money to have it filled, but I think it's still in my billfold."

"Praise the Lord," David shouted.

"Dig it out and we'll take it with us," Amanda said.

"But—"Alice began.

"It's taken care of, don't worry." Amanda smiled.

Alice followed Bill down the steps as David held on to him. Safely in their bed, she kissed his forehead and returned to the kitchen, anxious for her talk with Gloria.

Sensing Gloria and Alice's need to be alone, David volunteered to clean up from breakfast.

"You two go find something to do. I'm at loose ends until Jeff returns."

"Thanks, honey." Gloria gave her husband a kiss on the cheek.

Leading her into their apartment, Gloria softly closed the door, offering her one of the two easy chairs.

"How far along were you?" she asked.

"I was two weeks from delivery," Alice answered, placing her hands on her stomach. "We had named him William Thomas after Bill's dad. What about you?"

"Actually, I was only about four months. The baby had just begun to make himself known, although I hadn't felt a lot of movement yet."

"There was no pain; William Thomas was just gone," Alice mused. "My stomach was out to here one second and droopingly flat the next."

"It took me awhile to realize my baby was gone," Gloria said. "I had begun to show, but certainly not like you. In the horror of everyone disappearing it was about an hour before I realized that my baby wasn't inside me any longer." Tears gathered in her eyes.

"It still seems surreal," Alice said. "The only comfort I can get is to keep reminding myself that he is with Jesus. Jesus actually took him, so I know he'll be safe until I can join him."

Gloria nodded her head in agreement. "Amanda has several books on prophecy that we brought over with us. We spent an hour or so reading through them. Makes me wonder why we didn't pay more attention before."

"I know what you mean."

"The Bible is clear on what was going to happen. And those books pretty much cover everything up to this point anyway. But now that it has happened, reality kind of slaps us in the face," Gloria said.

"At least we found refuge here."

"Yes," Gloria said. "Even in the emptiness of a church sanctuary we can help others."

"Be honest with me, Gloria," Alice asked, with fear once again etched in her face. "Are we truly safe here?"

"As safe as we would be anywhere else, at least for the time being."

"And Jeff is really a Christian and not just another spy?" Alice asked.

"Yes, Jeff is in a daily battle trying to do his job without being found out. His captain already suspects and has at least one other person spying on him."

"Do you know what that agent looks like so we can tell Jeff if he snoops around here?" Alice asked.

"All I know is that he's redheaded," Gloria said. "I honestly don't know how Jeff makes it through each day."

"We've got to find some way to help him," Alice said.

Gloria smiled when she looked at her friend and knew the wheels were turning.

"Alice, I am so thankful that God brought you to us." She gave her friend a hug.

"Me too."

"The others can't possibly understand our loss, but we'll be able to pray for each other when either of us begins to flounder," Gloria said.

As the two women hugged each other, David gave a soft knock on the apartment door. "Safe to enter?"

"Take your chances," Gloria called back with a wide smile.

"Jeff is back, so we're going out to check around the grounds. Just wanted you to know," David said.

"I better go check on Bill," Alice said. "Thanks, Gloria."

"Everything all right?" David asked quietly as he put his arms around his smiling wife.

"Yes, I'll tell you later." She kissed his cheek. "Please be careful out there."

"Not to worry, I have my slingshot," David said, patting his back pocket.

"Slingshot?" Gloria asked.

"Yeah. You know, David—giant—slingshot."

"Oh! Okay, mister David giant killer," Gloria laughed.

Bill had not only gotten over his headache, but was feeling well enough to join the other men.

Soon after the men left the building, Amanda and Sue returned from their shopping expedition. Sue was bubbling with excitement when she entered the kitchen with her arms full of grocery sacks.

"You're not going to believe this," she exclaimed.

"Probably not," Gloria laughed. "Just tell us, okay?"

"I think I've got a job."

"You're kidding," Alice said. "At the grocery store?"

"No." Sue was so excited she had a hard time talking without stumbling over her words. "When I took Bill's prescription to the pharmacy, they wanted to hire me on the spot when they found out I was a nurse."

"Why would they need a nurse at a pharmacy?" Gloria asked.

"Things have changed so much out there," Sue continued. "They have a clinic set up right there in the store. The nurse they had hasn't shown up for work in two days."

"Which means?" Alice asked.

"Don't even want to think about what happened to her," Sue advised. "But they want me in the morning."

"Another answer to prayer, if you ask me." Amanda piled the last of the grocery sacks on the counter.

"Praise the Lord," Gloria shouted.

Sue began digging into one of the sacks. "Here's Bill's medicine. Make sure he takes it faithfully."

"Oh, Sue, thank you so much," Alice said with tears in her eyes. "I thought I had lost him this morning."

"I know, but God obviously has other plans," Sue said.

FORTY-TWO

Bam! Bam! Bam! Angrily kicking the shed's back wall, Jeff's conversation with Bonnie Summers kept replaying in his mind.

Yesterday, Bonnie had answered his knock dressed in blue jeans and royal blue sweat shirt. Her blond hair hung free down her back and over her shoulders.

"Agent Howard," she exclaimed. "Is something wrong?"

"No, Agent Summers," Jeff assured her. "I just need to have a few words with you."

"Certainly, come in." She stood back to allow him inside. Jeff found her home to be simple yet comfortable.

"I'll get right to the point," Jeff said, taking the seat offered. "I've been watching Agent Wickes around you. When he arrived in your vehicle yesterday, I have to say I was concerned. Deeply concerned. I need to ask if he got out of hand with you in any way."

Jeff watched as Bonnie wilted into her chair. "Wow. I wasn't aware that anyone else knew." Her head fell into her hands.

"Listen, Bonnie, is it okay if I call you by your first name?" Jeff asked.

"Yes, sir," she replied, looking up at him. "We're not working, so it's fine."

"Thank you," Jeff said. "As you are well aware, Agent Wickes is in training under me and will soon have his own squad."

"He's planning on taking over your squad, sir," she interjected.

"I thought as much," Jeff said. "Tell me, how do you honestly feel about what's happened and how things are going now."

Turning her back on Jeff, she reached for a tissue before beginning to speak.

"During our training, I was so proud of being part of the W.S.F. But after everybody disappeared and we were put on active duty, I've been scared. I don't believe what we've been told about aliens taking everyone. And I die inside every time I have to use my weapon. Sir, sometimes I think I'm losing my mind."

Bonnie began dabbing at her eyes with the tissues. Jeff reached across the table and placed his hand on hers. He failed to notice that the tissues weren't even damp.

"Do you know that Agent Wickes is trying to get rid of you?" she asked.

"I've suspected it all along," he answered.

"I can tell you for certain that Wickes is your mortal enemy," Bonnie said.

"Thanks for the warning," Jeff said. "Now, can you tell me about yesterday?"

"When we were dismissed from inspection, he ordered my partner to patrol with someone else. He then ordered me into the passenger seat and we proceeded with what I assumed would be normal patrol. After we made our first round, he told me to park behind the main building where the school buses used to be built."

"What reason did he give?" Jeff asked.

"He said he'd received a report that people were hiding out back there, which was ludicrous," she replied. "When we parked, he leaned over towards me and began to tell me how I was going to be his second in command as soon as he managed to get rid of you."

"How did you respond?" Jeff asked.

"I was scared to death," she said. "But I asked him how he was going to accomplish that. He just said he was working on it but it would happen soon."

"I don't want to embarrass you, but I have to ask, did he touch you in any inappropriate way?" Jeff asked.

Bonnie took a deep breath before answering. "I had kept both my hands clasped around the notebook, holding it close to my chest. He reached over and pushed the notebook to my lap then proceeded to outline my badge with his finger."

"And then?" Jeff could feel his face heating up with anger.

"He laughed when I shoved his hand away and he said how he likes fiery women. He then retraced my badge, slower and with more pressure, only that time he left his hand on me and told me that I would soon be begging him for more. He doesn't know how close he came to dying right then."

Jeff smiled in spite of his rising anger.

"Anyway, I grabbed his wrist in a grip that had to have left bruises—"

"I remember the power of your grip, from training." Jeff laughed.

"I didn't say anything. I just tossed his hand back and stared out the windshield."

"Did he do anything else?" Jeff hated to keep after her, but he knew he had to know the whole truth.

"He told me that I'd come around sooner or later, one way or the other. I wanted to spit in his face," Bonnie said with a shudder.

"Thanks for sharing this information with me, Bonnie," Jeff said as he stood. "I know it was difficult for you and I won't bother you again."

"Believe me, it wasn't a bother," Bonnie said.

Jeff thought she looked as if she wanted to say something else.

"Is there anything else you want to talk about?" Jeff asked.

"I don't quite know how to ask you," she said, rubbing her hands together nervously.

"Just ask," Jeff said, sitting back down. "I'll try to answer the best I can."

"I'm tired of being scared all the time. I just wish I knew how you manage so well."

"I just try to do my job the best I know how," he said. "When I go home, I have my friends I can talk to and that helps."

"I don't feel safe here by myself anymore," she said. "And I don't have any friends since I've have to work every day."

"Would you consider moving in with us?" Jeff asked.

"In a church?"

"It's not a church so much anymore," he said. "It's open to anyone who needs a place to feel safe."

"How would it affect my job, living in a place like that?" she asked. "And what about the situation with Agent Wickes? Would it make it worse?"

"I can fix it with the captain about your job and Agent Wickes is your biggest threat as long as you live alone."

"Can I think about it for a couple days?" she asked.

"Sure, just don't wait too long, okay?" Jeff warned with real concern in his voice.

He thanked Bonnie one more time before leaving and advised her to keep her doors securely locked.

As all these things replayed in his mind, Jeff became more and more incensed. His kicks against the backside of the shed became more intense.

Bill and David, hearing loud thumping from the back of the shed, approached silently, one on each side. David looked around the edge of the shed and saw what Jeff was doing a few seconds before Bill.

"See a spider, did ya?" David called.

Jeff growled loudly before smacking his fists into the shed also.

"Whoa, man," Bill called, grabbing Jeff's arms. "Is it worth injuring yourself?"

"Would it help to talk about it?" David asked, worried about the look on Jeff's face.

Jeff shook his head. "No, I need to get busy; get my mind off it." Looking toward the woods, he said, "I haven't been back in the woods for a couple years. I keep wondering if there would be any place to hide, really hide."

"You mean like underground or something of that nature?" David asked.

Nodding his head, Jeff began to walk toward the woods. "You know how the cave system is around here. I know there's never been an entrance found that I ever heard of, but maybe if we search we might find something."

"I remember coming back here with the youth group many years ago." David had to walk quickly to keep up with Jeff. "I seem to remember a couple sink holes. That would be the first places I'd look."

"You're right," Jeff said excitedly. "If we could find even a small opening, we might discover something we can use."

"There, up ahead," Bill shouted, running to a smaller sink hole. "What do you think?"

"Let's dig around and see what we can find," Jeff said as they all fell to their knees and began clawing through the deep layer of rotting leaves.

Bill not only clawed the ground, but in several places he pounded his large fists against the wet dirt, listening for a hollow sound that would indicate an underground opening.

After minutes of intense searching, Bill lay back amongst the wet, rotting leaves. "I think we're out of luck here, boys."

"I agree." David sat back on his haunches.

"Let's look for the other sink hole," Jeff said. He jumped to his feet, not wanting to waste one minute.

David was pleased that his friend's mind was temporarily free of whatever had caused him so much anger. Although he now moved a bit slower, he joined in the new search for the second sink hole.

Bill, moving even slower, went in a slightly different direction so they could cover more area. Feeling his strength begin to ebb, he tried not to panic. He certainly didn't want to collapse out here in the woods.

David, suddenly realizing that he hadn't seen Bill for several minutes, began to worry, just as Jeff's voice echoed through the trees.

"I found it."

David darted in the direction of Jeff's voice, arriving almost simultaneously with Bill. "You okay, Bill?" he asked, huffing from his run through the deep leaves.

Bill fell to his knees at the edge of the large sink hole. "Yeah, just a little out of breath."

"Don't overdo it, Bill, we won't be able to haul you out of here fast enough." Jeff watched his black friend's labored breathing.

Bill bent over, shaking his head. "I'll be all right, just let me rest a minute."

Jeff and David set to work first by dragging their feet through the deep indention in the earth. Jeff fell to his knees in the center of the hole and began feeling with his hands.

When he felt the earth give beneath his knee, he yelped and began tossing wet clumps of leaves in all directions. "I think I've found something!"

David was at his side in an instant. Not wanting to miss out, Bill waded through the leaves to help. It didn't take long to clear off a spot approximately six feet in diameter.

"See where my knee punched through?" Jeff asked. "We need to see how deep we can dig there."

Bill sat back to look at the hole. "Promise me there aren't any snakes in there."

"Snakes?" Jeff looked at Bill in disbelief. "Snakes are the least of our problems, my man."

"Not mine," Bill said, remaining at the outer edge of leaves. "I'm terrified of snakes."

"I think it's too late in the season for snakes," David said.

"Not if you're digging into their nests," Bill said.

Even though the thought of snakes didn't bother him, Jeff sat back on the ground to contemplate what their next step should be. "How about—" he began just as an earth shaking clap of thunder caused them all to dive for cover.

"What was that?" Bill shouted.

"We've got to get back inside," Jeff said, hurriedly kicking the leaves back over the small hole. "We'll come back tomorrow with shovels and see where this goes."

"What's going on, Jeff?" David asked, helping cover the area with piles of dead leaves.

"I don't know," Jeff said as they quickly exited the woods. "I've been watching the sky lately and you wouldn't believe what's been going on up there."

"Such as?" David asked, trying to catch his breath.

Although no other sounds of thunder could be heard, Jeff stopped at the edge of the woods and pointed upward. "Look at those clouds."

Bill and David watched in amazement how the clouds sped across the sky while horrifying streaks of lightning bolted through them.

"My word," David exclaimed.

"What's happening?" Bill asked as he began walking quickly toward the church.

"Don't know except that even nature seems to be rebelling about what's going on down here." Jeff quickly unlocked the door so they could hurry inside.

Trembling, Sue, Amanda, Gloria and Alice huddled in the middle of the foyer, hoping whoever was coming in was their husbands.

Alice and Gloria ran and grabbed their husbands. Jeff quickly stepped over to put his arms around Amanda and Sue.

"What was that, Jeff?" Amanda asked.

"The sky's going crazy," Bill said, holding tightly to his wife.

"Believe it or not, that was a clap of thunder," Jeff said.

"Is it getting ready to storm?" Sue asked.

"No, there are just some really strange things happening in the sky," Jeff answered.

"We've got some sandwiches made if anybody's hungry." Gloria was reluctant to let go of her husband.

Slowly and quietly, the group made its way into the kitchen and just as quietly began to eat.

"How'd your meeting go?" Amanda asked.

"Oh, yeah, I need to tell all of you this." Jeff wolfed down the last bite of his peanut butter and jelly sandwich. "We might have another boarder next week."

"Your other agent?" Amanda asked.

"Yes, her name is Bonnie Summers."

"Can she be trusted?" David asked.

"I think I trust her," Jeff said.

"Do you know if she's a Christian?" Amanda asked.

"Probably not, but I think she could be won over easily," he said.

"Are you sure?" Bill asked.

"I'm almost positive," Jeff said. "Agent Wickes has been harassing her and she's scared. She also shared with me that she doesn't understand what's happened and she frightened about that."

"So you invited her to move in with us?" Amanda asked.

"Yes, she isn't safe by herself any longer," Jeff said. "I'm hoping we can show her how to become a Christian."

"I'll get a room ready," Gloria offered.

"We'll have to be careful what we say," Amanda said. "At least until we're sure about her."

"By the way, why are you men so dirty?" Alice asked.

"We'll let you know later," Jeff said.

"Honey, I think I need to rest awhile," Bill said to his wife. "I almost overdid it out there in the woods."

"I was afraid of that," David said. "Man, you've got to be more careful."

"I'll be okay after I rest awhile." Bill headed for the steps with his arm around his wife's waist.

"You're due for another pill in an hour," Sue reminded him.

"Don't worry, I won't let him forget," Alice smiled.

"I didn't think the day would ever come when I'd choose to take a nap, but for some reason, I feel drained," Jeff said. "Do you mind if I disappear for a while?"

"Not at all," Amanda said, watching him closely.

While Gloria put the food away and wiped down the countertop, David watched Amanda's face. "You okay?" he asked.

"Yes," she answered. "I'm just concerned about Jeff. And I'm really worried about Agent Summers living with us."

"Bill and I found him behind the shed trying to kick a hole in it," David said.

"What?"

"I don't think I've ever seen so much anger in a person before," David said.

"But why?" Gloria asked.

"I don't know," David answered. "I'm sure he'll tell us before the day is over."

"You know, I've been thinking," Amanda said. "With more and more people moving in, I think we need to find secure hiding places for our Bibles."

"I hadn't thought about that, but I think you're right," Gloria said.

"I've also been thinking about destroying Dad's books," Amanda said, looking at her friends.

"His prophecy books?" David asked.

Amanda nodded her head. "We've all read them and it's just one more reason to fear getting caught with them."

"You're probably right," David said. "We need to find some way of burning them, don't you think?"

"I'll ask Jeff when he wakes up. He'll know what to do."

"You sure you're going to be all right?" Gloria asked.

"No, but that's beside the point," Amanda said, giving her friend a sweet smile.

"I'm going to gather up those books and then find a hiding place for my Bible. See you all later."

Sue, who had been quietly listening to the conversation, followed Amanda down the steps. "I don't know what's happened to us in the last few hours, but I sense a deep heaviness on all of us."

"I can't explain it either, but I feel it too," Amanda said. "We probably need to do some major praying."

"Catch you later, girl," Sue said as she made her way to her own room.

"Yeah," Amanda answered. Without turning on her light, she quietly closed her door and collapsed onto the bed.

FORTY-THREE

When Amanda didn't make an appearance at dinner, everyone was concerned, especially Jeff. Normally he would have been working, but the schedules had been changed again.

"Do you think I should knock on her door or something?" he asked.

"She was in funky mood when I left her after lunch," Sue said. "And it certainly isn't like her to sleep this long."

"There's been a spirit of heaviness on all of us today for some reason," David said. "I think we need to join in prayer to get this spirit out of here."

"You're right, David," Jeff said. "I felt it and I know some of you felt it. There's only one way to keep these spirits off of us and that is to pray them away."

The group pushed their chairs back and formed a circle, clasping hands. As the prayers began, each person seemed to enter a different realm. There were no thoughts of time, dirty dishes, or each other as the intensity of the prayers rose.

Amanda's terrifying scream caused eyes to snap open and hands to break loose. Jeff was the first to reach the stairway.

"IN THE NAME OF JESUS, GET OUT OF HERE!" Amanda's voice could be heard all over the building.

Jeff burst through her door as a gust of cold air slammed him against the wall. Amanda slapped the light switch and grabbed Jeff, hanging on to him as if he was life itself.

"What was that?" he croaked.

Clinging to him, she shook her head, unable to speak.

The violent gust of icy air flew up the steps causing Sue and Gloria to stumble. Sue's injured ankle gave way and she tumbled down three steps. David caught Gloria as she also began to fall.

David was able to help Sue sit on the bottom step while Gloria scooted close behind her. Halfway up the steps, Bill and Alice clung to the railing.

"Would somebody please explain to me what just happened?" Sue shouted as she rubbed her throbbing ankle.

"It was awful," Amanda cried softly.

"The spirit of heaviness was exactly what we just felt rushing up the stairwell," David said.

"You're kidding?" Bill exclaimed.

David said, "I know all of us felt something powerful while we were praying, right?"

"Yes, I have to admit I'd never experienced anything like that before," Sue said.

"Satan's demons are on the loose now and we will probably see and feel more of what just happened," David said.

"So we need to pray them away," Bill said.

"That's right, or else they'll destroy us and this place," David said.

"Can you talk about it, honey?" Jeff asked.

"I was beginning to wake up when a horribly foul smell made me start gagging. When I opened my eyes I saw this—this—I don't think I can even describe it. It was so incredibly ugly and evil. His bony fingers reached for my throat and I yelled for him to get out in the name of Jesus."

"We heard that," Gloria said with a smile.

"When I said Jesus' name, it covered its ears and smacked into the door just as Jeff came in."

"I've never seen or felt a demon before," Jeff said. "In fact, it was just a matter of weeks ago that I didn't even believe in them."

"I think it's safe to say that we are all believers now," Bill said.

"Amanda, are you hungry?" Gloria asked.

"I feel a little hungry, but we just had lunch, so I'll wait a while," Amanda answered.

"Amanda, it's six o'clock," Gloria said.

"Six o'clock?" Amanda exclaimed. "That's impossible."

"She's right," Jeff said. "You slept practically all day."

"How could I?" she said. "I've never done that before."

"Come on upstairs," Jeff said, gently leading her from her room. "You can eat and we'll talk some more."

Almost afraid to be separated, the whole group climbed the steps and sat around the table chatting while Amanda ate.

"I think after what's just happened, we need to spend more time praying together," David said.

"I agree. It's imperative that we do so," Bill added.

Gloria, who had brought a bag of ice to place on Sue's ankle, offered her suggestion. "Why don't we just plan on at least two intensive prayer times each day?"

"Great idea," David said.

"How about after breakfast and before or after dinner?" Sue tried to make herself comfortable by propping her foot on another chair while holding the ice pack on her ankle.

"That should work, at least for me and my work schedule," Jeff said.

"Oh, Jeff, you don't know yet," Sue exclaimed. "I start a new job tomorrow."

"Awesome." Jeff smiled. "Where?"

"At the pharmacy," Sue said. "They've begun a clinic in the store and they need a nurse."

"That's great," Jeff said. "And you won't have to drive all the way to Bedford."

Even though all the lights were turned off by seven o'clock, the group continued to sit in the fellowship hall talking.

"Have you asked Jeff about the books, Amanda?" David asked.

"What books?" Jeff asked.

"David and I were talking earlier about finding a safe place to hide our Bibles. And I think we should destroy my dad's books."

"You're probably right," Jeff said. "We never know when someone will come in here looking for evidence against us."

"Is there any way we can burn the books without drawing attention to ourselves?" David asked.

"Probably not. Let me think about this for a few minutes," Jeff said.

"How many of us have Bibles?" David asked.

Amanda, Gloria, Jeff, and David held up their hands.

"Under no circumstances would George allow us to have one," Sue said.

"We were afraid to carry one with us when we left our house," Bill said.

"Okay, by tomorrow morning those of us who have Bibles will need to find secure places for them," David said.

"Is your father's name in any of his books?" Jeff asked Amanda.

"I don't think so, but I'll check."

"I think this is the wisest solution," Jeff said. "After we make sure his name is nowhere inside or outside, we'll box them up and I'll take them to Captain Mercett."

"Are you crazy?" Amanda cried.

"Probably," Jeff said. "But not about this. If I take the books to him and tell him we found them in the church library and we don't want trash like them around, he'll have more reason to trust me—hopefully."

"Oh, okay. I think I see where you're coming from," Amanda said.

"You're right, Jeff," David said.

"I hate to be a party pooper, but I'm exhausted," Gloria said after a long yawn.

"I agree," Sue said, standing gingerly on her aching foot. "Thanks for the ice, Gloria."

"See everyone at breakfast," Gloria said. David followed closely behind his wife.

It was time for Bill's last dose of medicine before turning in for the night anyway. After exchanging "good nights," everyone entered their own rooms.

Holding hands, Jeff and Amanda went into the sanctuary to talk and pray since neither of them was sleepy.

"I didn't realize how dark it could get in here with all the windows covered," Amanda whispered.

Remembering the candle that always sat on the communion table, Jeff felt his way until he found the small box of matches the pastor kept inside the pulpit. Amanda was surprised how much light shone from a lone candle.

"You sure it can't be seen from outside?" she asked.

"I don't think so," Jeff said as he sat in the middle of the front pew. Amanda scooted close to him, still frightened from her encounter with the demon.

"You okay?" he whispered.

"Yes, it's just going to take awhile to shake off that experience," she said.

"How about you?" she asked. "Are you okay? I'm really worried about you, Jeff."

"I'll be okay," he said, putting his arm across the pew behind her back. "I don't expect anything to be easy from here on out. We've just got to take it one day at a time."

"This Agent Summers, are you sure it's safe to invite her to say here?" Amanda asked.

"I hope I'm doing the right thing," he said. "I think you'll like her. You two are about the same age."

"How much longer do you have to put up with Wickes?" she asked.

"He's almost finished training. Hopefully Mercett will move him far away from us."

"And if he doesn't?" Amanda asked.

"I'll worry about that when that time comes," Jeff answered. "I can't spend my time worrying about what-ifs."

"I'm sorry." Amanda dropped her head. "It's just that—"

"I know. It's not a problem, okay?" Jeff said, lightly rubbing her back.

"What were you all praying about earlier this evening?"

"We were talking about the spirit of heaviness we all seemed to be under since lunchtime, so we decided to do some spiritual warfare. I've never prayed like that before," Jeff said.

"That's probably what made that demon show himself, don't you think?" she asked.

"You're right," Jeff agreed.

Out of the corner of his eye, Jeff thought he caught a hint of royal blue and shiny gold. *Am I imagining things?*

Without saying anything, Amanda slipped to her knees and bowed her head on the pew. Jeff slowly slid from the pew while searching the darkened corners at the back of the room and straining his ears to hear any hint of what or who might be lurking there.

Just as his head began to bow, he saw the shadow.

"Trust me," he whispered into Amanda's ear as he grabbed her, falling on top of her on the carpeted floor.

Completely startled by his moves, she failed to hear his words. Instead she struggled as Jeff's lips covered hers. Trying desperately to extract herself from the hold he had on her was futile.

Jeff's fingers quickly combed through her hair bringing her ear close to his mouth once more. "We're being watched," he whispered. "I love you, Amanda," he said in a louder voice.

At that same instant the sanctuary lights flashed on as a female voice shouted, "Stay right where you are."

"What?" Jeff yelled in mock surprise as he rolled off Amanda.

"Well, well, well."

Amanda began trembling when she heard the evil in Russell Wickes' voice, just like the demon.

"What do we have here?" he said.

"Oh, my," Agent Summers exclaimed. "Agent Howard, I am so sorry. I didn't know, sir."

"Agent Summers, do your job," Wickes shouted.

Jeff jumped up, reaching down to help Amanda. Her clothing was in disarray. Embarrassed and trembling in fear she slid onto the pew.

"What on earth do you think you're doing, Agent Wickes?" Jeff yelled.

"You, sir, are under arrest," Wickes said, his grotesque smirk exaggerated in the dim light.

"Are you insane?" Jeff barked.

"We caught you praying right here in front of this appalling building. I don't have to tell you what penalty awaits you."

"Praying? Praying?" Jeff shouted. "You have completely lost your mind."

"Oh, please," Wickes continued. "You're not going to weasel out of this one. Correct, Agent Summers?"

"Uh, sir—uh, I didn't see—" Agent Summers stammered.

"She didn't see any praying going on because there wasn't any," Jeff stated. "You are finished, Agent Wickes. I've had it with you. By the way, why are you working, Agent Summers? This was your weekend off."

"Agent Wickes called me in for extra duty, sir," Summers said.

"You?" Jeff shouted. "You have no authority to call anyone."

"Talk to the captain," Wickes said. His voice was losing a bit of gusto.

"Oh, don't worry, I most certainly will," Jeff said. "For your information, I had just asked my girlfriend to marry me and we were—uh—we were celebrating. The captain already knows about this girl and my plans for her."

"He does?" Amanda squeaked.

"Yes, he does," Jeff said in a softer voice. "I clear everything with the captain, and I most certainly will be seeing him first thing in the morning. Now get out of here."

"You sir, are under arrest," Wickes said. "The captain is crystal clear on what's been going on in here."

"Yes, he is, Wickes," Jeff said. "Every day I keep him up to speed on what each person is up to. I'm ordering you out of here. Agent Summers, you have my permission to spend the rest of the night here with us. I'll see that you get home in the morning."

"Your head is going to roll," Wickes hissed. "Captain Mercett has the blades sharpened and ready. You will be our first."

"I guess we'll see about that, won't we?" Jeff retorted.

As Wickes turned to exit the room, he spun around once more, "Tomorrow," he said, pointing at Jeff. "Tomorrow, your ruse will be over."

Jeff followed him to make sure he was out of the building and the door was securely locked. *How did they get in here?*

Returning to the sanctuary, he found Amanda bent over sobbing. Agent Summers, still wearing her glasses, was sitting beside her.

"Are you ladies all right in here?" he asked.

Agent Summers jumped to her feet as her boss approached. "I'm sorry, sir. I had no idea."

"Don't worry about it, Summers," Jeff said, setting beside Amanda and putting his arms around her. "I'll have it taken care of first thing in the morning."

"I told you he was your enemy," Summers said.

"Yes, you did," Jeff said. "But I already knew that. Can I ask how you got inside tonight?"

"He has a key," Summers said.

"Jeff, what are we going to do?" Amanda asked as she wiped her face with tissues.

"We'll talk about it later, honey. Right now I think we need to show Bonnie her room. Is that okay with you, Summers?" he asked.

"Yes, sir, that sounds great at this point."

As they exited the sanctuary, Amanda said, "Jeff, you know I—"

He cut her off quickly, "I'll take care of it first thing in the morning, I promise."

For some odd reason, he didn't want Agent Summers to know that he had lied about what had been taking place earlier.

Amanda led the way down the steps and guided Bonnie Summers to the last available room in the basement. "The restrooms are at the end of the hall. There's a shower if you care to use it. We usually eat breakfast together upstairs. I'll bring some extra clothes in a few minutes."

"You sure you're okay?" Bonnie asked as she stepped into her small but comfortable room.

"I will be." Amanda smiled. "You make yourself comfortable and I'll be right back."

Bonnie turned to inspect her room while Amanda hurried to her own room to dig through her things for something their new boarder could wear since they were close to the same size.

She found the light on and Jeff waiting for her when she returned. "I'm going to find something for her to wear," was all she said.

After she took Bonnie the clothing, she returned to her room, closed the door and sat on the edge of her bed.

"Amanda, I deeply apologize for what I did to you up there," Jeff said, falling to his knees in front of her. "I tried to whisper to you, but it happened so suddenly you apparently couldn't hear me."

"How did you know?" she whispered.

"At the last second I saw Wickes' shadow and I didn't have time to do anything else."

Amanda nodded just as a light knock sounded on her door. She immediately jumped from the bed as fear crossed her face.

"I'll answer it," Jeff assured her as he stepped to the door to find David waiting.

"What was all that racket about?" he asked quietly.

As quickly and simply as he could, Jeff shared with David the happenings of the last hour.

"And you think you can fix it with your captain before Wickes destroys you?" David asked.

"I'm fairly confident that I can not only fix my situation, but get rid of Wickes in the process," Jeff answered.

"So your other agent is here for the night?"

"Yes, and until we are certain about her, we have to be cautious," Jeff said.

Amanda was more concerned than ever because earlier he had been adamant that he felt safe with Agent Summers. She had been too frightened to watch and listen like she was in the habit of doing with new house guests.

"Can you let the others know tonight, just to be safe?" Jeff asked.

"I'll get right on it," David said. "Gloria and I will be praying most of the night about this. Oh, just so you know, I hid all of the Bibles and I have your books boxed up, Amanda."

"Thanks, David, I'll be taking those with me in the morning," Jeff said. "I'll be staying here tonight. I know the floor is hard, but I can stand it for one night."

"Good idea. See you in the morning." David quietly closed the door behind him. Jeff listened and was pleased that he could not hear the visits David made to the other doors.

"Jeff, you don't have to sleep on the floor. My bed is big enough for us both. I think we can be adult enough to keep to our own sides," Amanda said.

"If you're sure," Jeff said. "I'm just so sickened by what I did to you—"

"It's over, you were trying to save our lives," Amanda said as she kicked off her shoes and crawled into one side of her bed.

Jeff turned off the overhead light, but left the small lamp burning. When he settled onto the opposite side of the bed, he could feel Amanda trembling.

"I am still so scared, Jeff," she whispered as tears ran from the corner of her eyes onto her pillow. "Until I see you safely back here from meeting with your captain I won't be able to breathe."

"Would you let me put my arms around you and just hold you so you'll feel safe?" Jeff whispered.

She leaned her back against his chest as his arms encircled her. Several long minutes later, they both fell asleep.

FORTY-FOUR

Hearing activity upstairs and smelling fresh brewed coffee, Bonnie slipped from her room. Dressed in Amanda's clothing, she had just reached the stairway when Jeff opened Amanda's door and stepped out.

"Good morning, Bonnie," he said. "I hope you were able to sleep well."

"Yes, I did," she replied. "Everything was dark and peaceful; quite a change from my house."

"Good," he said. "Have you given any more thought to moving in with us?"

"I'm giving it serious consideration, sir," Bonnie said as she walked into the fellowship hall.

Gloria turned to smile at her while the rest of the group acknowledged her presence in their own ways.

"Please, have a seat," David offered.

"Thank you," Bonnie replied. Jeff pulled out the end chair and Bonnie chose the one next to him, where Amanda usually sat.

"Sleep well?" Sue asked as she reached for a box of cereal.

"Yes, I did. Thank you," Bonnie answered with a sweet smile.

"Not quite like home, but it's comfortable and, for the time being, safe," David said.

"Actually, I was thinking that you have a very good setup here. The rooms downstairs give privacy and yet we are all close enough to help if there should be any trouble."

"Good morning, Amanda," Gloria called as she carried a plate of toast to the table.

Amanda's eyes saw that her usual chair next to Jeff was now occupied. Without hesitation, she pulled out the chair on the opposite side of Bonnie.

"Good morning, everybody," she said cheerily as she poured herself a glass of cold milk.

Hoping everyone remembered not to offer a blessing, she immediately reached for a slice of toast and began eating.

"I bet you have a big day, huh?" she mumbled to Sue.

"Yes," Sue said. "I have to leave shortly."

Although he hadn't eaten anything, Jeff stood and picked up his cup of coffee. "I'm going to change into my uniform for a meeting with my captain. I hope to be back in plenty of time to take you home to pick up some of your things, Bonnie."

Having just taken a spoonful of cereal, Bonnie nodded her head.

"I'm planning a job hunting expedition also, if you're okay with that," David said, turning to his wife.

"I don't have a problem with it," she said. "Will you and Bill be around, Alice?"

"I think so," she replied. "We've been talking about something that we'd like to run by all of you later this evening."

"Ooo, a mystery!" Amanda said.

"I have a job I'd like for someone to begin work on today," Jeff said.

"What's that?" Amanda asked.

"The library," he said.

"What about the library?" Bill asked.

"We need to start clearing out all the books," Jeff said. "I'm going to try to get permission today to burn all of them."

"Alice and I will get on it right away," Bill said.

No one openly expressed any regret. Until everyone was sure about Bonnie, it was quite obvious that caution was the word of the day.

"Okay, thanks," Jeff said. "I'll be back as quickly as possible. Bonnie, if you should decided to join us, we can move some of your things today."

"Thank you, sir," she said, wiping her mouth on a napkin.

Amanda followed Jeff to the outside door where he gave her a gentle hug and kiss before leaving. Into her ear he whispered, "Please pray for me."

"As we speak," she said, tenderly touching his face.

"You two have it bad," Bonnie said, causing Amanda to visibly jump. She hadn't heard Bonnie walk up on them.

"You startled me." Amanda laughed as she walked back into the foyer. "I've never been engaged before so it's kind of exciting."

"Are you still in school?" Bonnie asked.

"I was a junior before life changed so drastically. Jeff was a senior."

"I was a senior, also. Jeff and I were in some of the same classes," Bonnie said.

"So you've been in the W.S.F. for some time?" Amanda asked.

"Since my sophomore year," Bonnie said. "I sure did love it."

"Did?" Amanda studied Bonnie's face.

"Things have changed, that's for sure," Bonnie said.

"How so?"

"Reality always seems to change the color of things," Bonnie said as she sat in one of the foyer's deep-rose colored chairs. "I'm sure Jeff has told you the same."

"Actually, Jeff loves his job," Amanda lied. "He's always excited when he talks about it. I guess that's why Russell Wickes upsets him so much."

Bonnie was looking at Amanda in disbelief. "Really?"

"Yes," Amanda continued. "I don't know what he'd do if he couldn't keep his job."

"That's interesting," Bonnie said softly.

"So, you're having a hard time with it?" Amanda asked.

"I just didn't expect some of our duties to be so—so—I don't know, just so difficult," Bonnie said, rubbing her hands together.

What is it about her? I don't think I'm jealous, but something just isn't right. Amanda's thoughts caused her to miss Bonnie's last statement. "I'm sorry, what did you say was difficult?"

"Oh, nothing really." Bonnie stood and walked toward the steps. "I need to get my room in order before Jeff gets back. I'll catch you later."

"Yeah, see you," Amanda said, watching her go down the steps.

"Bill and Alice are in the library," Gloria called from the kitchen.

"Looks like you've got everything in order here, as usual," Amanda said, giving Gloria a hug.

"What do you think?" Gloria whispered.

Shaking her head, Amanda quietly answered. "I just don't know."

"Hm-m-m. We'll just be careful until we know." Gloria dried her hands on a towel. "I'm done here so I think I'll help Bill and Alice."

Amanda reached out and caught Gloria's arm. "Gloria, wait," she whispered.

"What?"

"I don't know if you heard what happened last night, but please pray hard for Jeff this morning."

Watching Amanda's eyes well up in tears, Gloria gave her a hug. "Don't worry, honey, we've all be praying for him."

"Thanks," Amanda said, wiping her cheek with the back of her hand. "I'm going to be in my room if you need me."

Stepping into the basement hallway, she saw Bonnie coming out of the restroom. "Need anything?" she called.

"I think I'm okay, but thanks."

Amanda walked into her room and closed the door. She wasn't sure where David had hidden her Bible, but she desperately wanted to read it. Instead, she knelt beside her bed and began to silently pray.

Having lost all track of time, she was startled when someone knocked on her door. Not wanting Bonnie to see her praying, she jumped up so quickly her knee bumped into the wooden frame of her bed causing her to yelp.

Jeff quickly opened her door. "You all right?"

"I bumped my knee," she laughed. "I didn't expect you back so soon."

"I wouldn't exactly call two and a half hours 'soon,'" he said.

"How'd it go?" she asked, just as Bonnie walked up to the door.

"Touch and go," he said, giving Amanda a look that told her he had more to say later. "How's your morning been, Bonnie?"

"Quiet, actually," she said. "I'm ready to leave if you are."

"Sure thing," he said. "Let me tell everyone so they won't worry."

"I'll tell them," Amanda volunteered. "That way you won't waste any more time."

"Thank you."

Jeff and Bonnie left in a matter of minutes. Amanda went upstairs to find the others.

Looking into the library, it saddened her to see almost all the bookshelves empty; especially knowing that all the books would more than likely be burned.

"I need to talk to all of you," she said. "Are you ready for a break?"

"I certainly am," Bill said.

"I'll go fix us something to drink while you're finishing up," Amanda said, going into the kitchen for cold drinks.

While everyone sat around the table resting, Amanda filled them in on the previous evening happenings. When she had finished, Alice was hugging herself while Bill fiddled with his empty paper cup.

Attempting to lighten the mood, Gloria said, "Engaged, huh?"

"Not exactly, but we're all going to have to go along with it until we're sure about Bonnie."

"I don't trust her." Alice's tone caused everyone to look at her.

"Why?" Bill asked.

"I don't know," Alice said. "I just don't trust her. In fact, I think I don't even like her."

"Is there anything specific you can pinpoint, Alice?" Amanda asked.

"I can't," she answered. "That's what's frustrating. On the surface, she looks and acts totally innocent."

"For some reason, I can't call this one," Amanda said.

"I know we have to always be careful, but I haven't picked up on anything with her. She seems like a sweet girl," Gloria said. "And Jeff said she is close to becoming a Christian."

"Let's just keep our guard up until we're all one hundred percent sure, okay?" Amanda said.

"Sure of what?" David asked, walking into the room. "I'm sure I'm hungry."

"Hi, honey?" Gloria said, getting up to greet her husband. "Alice, would you like to help me with lunch?"

"We were talking about Bonnie," Amanda said. "Some of us still have misgivings."

She proceeded to fill David in on the details of the previous evening.

"And Jeff isn't back yet?" he asked.

"He's back from his meeting with his captain, but he took Bonnie home to get some of her things."

"So, she's going to be staying here?" David said. His eyes told Amanda that he was worried.

"You're not sure either, are you?" she asked.

Shaking his head, he sat down at the table. "I really haven't been around her, so I can't say."

Amanda slowly walked into the kitchen to help finish lunch. Everything was on the table just as Jeff and Bonnie returned.

After wolfing down a quick lunch, the men helped Bonnie take her things to her room. Leaving her to arrange them the way she wanted, the men excused themselves to do some work outside.

FORTY-FIVE

His heart beating wildly, Jeff resolutely stepped up to Captain Mercett's office door, holding the thick report he had spent the better part of an hour typing.

Upon knocking, he heard Mercett's growl, "Enter." Trying to ignore raging fire in his captain's eyes, he stepped forward and handed him a thick, shiny blue and gold folder.

"Sir, I apologize for taking up your time but I feel it's my duty to bring you up to speed on a major incident which happened last evening involving Agent Wickes. It's a situation that has been building up for some time and came to a head last night."

"Every report up to this point has given glowing remarks on Agent Wickes. Why this sudden change?" Mercett barked. His large hand slamming done on the folder.

"If you would take a look at my report, sir, I think you would better understand how things have changed. I'll answer any questions you have concerning the report."

Without uttering another word and without offering a chair to Jeff, Mercett flopped open the folder and began to read.

Twenty long minutes later, Mercett closed the folder, stood and walked to where he could look out the darkened window to the gym floor below. Intertwining his large fingers behind his back, he stood quietly, seeming to contemplate what his next move would be.

Finally, without turning around, he spoke. "Agent Wickes was in here an hour ago with an altogether different story, Agent Howard."

"That in no way surprises me, sir," Jeff said bravely.

"And what would your recommendation be, Agent Howard?"

"Excuse me, sir?" Jeff asked.

"You've given me a quite detailed report of the last few days happenings with your trainee, but you didn't add your recommendations."

"Sir, I didn't think it was my place to make recommendations in this situation," Jeff said.

Slowly walking to his chair behind his large desk, Mercett continued, "I'm asking you now, what would you recommend I do with Agent Wickes."

"Uh—I think—" Jeff stammered.

"You think?" Captain Mercett barked.

"Sir, I would recommend that Agent Wickes be removed from my squad and possibly from the leadership training program. He is in violation of the sexual harassment code and is in violation of overstepping his authority in calling another agent in to work. He has exercised insubordination for attempting to arrest me for something that clearly was not happening, a situation for which I have kept you abreast of, sir."

"I see." Captain Mercett leaned back in his chair and crossed his arms across his stomach. "Done."

"Excuse me, sir," Jeff repeated.

"You having a hearing problem today, Agent Howard," Mercett shouted.

"No, sir," Jeff answered. "I've just never been in a situation such as this before, sir."

"And it won't be your last," Mercett said. "So is a wedding in the works?"

"No, sir, not if I can help it," Jeff said.

"But your report said you'd asked the girl to marry you." Captain Mercett's confusion showed on his face.

"I did," Jeff said. "I was allowed to stay in her room last night, so what's the point of a wedding, sir?" Jeff said with a feigned smirk.

"I see," Mercett said.

"Sir, about Agent Wickes," Jeff began.

"I'll see to his removal," Mercett said, putting an end to that subject. "What else is going on in the old church?"

"We're trying to eradicate everything religious from the building, sir. By the time I return this morning, most of the library's books will be piled out in the yard," Jeff said. "I would like permission to burn them. It will make quite a large fire, sir."

"Granted," Mercett said.

"I brought a box of some of the books for your inspection, sir," Jeff said. "They have to do with prophecy or some such nonsense."

"And your point in bringing them to me?"

"We already had them boxed up and in my truck before we started on the library, sir," Jeff said.

"Leave them here and wait until tomorrow to burn the others," Mercett said.

"Do you have any recommendation for a replacement for Agent Wickes?"

"Actually, sir," Jeff began. "I believe Agent Bonnie Summers would make an excellent choice, sir."

"Send her to my office first thing Monday morning," Captain Mercett said. "Dismissed."

"Thank you, sir," Jeff said as he saluted and spun around toward the door. With the door opened, he scooted the box of books inside and shoved them against the wall.

"If you would like me to destroy these with the others, I'll be glad to return for them, sir."

"That won't be necessary."

Even though his meeting with Captain Mercett went far better than he anticipated, Jeff didn't trust his superior officer. Things had gone far too smoothly.

What he didn't see, or even suspect, was the speed at which Captain Mercett began digging through the books. And what he would never know was the hours Mercett spent during the remainder of the weekend, reading each and every one of the books.

FORTY-SIX

"What do you think?" David asked as he tossed the shovel aside.

"This sink hole doesn't look promising at all," Jeff said dejectedly.

"It's not even a large enough hole to hide supplies in let alone any one of us," Bill said. "Not that I was looking forward to crawling down any ole snake hole in the first place."

"All we have is the church building to hide out in," Jeff said, leaning on the shovel handle.

"Jeff, you should know the answer to this," David said. "Are we able to travel? Will they let us move from state to state? Can we fly? Can we ride the bus? How restricted are we in our travel options?"

"Whoa," Jeff laughed. "One question at a time, please."

"Those are good questions," Bill said. "If we could get far, far away from here, we might have a chance of surviving longer."

"What's going on here is going on everywhere," Jeff said. "But, yes we can travel if we have the money. However our IDs have to be in perfect order."

David rested his head on his knees.

"Home sweet home," Bill moaned.

Seeing no point in covering up the clearing they'd made with their shovels, three dejected men scuffled through the thick, rotting leaves back to the storage shed, tossing their shovels inside, not bothering to hang them in their normal place.

Because all doors except one had been secured from the inside, they tramped through the west door in their muddy shoes across the foyer carpet and into the fellowship hall.

Gloria was standing in the kitchen folding clean kitchen towels when she looked up to see her husband and two friends drag themselves to the table and plop down into the chairs.

Despair shrouded the room. Gloria didn't know what to say, so she made a pot of strong, hot coffee. When the men had warm mugs sitting in front of them, they seemed to breathe easier again.

"No luck?" she asked as she rubbed her husband's shoulders.

David shook his head without answering. As he brought the hot coffee to his lips, an unseen hand shoved his mouth into the hot liquid.

"Gloria, why'd you do that?!" he yelled. Gloria stumbled backward into the chairs behind her.

"I didn't," she cried, running to the kitchen for a cold, wet towel.

"She really didn't, David," Bill said.

David, holding his hand over his burned mouth, mumbled, "Somebody sure did and she was the only one behind me."

As Gloria handed him the towel, he grabbed it, dodging her effort to help. Tears were running down her face as she ran from the room. Reaching the top of the steps, that same unseen hand gave her a shove.

Her scream caused David to jump up so quickly the metal chair clanged to the floor. When he got to her, Gloria was curled up hugging her knee. Her sobs came from her broken heart.

David knelt beside her, picking her up into his arms. "I'm sorry, Gloria. I am so sorry. Please forgive me."

Bill and Jeff hovered closely, making sure that Gloria wasn't seriously injured. Amanda ran up the steps with Bonnie right on her heels.

"What on earth?" Amanda exclaimed.

"Someone pushed me." Gloria sobbed.

"What?" David exclaimed, pulling back to look into his wife's face. "No one was near you."

"Nobody pushed you either," Bill said.

"Would someone tell me what's going on here?" Amanda said.

Jeff told her what had taken place with the coffee and then Gloria's tumble down the steps.

"What was going on before all this took place?" Amanda asked.

Jeff glanced quickly at Bonnie before speaking. "We men had been working on a project that just wasn't coming together and so we gave up and came inside. To say that we were disappointed would be a serious understatement."

Still holding her knee, Gloria pulled away from her husband, her eyes wide. Quickly swiping away tears, she said, "Wait! Remember yesterday?"

"What?" David asked. His blistered lips ached.

"The spirit of heaviness," Gloria said, looking around the group. At this point she didn't care about Bonnie finding out. "When you guys came in there was a terrible spirit of despair on each of you."

"That's it," Amanda shouted.

Alice, who had heard the commotion from the library, joined the group. "We all remember what we had to do about the first one."

"What on earth are you people talking about?" Bonnie said.

"Right now we have some very serious, dangerous warfare to do to get rid of another evil spirit," Jeff said.

"Evil spirit?" Bonnie asked, giving the group an incredulous look.

"Bonnie, you won't understand this, but there is an evil spirit in this building and we are going to pray it out of here," Jeff said.

"You mean you really do pray, just like Agent Wickes said?"

"Yes," Jeff said. "We have all become Christians since the rapture. You asked how I was able to face each day. This is how. I wouldn't be able to survive if I didn't know Jesus as my savior."

As soon as he said the word *Jesus,* every opened door inside the church building slammed, causing the entire group to gasp and grab each other.

"You've got to be kidding me," Bonnie exclaimed.

"No, Bonnie, it's true. Would you like to know how to become a Christian?" Jeff asked.

"You know what happens to Christians. How can you ask me that?" she said.

"Because we want you to know the peace that we experience because we belong to God," Jeff said.

"I don't know, Jeff. Let me think about it, okay?"

"These are very real, very evil, and very dangerous beings," David said. "And they will do anything possible to keep you from becoming a believer."

"So now I have something else to worry about," Bonnie said.

Amanda didn't miss the hint of ugliness that crept into Bonnie's voice.

"While you're thinking, we have to try to keep you safe while we pray," Jeff said.

"And how do you propose to do that?"

Gloria and Alice heard the ugliness this time.

"We're going to walk you to your room and shut you in while we pray for one of God's warriors to stand guard at your door," David said.

"God's warriors?" Bonnie exclaimed. "Are you all insane?"

There was no mistaking it any longer. Deathly quiet settled over the group as even the men could no longer ignore her attitude.

"I told you that it would be difficult for you to understand," David said quietly. "But, we would still like for you to allow us to do what we can to protect you, okay?"

"By all means, please." She regained her innocent look when she realized how the others were looking at her. "If this is as bad as you say it is, I don't have the power to protect myself."

"Okay, then," David said, leaving his wife's side to follow Bonnie downstairs. Jeff and Bill followed so they could pray outside her door.

Without a word passing between them, the ladies looked at each other, knowing that Bonnie Summers was a serious threat to their lives.

Taking the steps two at a time, the men joined the women in a prayer circle that they trusted would rid them of yet another evil, tormenting spirit.

Before the prayers began, Gloria looked up at her husband, "David?" she asked quietly.

"I know," was his only response.

"I'm sorry," Jeff said. "Let's pray."

Just as before, when their prayers began around the hand-clasped circle, they felt a surge of divine power.

The doors began to rattle. Bone-chilling air began to slap against the back of their legs as they called on the power of Jesus' name.

Like a vacuum, the cold air suddenly sucked back down the steps. The prayers momentarily stopped. Each person looked at the other as an unholy quiet enveloped the foyer.

Still clinging to each other's hand, they heard Bonnie's and an unearthly voice reverberating through the heating ducts.

"Do you still belong to us?" the spirit hissed.

"You know the answer to that, now get out of here and go torment those Christians upstairs," she hissed back.

Jeff's head dropped. Alice's and Gloria's hands began to tremble. Amanda had an overwhelming desire to wrap her arms around Jeff but knew their circle must not be broken.

"It will be back; we need to continue to pray," she whispered.

David immediately began praying. Icy cold assaulted them from behind; Amanda began chanting out loud, with the group picking up the pattern.

"The blood of Jesus. The blood of Jesus. The blood of Jesus." Their chant became louder and louder.

Suddenly a violent shove knocked Gloria to her knees, although she refused to stop chanting Jesus' name.

Considering Gloria to be the weak link, it karate chopped her and Alice's clasped hands causing both ladies to squeeze even harder, refusing to let go.

"On the count of three," Jeff said. "One. Two. Three."

"IN THE NAME OF JESUS, COVERED BY JESUS' BLOOD, WE COMMAND YOU TO BE GONE, SPIRIT OF DESPAIR!" Without prior prompting, all six voices joined in the spiritual command.

A horrendous, earsplitting scream echoed through the foyer. Each person grimaced but continued to call out the name of Jesus.

Plywood covering the double east doors splintered as the evil spirit screamed through the wooden opening.

The group fell to their knees, giving thanks to Jesus. Their praise continued for several minutes. Satisfied that the spirit was entirely gone, they opened tear-filled eyes and surveyed the damage.

"Someone should go check on Bonnie," David said.

"I'll do that," Amanda offered.

Gloria could see in her eyes that Amanda was going to inflict serious bodily injury to Bonnie. "Jeff, why don't you go with her?"

Jeff and Amanda walked down the steps, hand in hand, and knocked on Bonnie's door. Without waiting for a response, Amanda pushed the door open.

"You okay?" she barked.

Bonnie was equally startled as she tossed down the magazine she was reading.

"Done already?" she asked, sheepishly.

Looking at his watch, Jeff said, "This was a bad one, it took an hour. Are you sure you're all right?"

"Your prayers at her door certainly worked," Amanda said. "She's not worried one little bit."

Not having a clue that the group had heard her conversation with the demon, Bonnie replied sweetly, "That's right, Jeff. Thank you so much for protecting me." Stepping past Amanda, she gave Jeff a tight hug.

Jerking away, Jeff said, "Sue will be home from work shortly. Gloria is beginning dinner."

Amanda had never seen Jeff struggle for words before.

"Would you like to help us with dinner," Amanda asked her, wanting Bonnie where they could watch her.

"I'm not much on cooking, but I'll do what I can," Bonnie said, giving Amanda a look that only the two of them understood. "Give me half an hour and I'll be up."

Amanda took the initiative in leading Jeff up the stairs and into the kitchen where she and Gloria began making as much noise as possible with plates, pots and pans.

David and Bill were feverishly working to repair the doors the spirit had demolished.

Amanda kept her eye on Jeff as he sat at one of the tables with his head in his hands. Up until this point in time, she had never seen Jeff when he was not in control of himself or any given situation.

God, you've got to help him.

"She said she'd be here in thirty minutes," she whispered to Gloria.

Gloria, clearly angered, nodded her head as she continued to clang the silverware and cooking utensils.

Clasping her hand over Gloria's, Amanda whispered, "This won't help, friend."

Gloria turned to speak to Amanda just as Sue entered the fellowship hall.

"Hi, everybody, I'm home," she called. Stopping in her tracks, she knew something was wrong. "Oh, no! What's up?"

"What'cha got there?" Amanda asked, quickly walking up to her friend who was holding a full, brown paper sack. "Tell you in a minute," she whispered.

Sue walked over to the long kitchen countertop where she dumped out the contents of the sack. "Goodies," she said, looking from Gloria to Amanda.

"Well, look here, Gloria!" Amanda announced, holding up a small yellow box.

"How'd you know?" Gloria exclaimed, limping over to the counter.

"Know what?" Sue asked. "And why are you limping?"

"Oh, I had a little tumble," Gloria said. Opening the box, she pulled out an elastic knee brace which just happened to be her size.

"Let me see," Sue said.

Gloria was shocked at how swollen her knee had become.

"Oh, my," Sue said. "Let's get you off your feet and put some ice on this knee before we put a bandage on it."

"But—" Gloria complained.

"No buts, girl," Sue said. "This does not look good."

Amanda and Sue led Gloria to a chair that looked comfortable. Once Gloria's leg was propped up on another chair, Amanda returned to the kitchen to make an ice pack.

"We had another visitor today," Jeff informed her. Amanda was pleased to see the look of authority beginning to return to Jeff's eyes.

"Good or bad?" Sue asked.

"Worse than the last," Jeff said.

Sue looked at Jeff, then at Gloria and Amanda. "You mean—"

"Yes," Amanda said. "I think this one's name was 'despair' and he was very determined and horribly evil."

"He pushed me down the steps," Gloria said.

Bill, Alice and David entered the fellowship hall at that moment. Sue was shocked to see David's face.

"What on earth?" she said, walking up to David to inspect his mouth.

"The demon shoved his mouth into a cup of hot coffee," Gloria said.

"Sounds like I missed an eventful day." Sue dug through the items on the counter, finding the burn ointment that just happened to be there.

"Keep this on your lips as much as possible," she told him.

"Did you buy all this stuff?" Amanda asked, searching through the pile of medical supplies.

"No, they were going to throw it all out," Sue said. "They were more than willing to let me have what I wanted; and I wanted it all."

"Dinner ready yet?" Bonnie asked, bouncing into the fellowship hall.

"We need extra help," Amanda said with a definite clip to her voice. "Gloria's going to be off her feet for a while."

"I'm sorry, Gloria," Bonnie said sweetly. "Okay, tell me what I can do."

"Me too," Alice said.

While Sue found a place to store her newly acquired supplies, the other ladies began preparing dinner.

"I've only been off work for two days now," Jeff said. "It seems like two months. I'll certainly be glad to get back to work Monday morning."

"I know what you mean," Bonnie said as she prepared a large salad. "This is the first entire weekend I've had off and it seems like a week."

Amanda's jaws ached from clinching them so tightly.

"What's on the agenda for tomorrow?" Bill asked.

Crossing her arms across her chest, Amanda turned from the stove to watch Jeff who was now standing. When she saw the look of determination on his face, her own face relaxed and her arms fell to her sides.

"Immediately following breakfast we'll have a praise and prayer service."

"Ouch!" Bonnie squealed, dropping the paring knife she had been using. Grabbing a towel, she squeezed her finger to stop the drips of blood.

Sue grabbed the first aid kit. "Here, let me take care of that."

It was Amanda's turn to smile sweetly. "And then?" she prompted.

"After that we'll have a huge bonfire. By the time that calms down, it should be around lunchtime and we'll just roast us some hot dogs. How does that sound?"

"A picnic," Amanda exclaimed. "Sounds great."

Gloria was getting a kick out of Amanda's excitement. David, sitting close to his wife, couldn't help smiling also.

On the pretense of checking her injury, Jeff walked over to Bonnie and Sue. "Is it very bad?"

"Just a little cut," Sue said. "But you know how they like to bleed. I'll finish the salad, Bonnie."

"Thanks," she said.

"Is there anything else you need from your place? How about all your uniforms and things?" Jeff asked.

"No, I think I have everything," Bonnie said, standing as close to Jeff as possible.

"I can't thank you enough for everything, Jeff."

"Not a problem," he said, taking a step back.

"The lease is up on my house in two weeks," she said. "I'd like to check one more time for anything that I might want later. It's not safe to leave a place empty these days, you know."

"You're right about that," he said. "The guys and I will plan on going with you tomorrow."

Amanda was watching this exchange. When she heard their plans for tomorrow her eyebrows went up as she turned back to the stove.

"That'd be great," Bonnie said as she followed Jeff to the table and pulled out the chair next to him. "If there's anything I can do, just shout," she added.

"How about setting the table?" Amanda called, not bothering to turn around.

Gloria bit her lower lip to keep from smiling.

"I should be able to do that," Bonnie answered.

"David, would you help me with something?" Jeff asked as he walked toward his room, which was located at the back of the fellowship hall.

"Sure thing," David said. "Be right back." He kissed Gloria on the top of her head before following Jeff.

Placing two pillows over the heater vent in his room, Jeff sat on the edge of his bed. David pulled the one chair in the room close to him.

"I don't know how, when, or where, but Bonnie will have to be dealt with," Jeff said.

David nodded his head, knowing full well the toll it was taking on his young friend who had to "deal with" yet another person.

"What can I do to help?" he asked.

"At the moment, just pray," Jeff said. "I have an idea that I think will work, but I'll need help after the fact."

"Understood," David said.

"We haven't had the opportunity to talk about it, but is the place you hid the Bibles completely safe?"

"I think so," David said. "Can I ask why?"

"I just wondered if there is a place to hide something forever," Jeff said.

"If you think we have time before dinner, I'll show you and see what you think," David said, standing.

"Let me check with the girls," Jeff said. "I'll have Amanda keep Bonnie upstairs while we're out of the room."

"Do you think moving the wall would be too big of a job?" Jeff asked as they walked up to the dinner table.

Realizing his friend's question was a camouflage, David answered, "Shouldn't be. With Bill and me helping, it shouldn't take long at all."

"What shouldn't take long?" Gloria asked. She had sat with her leg propped up for about as long as she could stand it. She found no enjoyment watching everyone else being busy while she sat idle.

"Oh, a little construction project," David said. Making sure Bonnie was in the kitchen, he bent to give his wife a kiss, whispering in her ear in the process. "Gotta go to the basement for a few minutes."

Looking up into his eyes, Gloria knew she shouldn't ask any questions. "Love you," she said, nodding her head slightly.

"I don't want to rush you, but how much longer before we eat?" Jeff asked.

"Twenty minutes should do it," Alice said.

"Good," Jeff said, sneaking a couple crackers to munch on. "David and I are going to check the leak by the washing machine. We'll see what it needs now and possibly fix it after dinner if it's not too complicated."

While Bonnie carried a stack of plates to the table, Jeff gave Amanda a hug, whispering in her ear. "Keep her up here."

Nodding, Amanda continued stirring the spaghetti sauce. "This smells really good so you better not make us wait."

"Better watch her, Jeff," David called as he headed for the steps. "She's practicing for her wifely duties."

"Funny," Gloria called.

While Bonnie was placing the silverware beside the plates, she announced, "I've got a headache that won't go away. I'm going to run to my room for my medicine."

"Not necessary," Amanda called out. "Here's a brand-new bottle Sue brought in today." She grabbed the plastic container of pain medication and set it on the countertop. "I'll get you a glass of cold water."

Gloria, helping Bonnie with the silverware, didn't miss her angry scowl.

"Those nagging headaches can be the pits," Gloria said.

Slapping the last fork onto the table, Bonnie remarked, "The 'pits' is exactly what I had in mind."

Gloria's lips spread into a wide grin as Bonnie stomped into the kitchen to grab the medicine bottle, popping a little white pill into her mouth and washing it down with the cup of water Amanda had left for her.

"Why don't you sit in one of the easy chairs by the TV until you feel better?" Sue suggested. "By the time we finish up here you should be feeling much better."

Not needing a second invitation, Bonnie dropped into the softest looking chair which also just happened to have its back to the kitchen. In frustration, she kicked the hassock across the floor.

"You okay?" Amanda asked, smiling.

Seething with contempt, Bonnie squeezed her eyes shut, not bothering to answer. *It's going to be a real pleasure getting rid of you, Amanda. A real pleasure.*

FORTY-SEVEN

Soon after the kitchen was back in order, Bonnie excused herself from the group. Always careful to act sweet and innocent around the men, she smiled and assured everyone that she was feeling better; she just needed to rest awhile.

"Let's set in the easy chairs tonight instead of these hard ones," Gloria said. "My bottom has had it with metal chairs for one evening."

Everyone laughed as they moved around the large screen TV which had not been used since they moved into the church building. Jeff kept them briefed on everything they needed to know so they had no desire to listen to the TV.

Jeff made sure he sat as close to Amanda as possible, having arranged with David to dominate the conversation so he could whisper to her without any chance of being overheard.

"You know what I'd like to do?" Gloria asked. "Since the rapture happened, I don't believe we've sung any songs. I think it's about time we remedied that."

"You're right," Sue said excitedly. "We've been so overwhelmed by everything else that singing just hasn't been high on our to-do list."

"What if someone outside should hear?" Bill asked.

"We don't have to raise the rafters," David said. "Who wants to choose the first song?"

"Oh, please, let's sing 'Amazing Grace,'" Alice said.

"You start us off, Alice," David said.

Everyone began singing except Jeff, who leaned over to whisper to Amanda. "Sometime this evening I will be alone with Bonnie for a while."

Amanda pulled away to look into Jeff's eyes, wondering why he would tell her something like that.

"And you're telling me this for what reason?" she quipped.

As soon as the words escaped her lips, she regretted them. Taking a good look into his eyes, she saw the truth.

"Oh, Jeff, I'm so sorry," she said, grabbing his hand. "I'm so sorry."

"Okay, how about another song," David asked when all five verses of "Amazing Grace" had been sung.

"How about 'His Banner Over Me Is Love'?" Gloria said.

"Start us off, honey," David said.

As the singing began, Jeff whispered to Amanda who didn't pull away from him this time.

"I don't know what excuse I'll use to get her alone, but I don't think it will matter to her."

"You're right in that department," Amanda said.

"David and I have it all planned out—" Suddenly the singing stopped. "Oops."

"Okay, lovebirds," Sue said. "It's your turn to choose a song."

"Hm-m-m. How about—"

Bonnie's unexpected appearance stopped Amanda.

"I really don't want to spoil your fun, but if I could hear your beautiful singing downstairs. I'm concerned anyone listening outside can too." Bonnie pulled up a folding chair next to the loveseat Jeff and Amanda were occupying.

"Maybe you're right," David said. "It just felt so good to sing again, we simply forgot."

"I understand, but I don't want us to get in trouble. By the way, those songs were really nice," Bonnie said. Turning in Jeff's direction, she laid her hand on his arm before speaking. "Jeff, apparently I left my family photos at my place. Would you run me over there to get them?"

Jeff pulled his arm away on the premise of looking at his watch. "It's too late, now. It's lights off in half an hour. I'll take you first thing in the morning if that's okay."

"Certainly, that's not a problem," she said, smiling sweetly at him. "I didn't realize what time it was."

"I tossed a load of clothes in the washer a few minutes ago," she said. "I assumed it was safe since I didn't see any leaks."

David's and Jeff's eyes met. "Actually, we fixed the leak before dinner. It was just a loose hose," David said.

"My dad hated working on plumbing jobs around the house," Bonnie said, continuing to dominate the men's conversation. "Mom always had to hire that work out."

"Are your parents still around, Bonnie?" Gloria asked, realizing that they hadn't learned anything about this girl's family or life.

"Actually, they left on a cruise before I was put on active duty," she answered. "I haven't heard from them so they must be having the time of their lives."

"Wow. A cruise," Gloria said. "I always wanted to do that."

"That's news to me," David said, giving his wife a strange look.

"I never told you because I knew we couldn't afford it," she said, touching his cheek. "I settled for our occasional trips to the beach."

"I always wanted to go out west," Alice said.

"I was planning on taking you for our tenth anniversary," Bill said.

"Get out." Alice laughed.

"Really. I really was," Bill said. "I had already started a savings account for it."

"How'd you do that without me knowing?" Alice asked.

"I have to admit it has been difficult getting anything past you." Bill smiled.

"How about you, Sue?" David asked. "What was your special dream?"

"An Alaskan cruise," Sue said with a far-off look in her eyes. "George kept telling me that he wasn't going to freeze his—he wasn't going to freeze to death just to ride a boat through a bunch of overgrown ice cubes."

"Overgrown ice cubes," David laughed. "That's funny."

"I might still go," Sue said. "Now that I've got a job I can save up and go by myself."

"Maybe we could all go together," Gloria said.

"Wouldn't that be fun?" Sue said.

"How about you, Amanda?" David asked.

"I don't know," she said. "I didn't think much past graduating from high school. I was trying to convince my dad to let me go to Florida with some girlfriends."

"Well, I'm doing what I always dreamed of doing," Bonnie said. "Nothing makes me happier than putting on that beautiful uniform and keeping an eye on our community."

She couldn't see Amanda rolling her eyes in disgust.

"Time for lights out," Jeff announced.

Bill walked to the row of light switches and gave them one big chop. The fellowship hall windows were not covered like the ones in the sanctuary so some light still filtered through the stained glass.

"Too bad we can't build a fire and roast some marshmallows," Gloria said.

"Hey, we can do that tomorrow," Amanda said.

Jeff walked into the kitchen to get a bottle of water. "Anybody want anything?" he asked.

"Is there any diet soda?" Bonnie asked, moving to the loveseat.

"Actually, there's only iced tea, bottled water or milk," Amanda said.

"I'll take some iced tea," Bonnie said.

"You know, since the library is empty, we could make another room in there in case we get any more boarders," Alice said.

"It's kind of small, don't you think?" Bill asked.

"Sure, but if the shelves were removed, there would be enough room for a single bed, a dresser and a chair," Alice said.

"There's a single bed in the storage shed," Amanda said. "It's one from my house."

"Thank you, Amanda," Bill said. "Now I have more work to do."

Amanda laughed as Alice playfully hit Bill's arm. "You're welcome, Bill."

Jeff handed a large paper cup of iced tea to Bonnie before sitting next to David and Gloria on the couch. After he was seated, everything became quiet for several long minutes as everyone seemed to be lost in their own thoughts.

As Jeff drained the last drop of water from his bottle, he kept fiddling with the lid. "Bonnie, we've all been praying for you today, hoping that you would be ready to ask Jesus to come into your heart."

Becoming choked on her last swallow of tea, Bonnie spluttered and coughed.

"That's right, Bonnie," Gloria added. "Jeff's your squad leader. If he can fool everybody, I'm sure you can too."

"I don't know," she said, bending the rim of her empty paper cup back and forth. "If they ever found out—"

"I've come to the point that if I had to die, it'd be worth it because I know I'll be going to Heaven," Jeff said.

"But, you know what they have in store for any one of us who might become a Christian," she said.

"Yes, I know that," Jeff said. "I also know that nothing is a sure thing any longer. That is, nothing except Heaven and Hell. And I have no intentions of going to Hell for any reason."

Bonnie slowly nodded her head. She hadn't noticed David getting up and leaving the room a few minutes earlier. Suddenly he reappeared and sat on the folding chair she had vacated.

"Let me show you some verses here in the Bible, Bonnie," David said, opening his Bible to the book of Romans.

The sudden appearance of the Bible in close proximity to her was more than Bonnie could stand. She jerked her arm away causing the paper cup to pop out of her hand and land on Amanda's foot.

Quickly reaching for the cup, she said, "I'm sorry. Here, I'll throw it away."

"No," Amanda said, patting Bonnie's leg. "I'll get rid of it for you so you can listen to David."

Unable to escape, Bonnie leaned forward with her elbows on her knees and her face cupped in her hands.

"See here? Chapter three of Romans, verse twenty-three tells us that *all have sinned and come short of the glory of God.* That's each and every one of us, Bonnie. But the Bible doesn't stop there. In chapter six, verse twenty-three we find the words, *the wages of sin is death, but the gift of God is eternal life through Jesus Christ our Lord.* We don't have to die and go to Hell because Jesus died for us on the cross and shed his blood so that we could be saved.

Chapter ten, verse nine tells us that *if we confess with our mouths and believe in our hearts that Jesus rose from the dead, we will be saved.* Would you like to confess your sins now and believe in your heart that Jesus died and rose again for you?"

"No, I don't," she stated, standing quickly. "I don't mean to sound rude, but I've tried to tell you that I'm not ready for this."

All eyes were on Bonnie as she walked toward the steps. "I think I'll go to my room, now. This has been a very long day. Good night, everybody."

"Good night," everyone said.

Jeff stood slowly, looking at Amanda in the darkening room. Tears began to well up in her eyes.

David slowly closed the Bible, stood and put his hand on Jeff's shoulder. "Everybody gather around, we need to pray for Jeff," he whispered.

As quickly as possible, everyone gathered close, placing their hands on Jeff as David whispered a prayer.

"God, Jeff needs your wisdom and guidance for what he needs to do. Please go with him. Amen."

Each group member added their "amen," as Jeff made his way down the steps. Amanda sank onto the couch crying softly. She, David and Jeff were the only ones privy to what would be taking place.

Bill, Alice, Sue and Gloria quietly took their seats, not knowing what to say since they didn't know what was going on. Gloria chose a seat next to Amanda, putting her arm around her young friend.

"We need to talk about something to make everything seem normal," David whispered. "I'll fill you in on the details later."

"Sue, how was your job today?" Alice asked brightly.

"It was good, actually," Sue said. "It feels great to be a nurse again. We were busy, especially early afternoon."

"I wonder why?" Bill said.

"Probably because that's when most people feel safe to be out," Sue said. "You know, Bill, they were talking about needing someone to keep the shelves stocked. Maybe that'd be a good job for you."

"What do you think, honey?" Bill asked his wife.

"I'd rather have you here with me," she said. "But we all have to do our part to help out financially, so go for it."

"I'll ride in with your tomorrow, if that's all right," he said to Sue.

"That's fine with me," Sue said.

"I just remembered something," Gloria began. "Earlier today you told us that you and Alice had something to run by the rest of us. What was that?"

"Oh, that," Alice said. "We almost forgot, didn't we?"

"We were mulling over the possibility of teaching, or tutoring, adults in math or science or something. What do you think?" Bill asked.

"I'm not sure that would be safe," Amanda said after a few minutes of contemplation.

"Why's that?" Bill asked.

"I'm not real sure," Amanda said. "I just have a feeling in here," she pointed to her chest, "that it's just not the right thing to do."

"We certainly respect those feelings, Amanda," Alice said. "You may have just given us a few more months, or years, of life."

"Let's hope so," Gloria said. "I hope you all won't end up getting upset with me for not working. I just have no desire to leave this building."

"It's not a problem for me," Amanda said.

"Somebody needs to be here to keep an eye on things," Sue said.

"And we surely don't have a problem with that, Gloria," Bill said.

Hearing a rattling noise on the back side of the building, Bill got up to investigate.

"What is it?" Alice asked.

"I believe the wind has picked up again," Bill said.

"I think you're right," David said. "I can hear it now."

An hour passed before Jeff scuffed into the fellowship hall. Amanda immediately went to his side, guiding him to the couch. His friends had not seen Jeff Howard's shoulders so slumped before.

David looked through the darkness at his young friend, concerned for the load of guilt that his friend was carrying. Realizing Jeff's inability to speak, he began to fill everybody in on the story he and Jeff had concocted earlier. They had made the decision to give out as little information as possible just in case any one of them should be questioned by the authorities.

"Bonnie won't be joining us again, will she?" he asked Jeff.

Jeff shook his head.

"What do you mean 'she won't be joining us'?" Alice asked.

Swallowing hard, Jeff began to speak.

"I tried to speak with her about what we heard earlier between her and the demon. She became irate and advised me that she was out of here. I tried to stop her, but she filled a bag with her personal belongings and made me unlock the door for her."

"You mean she left the building? After curfew?" Sue asked.

Jeff nodded his head. "She called somebody on her cell phone. They were here to pick her up in a matter of minutes."

"Oh, Jeff," Gloria cried. "What if she reports us?"

"There's nothing we can do about it now except pray," Jeff said. He felt sick inside, not only because of what he had done but how he had to lie to his friends about it.

"Let's all turn in early tonight," David said. "We've taken an emotional beating today and haven't a clue what we're going to be facing tomorrow."

"Good idea," Bill said. "Let's pray together first, okay?"

The group of friends held hands in a circle as David, Bill and Sue offered up prayers. When they were finished they all descended the steps together.

Amanda didn't question him as he followed her into her room, kicked off his shoes, and climbed onto her bed.

Tonight the small table lamp remained off. Blinding darkness engulfed them. Fully dressed, she snuggled into the exact position as the night before, only this time it was Jeff's tears that dampened the pillow.

"When you're ready, I'm listening," she said softly. Eventually his arms around her began to relax.

The moment she felt herself slipping into the realm of sleep, she heard him whisper, "Please turn on the lamp."

Moving quickly, her hand reached out to twist the small, black knob. Soft light danced gently across the room.

"I want to tell you about it," Jeff said.

"You don't have to, you know."

"I need to tell you," he said, his arms tightening around her.

"Okay, I'm listening," she said. She sat up and crossed her legs.

Sitting up, Jeff scooted until his back was against the wall; he began his story.

"When I got to the bottom of the steps, she was waiting for me, as if she knew I would follow her. It was crystal clear what her intentions were. I told her to go into the restroom."

"Was she scared at that point?" Amanda asked.

"Are you kidding?" he said. "The comment she made was, 'why, Jeff, I didn't know you Christians knew how to really enjoy sex.' I wanted to vomit."

"So she didn't have any qualms about anything?"

"No," Jeff said, shaking his head. "I told her to go on in and I'd be right there. When David and I were downstairs earlier, I had gone into her room and found her weapon. So when she went into the restroom I hurried into her room, grabbed her weapon and followed her. By the time I got in there, she had her blouse completely unbuttoned. Like I said, I wanted to puke. I immediately pointed the weapon at her and told her to back away from me. Her face turned white as she backed up against the wall." Jeff paused for several seconds.

"And?" Amanda gently prodded.

"Oh, she bounced back quickly. Her face twisted into an evil mask. She told me that Captain Mercett already knew about what was going on here. She said that Russell Wickes was an inept weenie and that she was not only the captain's real spy, but his special agent, if I knew what she meant."

"Did you believe her?" Amanda asked, nervously rubbing her hands together.

Jeff shrugged his shoulders. "I just let her talk. We need all the information we can get. She began to offer me a position by her side with no more need to fear the head office. In fact, she even had plans to use this building for their headquarters."

"No," Amanda whispered hoarsely.

"Amanda, I just can't do this any more," Jeff said, rubbing his hands through his blond hair.

"I told you that you didn't have to tell me," she said, reaching over and touching his forearm.

"No, not that," he said. "I can't play this game anymore. I became a W.S.F. agent with excitement. I looked forward every day to our training sessions. That's how I advanced so quickly. Everybody knew I had made the Security Force my life. I didn't have a clue. I didn't have a clue."

"You weren't a Christian then, either," Amanda said softly.

"That's right," he said, looking at her. "And I don't want to go back to not being one, but this charade is too much. I'm going to lose my life anyway so it may as well be soon."

Amanda dropped her head, shaking it slowly as tears ran down her cheeks. "You can't. You just can't."

An uneasy quietness settled into the softly lit room. Only Amanda's occasional sniffs broke the silence.

Minutes later, Jeff cleared his throat and continued, "Anyway, when Bonnie saw that her words weren't going to change my mind, she pulled off her blouse. When she reached back to unhook her bra, I—I—"

Amanda scooted next to him, wrapping her arms around him as he sobbed against her hair. They cried together for yet another lost life, the bleakness of their own present life, and for the life they would never have.

Amanda finally pulled away and reached for the box of tissues on the bedside table. Snatching a handful, she handed them to Jeff then sat with her back against the wall next to him.

Suddenly remembering something he had told her earlier about his weapon, she leaned forward where she could look in his face.

"Jeff, your weapon. How will you explain that it was used again?" she cried.

Placing his hands on her arms, he tried to calm her. "It's okay, it wasn't my weapon. Remember, I said I got hers from her room."

"Oh, yeah," she breathed, putting her hand over her heart. "Phew, that scared me."

"Obviously," he laughed. "David and I figured it all out earlier. We found a place to hide her weapon where no one would ever think to look. I've already put it there. Tomorrow, during the bonfire, we'll burn her uniforms and some of her personal items. Her makeup and things like that, we'll divide up between you ladies."

"I don't want any of that stuff," Amanda said.

"Just as a way to hide it in plain sight," Jeff said.

"Okay," she responded. "Just don't expect me to use any of it."

"First thing tomorrow morning I will tell Captain Mercett that she left during the night and I've been unable to make contact with her."

"Will he believe your story?"

"Who knows," Jeff said. "He'll no doubt want me to come to his office where he'll inspect my weapon. He'll never find hers."

"So, it's more just wait and see, huh?" she said.

"I'm afraid so," he replied. "I keep thinking about that guillotine. I've pretty much convinced myself that when the time comes, at least it will be quick and virtually painless."

Amanda began to rub the back of her neck while she grimaced.

Jeff laughed a little as he glanced at the digital alarm clock. "It's going on one o'clock. We'd better try to get some sleep. I'll go to my room, if you want."

Amanda shook her head slowly. "I don't know if I'll ever be able to sleep alone again. Please stay."

As they both settled back into their original positions, Amanda asked, "Can we keep the light on?"

"It won't bother me," he replied.

Amanda watched the red digital numbers slowly roll over and over. Tears seeped from her eyes, making a damp spot on her pillow.

Much later, Jeff spoke ever so softly. "Are you asleep?"

"No," she whispered.

"I realize our time here on earth is going to be short, but I've been thinking that it would be so wonderful to consider ourselves husband and wife."

"Jeff," she said with a worried tone.

"No, not that way," he assured her. "I'll never ask that of you. It's just that my mind, my heart, my life belongs to you and will continue to do so until 'death do us part.'"

Feeling much more at peace than he had in weeks, Jeff slipped into a deep, peaceful, rest-giving sleep.

Long minutes later, Amanda flipped her damp pillow over, pulled the pink, soft blanket over her shoulders and drifted into a dream-filled sleep.

FORTY-EIGHT

Violent blasts of wind crashing into the sides of the building awakened everyone. When the building began to shake from the bottom up, Amanda fell from the bed. Jeff struggled to reach her as the concrete floor rolled as if it were a sheet shaken in the breeze.

"Jeff! Amanda!" David shouted above the rumble of the earthquake and howling, wind. "Jeff! Amanda!"

"We're okay," Jeff shouted back. "Grab my hand, Amanda."

Wobbling along the moving floor, they made it to the door. Jeff had to jerk with all his might to open it.

Jumping across the hallway, they joined their friends in a huddled mass of trembling bodies in the stairwell. Terrified, no one was able to speak or even cry.

An abrupt unearthly quiet squeezed their eardrums. The earth stopped rolling. The wind ceased howling.

Jeff began to shine his flashlight around the group, making sure they were all accounted for.

"I can't promise, but I think it's safe," he said quietly.

Jeff, David and Bill stood first.

"Everyone, all right?" David asked, reaching for his wife's hand.

One by one the women began to stand, except Sue.

"Sue," Amanda exclaimed. "Sue, are you okay?" She knelt beside her friend, terrified because Sue was not responding.

"Let me see," David said, gently moving Amanda away.

Gloria put her arm around Amanda as tears began to run down both faces.

"Help me stretch her out," David said.

Jeff and Bill helped David get Sue stretched out on her back. The ladies cried as they prayed out loud for Sue.

David felt Sue's neck for any hint of a heartbeat. Feeling nothing, he laid his head against her chest. He slowly sat back and shook his head.

"Her heart must have given out," he said softly.

Alice, Gloria and Amanda clung to each other, sobbing. The men wrapped their arms around the grieving women.

Minutes later, everyone began to pull away as they realized they would have to make some serious decisions now.

"They won't let us bury her. I'll have to take her to the hospital and make a report for the captain. I have to call him anyway about Bonnie," Jeff said.

With fresh tears in her eyes, Amanda asked, "Can we fix her up first, please?"

"I don't see why not," David said. "You ladies do what you have to do. We'll make something to carry her upstairs."

Not knowing when the electricity would be restored, Jeff shined the flashlight onto his watch to see how long it would be before he'd be able to contact his captain.

"It's four o'clock," he said. "I'm going up and check for any damage. I'll try to check outside also."

"Bill, let's look around and see if we can find something to carry Sue on," David said.

Amanda stayed with Sue's body while Alice and Gloria made their way to her room to find what they would need to prepare her before she'd be taken from them.

Approximately forty-five minutes later, Sue was made beautiful by her grieving friends and had been placed on the makeshift stretcher by the men. Needing comfort and support, the group sat close together in the fellowship hall.

"Find any damage?" David asked.

"Three of the sanctuary window coverings need to be replaced. The window over there," Jeff pointed to the far end of the room, "is broken. That's all I've been able to discover so far. When daylight gets here, I'll check outside."

Feeling cold air moving around her feet, Amanda whispered, "David, please go get a Bible."

Without hesitation, David jumped up and ran down the steps with Gloria right behind him. "I'll get some blankets," she called out.

"I'm afraid we have visitors," Amanda continued to whisper.

"What makes you think so?" Jeff asked, not feeling or sensing anything.

"I feel ice-cold air swirling around the floor," Amanda said quietly.

"It's not that I don't believe you, Amanda, but is there anything else that makes you think so?" he said. "Because it's going to get very cold in here without the furnace working."

"Do you feel anything?" Amanda asked Bill and Alice.

Shaking her head, Alice said, "I don't think so, other than being cold and scared half to death."

"You'll have to forgive me for being paranoid," Amanda said. "But it won't hurt to be prepared."

When everyone was wrapped snuggly in a blanket, Amanda tenderly held on to the Bible David handed her. With her eyes closed, she touched the Bible to her forehead as she silently prayed.

No one spoke as they watched Amanda. David had his arm firmly around Gloria's shoulders. Bill and Alice held tightly to each other.

Jeff refused to touch Amanda or speak to her, knowing that something incredibly important was going on with her.

Many long minutes passed until Amanda removed the Bible from her face, laying it on her lap and folding her hands on top of it. Quiet sobs that sounded like short gasps continued for several seconds.

Everyone remained quiet, waiting.

Regaining enough composure to speak quietly, she began to speak.

"I am so new at this Christian thing. Almost everything I've learned has been during this time after the rapture. I've read and re-read the Bible, searching for meaning, searching for answers. Thankfully, I've discovered what I missed. I understand the life we have been left with. I just now realized that even though I have become saved, I have not used what I've been left with to help others find salvation. My fear has kept me imprisoned in this church building.

"Jeff leaves here almost every day never knowing if he'll make it back home or not. I can't even imagine the terror he lives with every time he puts that uniform on and goes to work. And, as far as I know, he's the only one that's tried to get others to become saved.

"Sue couldn't wait to get out and find a job. I'm sure she probably, in her own way, tried to witness to everyone she could. What have I done? If I don't do my part in helping people find refuge in this empty building, what good have I done? Beginning today, I will no longer waste what I've been left with. I'm going out those doors and try to find others who are looking for safety. I can't take this with me," she held up the Bible, "but I've been trying to memorize verses, so I have them hidden in my heart. They can't take that away from me."

Jeff's usual stalwartness cracked slightly as tears slipped from the corners of his eyes, sliding down his handsome cheeks.

"It's not just you, Amanda," David said. "I'm equally guilty."

"I've been so caught up in surviving that I forgot about the rest of the world," Bill added. "Honey, you up to stepping out?"

"I can't wait," Alice said. "Living in this building, scared to death all the time is driving me insane anyway."

"I still think I should stay around here," Gloria said. "Someone has to be here to welcome in those you send our way."

"You're right, Gloria," Amanda said. "So, please don't feel guilty about that.

"Besides, I don't have to stay right here in the building. I can be outside watching and waiting and showing them the way in."

"Just be careful; be wise," Jeff said.

"It's getting daylight," Amanda said, looking toward brightened windows. "Today will be the most dangerous so far for you, Jeff, especially if what Bonnie told you was the truth. Let's pray for him."

The group gathered around Jeff, laying their hands on him, and praying for God's protection to be upon him.

When the prayers were finished, Jeff checked his watch. "I have a few more minutes before I can call the captain. I'll check around the building while I wait."

Just as he walked out the door, the lights flickered on. Gloria immediately began preparing a pot of hot coffee and breakfast.

Returning to the fellowship hall later, Jeff reported to his friends that a tree had fallen on the storage shed, several cars in the parking lot were heavily damaged, and the church steeple was nowhere to be found.

FORTY-NINE

Unable to control the tremor in his finger, Jeff punched Captain Mercett's number into his cell phone. The call was answered so quickly, he nearly forgot the words he had been practicing for this conversation.

"Captain Mercett, Agent Howard here, sir."

"Is there a problem?" Mercett growled.

"Yes, sir, I'm afraid so," Jeff began. "I've been outside checking storm damage and since I came inside I have not been able to locate Agent Summers. Could I ask, sir, if she has been in contact with you or with anyone in headquarters?"

"Not that I'm aware of," Mercett answered. "Has there been a problem with her?"

"Negative, sir," Jeff lied. "She retired approximately an hour before I did, sir. I expected to see her at breakfast but she's not here. Her uniforms and weapon are also missing, along with some of her personal items."

"No note, no message, not any type of communication?"

"No, sir," Jeff said, putting a worried edge in his voice. "I'm quite concerned, sir. This is not like Agent Summers at all."

"Let me do some checking," Mercett said.

"Thank you, sir," Jeff said.

"Do you have any ideas?" Mercett asked.

"No, sir," Jeff said. "I do have one concern, though. I have no idea where Agent Wickes is at this time, but he did make threats. I would hope that he had nothing to do with her disappearance."

"Highly unlikely," Mercett growled. "Anything else?"

"Yes, sir, I'm afraid so," Jeff said with a sigh. "One of our group, Sue Zoller, apparently had a heart attack during the earthquake. Shall I transport her to the hospital?"

"George Zoller's wife?" Mercett asked, surprised.

"Yes, sir."

"Transport her," Mercett said. "Anything else?"

"No, sir, that's all, sir." Jeff heard the other phone click off abruptly.

Not realizing how his body had been trembling during his phone conversation, Jeff now had difficulty walking. Amanda noticing his peaked face, immediately walked over to put her arms around him.

"Bad?" she asked.

Nodding his head, Jeff replied, "It's what he doesn't say that worries me."

"How'd he react to your news about Bonnie?" David asked as Jeff joined them at the table.

"He said he'd so some checking," Jeff said. "Are the uniforms hidden well?"

David nodded his head.

"Okay, men," Jeff said. "We have to get Sue to the hospital. Will you girls be okay until we return?"

"Not a problem," Gloria said, finishing up the breakfast dishes.

"We should be back within the hour," David said.

The women followed Sue's body to the door as the men carried her out. Amanda was careful to lock the door after them.

"I keep thinking that she's the lucky one," Alice said.

"You're probably right," Gloria said.

"So what do we do for an hour?" Amanda asked.

"We all left our rooms so quickly, we should check to make sure everything is okay," Gloria said. "And then, if one of you would volunteer, my hair desperately needs to be trimmed."

Amanda picked up the back of Gloria's hair and let its silkiness slip through her fingers. "It has gotten a lot longer since we've been here."

"It's been years since my hair has been this long," she said.

"I think it's pretty," Alice said. "You should leave it that way."

"You think so?" Gloria asked.

"Sure, just trim it a little," Alice said. "I don't know about you, but I have no desire to visit another beauty salon."

"You're right," Gloria said. "I'll let you both work on it. One gets this side and the other gets that side."

"You could be very sorry, you know," Amanda laughed.

"We could use a good laugh," Gloria said as she headed for her apartment.

Straightened their rooms became more difficult large cracks across the floor and in the hallways. Gloria picked up a hairbrush, comb, and a pair of scissors before hurrying from her room. Like thunder, a loud pounding began on the front door causing her to drop the scissors. The sharp point barely missed her big toe.

Amanda ran up the steps past Gloria. Alice followed at a safer distance. Taking a deep breath and saying a quick prayer, Amanda unlocked the door just as two W.S.F. agents were ready to force their way in.

"We have orders to search for evidence in the disappearance of one of our agents," one of them barked as they pushed past the ladies.

"Oh, thank goodness, you're here. Bonnie—un, Agent Summers was here last night and we had such a good time. Then this morning, she was just gone," Amanda said. She thought she sounded convincing.

"She didn't leave a note or say anything?" the female agent asked.

"Not that I know of," Amanda said. "In fact, we all thought that she and Jeff—uh, Agent Howard were getting along really well, if you know what I mean."

Seized by panic when she saw Alice's eyes widen at her last comment, she tried to give her a look that would encourage her to go along with the story.

"I was embarrassed," Alice stated.

"Is that so?" the male officer said. "Was Agent Howard putting the moves on her?"

"Oh, no, sir," Alice continued. "I'd say it was pretty much equal."

The female officer seemed offended by the ladies' giggling.

"I understand that one of you is engaged to Agent Howard," she commented.

"That would be me," Amanda said, holding up her hand.

"And how did you feel about what was going on between them?" she asked.

"Actually, I had already gone to bed with a migraine. I didn't know about it until this morning," Amanda said.

"So you failed to see the two of them together?"

"Apparently," Amanda said. "I have been told what went on and I have every intentions of having a heart-to-heart with him when I get the opportunity."

"You haven't seen him today?"

"One of our group had a heart attack and died during the storm last night," Amanda said. "Jeff's captain ordered him to take her body to the hospital first thing this morning. The other men helped him."

"I see. We'll search this entire building, beginning with Agent Summers' room," the female agent advised.

"Certainly," Gloria said. "Follow me." As she led the agents to the basement, she chatted amicably about the previous night's storm. "I have to tell you, I was terrified."

"Uh-huh," the male officer said as they entered Bonnie's room. "Excuse us and let us get our work done."

"Certainly," Gloria repeated. "There's hot coffee upstairs anytime you want to take a break."

Neither of the other ladies knew anything about the details of Bonnie's disappearance, especially about her weapon. When they gathered in the kitchen with the intentions of trimming Gloria's hair, Amanda had to let Alice do the work because her hands were trembling so.

Acting nonchalantly about the search, Amanda hopped up on the kitchen island countertop and sat cross-legged watching the hair trimming process.

The ladies giggled and girl-talked until they thought they'd drop. Suddenly Jeff rushed in with David and Bill on his heels.

"Where are they?" Jeff asked.

"They're searching the building, ole lover boy," Alice said with a wicked smile.

Jeff's eyebrows lifted as he quickly looked at Amanda, who gave him a wink.

Amanda exclaimed as she hopped off the counter, "I want a word with you, Jeff Howard."

"You'll have to wait your turn," he barked back at her before leaving the room in his quest of the W.S.F. team.

"I guess the honeymoon is over, huh?" Gloria said with a laugh.

"The honeymoon will not take place until he comes up with a very good explanation." Amanda continuing to speak loudly, hoping her voice would travel through the heat vents.

Jeff discovered the W.S.F. team searching the laundry room which was located next to the dark, dirty furnace room.

"Have you found anything?" he asked.

"Negative, Agent Howard," the male agent said. "We're done with all the rooms down here. We'll be checking the rooms upstairs shortly."

"I just don't understand," Jeff said as he stood back out of their way.

"We had an exceptionally good evening. Why would she leave without saying anything?"

"Everyone else felt the same way?" the female agent asked.

"Yes," Jeff said. "She just fit in like a glove."

"We understand she fit in your glove very well."

Almost caught off guard, Jeff began to understand why the ladies were acting like they were. Giving a crooked grin, he said, "Well, you know how it is sometimes."

"Your girl's not too happy about it."

"Ah, she'll get over it," Jeff said. "I'll pick up her engagement ring next week. She'll be eating out of my hand in no time."

"Regular Romeo," she sneered.

Jeff returned to the kitchen, reaching into the refrigerator for a can of soda. Popping the top, he whispered, "Thanks, guys."

"Not a problem," Alice answered with a smile.

"Well, what do you think?" Gloria sang out as she walked up to David.

"Pretty," he said. "I'm glad you're letting it grow again. I like it that way."

He wrapped his arms around his wife, holding her close as he nuzzled her neck. Whispering into her ear, he asked, "You all gave them this story?"

"Yes, I love you, too," she said, smiling into her husband's eyes.

The six friends sat around until the W.S.F. finished their search.

"Agent Howard, we'll make a report to the captain, but we've been unable to find any sign of Agent Summers."

Jeff shook his head as he pursed his lips. "I'm truly concerned for Agent Summers. It just doesn't make sense."

"We'll keep checking, sir," the male agent said.

"Thank you," Jeff said as he held the door for them. "I'll be back to work in the morning if you should find anything."

He watched until the shiny, black SUV disappeared in the distance. Turning back into the foyer, he motioned for everyone to follow him. Grabbing a piece of paper from the top of the piano, he began to write.

WE ARE NO LONGER SAFE HERE.
I'M SURE THEY'VE LEFT LISTENING DEVICES.

David smacked his fist onto the table so hard the legs bounced on the floor.

"Let's get rid of that pile of detestable books," Jeff said as he walked toward the door.

"I'll get the last box of books and meet you out there," David said. Jeff knew he was going to get Bonnie's things from where ever he had hidden them.

Jeff had already started the fire by the time the entire group gathered around the flames. He felt safe talking around the roaring fire. David placed the items in a spot where the fire would be the hottest.

"Would someone please tell me what I was supposed to have done last night?" Jeff asked.

"You don't remember how you and Bonnie carried on while Amanda was in bed with a migraine?" Gloria said, laughing.

"Oh, great," Jeff said. "No wonder you want to have a talk with me. And now I have to buy a ring to appease you."

"Better make it a big honker," Alice said, joining in the laughter.

"What are we going to do?" Amanda asked. She didn't feel up to joining the fun. "This was our safe place."

"They didn't search the storage shed," David said. "Maybe we can make it habitable."

"Do you not see that tree lying on it?" Gloria asked.

"Just a natural decoration," he said.

"We've got the TV, CD players and radios," Jeff said. "We'll have to keep them playing loudly, especially when we're praying and reading the Bible."

"Will that work?" Amanda asked.

"If we're careful," Jeff answered.

Having brought hoes and shovels from the shed, each group member did their share of digging through the burning books, making certain that everything was burned thoroughly.

By late afternoon, all that remained was a pile of warm ashes. Jeff and David had made sure no telltale signs of blue and gold remained.

When the ladies retired to the kitchen to begin dinner, Jeff spoke seriously to David and Bill.

"When I go to work tomorrow, there's a very real possibility that I won't be coming back. Too many things have taken place. My captain didn't trust me to begin with so I don't think I can fool him any longer. Promise me that the two of you will watch over Amanda as much as you can."

"I'm not going to quit trusting God for your protection," David said, slapping Jeff on the back.

"That makes two of us," Bill said. "And the Bible says that when two or more agree on anything, it will happen."

"That was before the rapture," Jeff said. He leaned heavily on the shovel handle, staring at the pile of ashes.

"I won't accept that," Bill said. "I choose to hold on to God's promises as long as I still have my head."

Jeff and David both looked at him and laughed.

Making certain the fire had burned itself out and there were no signs of uniforms, the men left the tools and made their way into the building. After washing up, they sat at the table and enjoyed a quiet meal.

One of the ladies brought a CD player to the kitchen and was playing a CD by Randy Travis.

Jeff spoke softly to Amanda. "You realize that I may not be returning home tomorrow?"

"I won't accept that until it happens," she said.

"Let's go check the basement?"

Jeff knew they needed to double-check certain areas of the basement.

"Be right there," he shouted back. "Bill, would you take care of the trash for the ladies?"

After a thorough search, David and Jeff were satisfied that nothing had been discovered—this time.

FIFTY

Months passed without any significant incident happening to the group. Amanda was working as receptionist at the same clinic where Sue had worked.

One of her duties was to accompany women to the restroom for urine samples, making sure no specimens were contaminated. Although this was an unpleasant duty, it gave Amanda the opportunity to witness. Even though the ladies were terrified, many gratefully accepted the gospel truth Amanda shared with them.

Although Jeff was amazed that Captain Mercett had promoted him, the strain of waiting for the proverbial shoe to drop began to show on his young face. His responsibilities entailed receiving reports from all the squads in their district, filing them appropriately, and supplying the captain with a daily, weekly, and monthly summery.

No longer required to go out on patrol or oversee one squad, Jeff felt somewhat at ease that his replacement was the same female agent who had searched the church. She seemed competent, fair, and displayed a hint of compassion. *When the time seems right, I'll witness to her.*

David had been hired as day maintenance at the hospital. Bill was a cashier at the grocery store. Gloria and Alice stayed busy in the church building with the dozens of people who discovered a place of shelter with the group.

All residents were aware of the possibility of listening devices, so everyone was careful where they talked about God or prayed. Almost everyone who came through the doors had become Christians through the efforts of Amanda, David or Bill.

No new residents were allowed to room in the basement with the original group. Most found places to sleep on the sanctuary pews. Everyone pitched in with cleaning, cooking and laundry duties.

Never seeing small children still seemed strange, even after such a long time. Gloria and Alice discovered that several of the women had also experienced the rapture of their unborn babies and were able to minister to them.

Keeping his word, Jeff bought Amanda an incredibly beautiful ring. She wore it with pride, knowing that it would be the closest she would come to that particular kind of happiness.

Even though life seemed to have leveled off to a certain degree, no one in the original group ever let their guard down. Even when the sun was allowed to shine, this band of believers lived under an ever thickening cloud of doom.

All on the same day, Jeff, Amanda, Bill and David were given orders to report to their supervisors immediately upon arriving at work the next morning. Blinding terror pushed them toward home.

Without a nod, without a word, David and Bill crossed the parking lot together, shoving through the doors. Entering the fellowship hall, they discovered most of the tables occupied by residents enjoying dinner.

Each man walked up to their spouse, hugged them and whispered in their ear.

As they did most days, Amanda and Jeff drove into the parking lot around the same time. Jeff didn't miss the fear in Amanda's eyes nor the tremble in her hand as he tenderly clasped it. As soon as they entered the building, Amanda hurried down the steps to her room. Jeff walked into the fellowship hall to find the other two couples hugging each other.

"As soon as you finish up in here, meet in Amanda's room," he whispered.

Feeling nauseated by the smell of food, Bill and David went directly to their rooms. Jeff followed them downstairs and entered Amanda's room.

Finding her sitting on the floor by her bed shaking like the last leaf of fall, Jeff knelt in front of her forcing her to look at him. "You too?" he whispered.

"What does it mean?" she asked quietly, her CD already playing.

Shaking his head, he sat on the floor beside her. "I don't know. By the looks of the others, they were given the same word as us."

Feeling Amanda's trembling become more intense, Jeff pulled a blanket off the bed and wrapped it around her. Tears began to spill from her eyes.

"I'm sorry," she said, leaning her head against his shoulder.

"Don't apologize," he said. "We're all scared."

Without knocking first, Bill and David entered Amanda's room. They each sat on the floor across from the couple.

"We have to report to our supervisors first thing in the morning," David said softly.

"What do you think it means?" Bill asked.

"I don't know," Jeff said. "I've been ordered to report to the captain immediately when I get to work."

Gloria and Alice knocked lightly before entering.

"Done already?" David asked.

"We asked some of the others to take over for us," Gloria said, sitting close to her husband. "Tell us what's going on?"

"We don't know exactly," Jeff said.

"We all have to meet with our supervisors immediately when we go to work tomorrow," David said.

Alice gripped Bill's hand as she too began to tremble. "Do you think you're going to be arrested?"

"I don't know what for," Bill said.

"Okay, let's try to think about this rationally," David said. "We're all so scared we haven't stopped to try to figure it out."

"Is there anything special about tomorrow?" Gloria asked.

"It's payday for me," Bill said.

"Me too," Amanda said.

"And me," David.

"That's got to be it," Gloria said. "Maybe each of you will get a raise. Wouldn't that be great?"

"But isn't it odd that all of us would get the same message?" Amanda asked.

"In my position, I'd know about any raises that were coming down," Jeff said. "In fact, I should know about anything new and I have heard nothing."

"We're going to drive ourselves crazy trying to figure out what we have no way of knowing," Amanda said.

"Amanda's right," Jeff said. "Let's pray about it and try to trust God with it?"

"Makes sense to me," David said.

After a long, desperate prayer time, everyone sat quietly. Every set of eyes were damp with tears.

"Listen, my friends," Amanda said. "Since there's no way of knowing what we're facing tomorrow, I want you to know that I love all of you. If the worse happens, we have the hope of seeing each other in Heaven."

"Ditto," David said.

"Me too," Gloria said.

"Us too," Bill said. Unable to speak, Alice shook her head.

"I'm thankful God put us together," Jeff said. "It seems it's been a lifetime ago since we failed to hear the trumpet, but I certainly won't miss Heaven the second time around."

Amanda slowly extracted herself from the blanket and stood up. "If you all don't mind, I am going to bed. I can't stop shaking and if I can't get control of myself I'll miss my meeting in the morning."

After hugs and kisses, everyone left for their own rooms. Jeff made his way upstairs to make certain the door was securely locked and all lights were extinguished. All residents knew the importance of no lights and as little noise as possible.

When he returned to Amanda's room, he discovered her buried under three blankets.

"You weren't kidding, were you?" he whispered.

Settling onto the bed, he snuggled close to her back, wrapping his arms around her, trying to give her the security she needed.

Even though they had not exchanged any words, Amanda's mind was working feverishly as she tried to cover all bases for all possible scenarios. So intent on her thoughts, she failed to notice that her trembling had stopped.

Feeling her body relax and assuming that Amanda had finally fallen to sleep, Jeff was startled when she began talking.

"Jeff?" When she said his name, she felt him jump.

"I thought you had finally fallen asleep," he said.

Afraid to turn up the volume on the CD player, Amanda sat up, pulling one of the blankets loose to wrap around her shoulders, she crawled to where she could sit with her back against the wall. Jeff followed suit.

Pulling the blanket over their heads, she began to share some of her thoughts. "Jeff, I need you to tell me something."

"Anything," he said. "What's going on in that pretty head of yours?"

"I need you to show me where you hid Bonnie's weapon."

"You what?" he exclaimed.

"Sh-h-h!" she said, holding her finger to her lips. "This is important, but I need to know."

"Oh, Amanda," he said, rubbing his forehead. "I can't. It's too dangerous for anyone but me to know."

"I've been thinking about this for a long time and after tonight I think I've come up with a plan in case the worst happens to you or David or Bill," she said.

"It will only get you killed, Amanda," Jeff said, grasping her hand.

"Can you please trust me on this?" Her eyes begged as much as her words. "There may come a time when I will need it. I realize that if that time should ever come, I'll only have one chance."

Looking into her determined face, desperately not wanting to give in to this request, he knew he had to trust her.

"Tomorrow," he said. "Tomorrow, I'll show you."

"Thank you," she said, giving his cheek a kiss. Watching his head drop and his lips tighten, she lifted his chin with her finger. "I promise you, Jeff Howard, you can trust me with this."

"Okay, honey," he said.

Silently she moved to her side of the bed, scrunching down under the covers. He moved slowly to his usual side of the bed. Lying on his back, his mind tried desperately to accept whatever might happen to them in the coming days.

FIFTY-ONE

After nibbling through breakfast, each one said their good-byes as if they may not see each other again on this side of Heaven.

Immediately upon arriving at the W.S.F. headquarters, Jeff walked up to the captain's door and knocked.

Without preamble. Captain Mercett shoved a blue and gold folder across the desk ordering him to read it. "When you've finished, make copies and distribute them to each squad leader in the district before the day's end."

Quickly reading the contents of the enclosed memo, Jeff nodded his head. He was certain the captain could surely hear the tom-tom beat of his heart.

"I'll get right on it, sir," he said.

"The minute you finish the distribution, I expect you to return here to become the first in my district to receive the implant," Mercett's gruff voice commanded as he watched Jeff's face.

"Sir, I've been expecting this for some time," Jeff lied. "My fiancée and I have discussed it and we want to do this together. Would that be possible, sir?"

It was obvious that Captain Mercett wasn't expecting this reaction. "Tomorrow at the latest. Dismissed."

Jeff silently thanked God for the short reprieve. His day was spent wondering how he would avoid following this order.

What now, God? I can't hide any more. My time has come. Please give me the courage to face tomorrow.

Gloria and Alice were shocked to see Amanda's glazed eyes when she walked into the kitchen. Like flashing neon signs, they blinked, "terrified," "terrified," "terrified."

Because many of the residents were milling around in the large fellowship hall, oblivious to impending doom, the ladies had to communicate through whispers and knowing looks.

"When the men come home—" Amanda's eyes blinked. She seemed to forget what she wanted to say. Taking a bottle of water from the refrigerator, she went straight to her room.

Just as she descended the stairs, Bill and David entered the fellowship hall. Alice had already started for the basement when her husband reached for her hand and they descended the steps together.

David walked into the kitchen, hugged Gloria and whispered in her ear, "Come to the apartment." Without any argument or questions, she followed.

While the two couples spoke quietly in their own rooms, Amanda buried her face in her pillow, too dazed and frightened to cry.

Captain Mercett had given Jeff permission to leave work early, with the understanding that he and Amanda would return the next morning.

Quietly opening Amanda's door, he found her curled into the fetal position facing the wall.

"Amanda," he cried softly as he tenderly cuddled her.

"I'm okay," she whispered back.

"Our days of hiding are over," he said.

"I know," she replied, turning to face him. "Would you get the others?"

Jeff got up and left the room, returning with both other couples.

As everyone sat in a circle on the floor, no one knew what to say.

"As I just told Amanda, our days of hiding are over," Jeff said. "Amanda and I have until tomorrow. How about the rest of you?"

"I was given the option of taking the implant or losing my job," Bill said. "I walked out."

"Same here," David said.

"What do you mean, we have until tomorrow?" Amanda asked.

"Captain Mercett ordered me to be the first to take it. I told him that you and I had already discussed it and wanted to do it together."

Amanda nodded her head.

"The decision has to be a personal one for each of us," Jeff said. "I can only answer for myself."

"There is no question for me," Amanda said. "I refuse."

Each other member repeated, "I refuse."

"The memo I had to distribute to each squad in the district said that everyone would have to take the implant if they wanted to survive. No food, fuel, shelter, or medicine would be available to anyone without the implant," Jeff said.

"Which means every single one of our residents?" Gloria asked.

"I'm afraid so," Jeff said. "How about our hidden supplies? How long do you think they will last?"

"Not long with the number of people we have here," Amanda answered.

"By the end of this month our buying power will end," Jeff said.

"I hate to sound stupid," Alice said. "But what's so wrong with having the computer chip implanted? It's supposedly just a tiny thing."

"If we allow the chip to be put in, we will no longer be allowed into Heaven. On the chip is what the Bible calls the 'mark of the beast.' It means we either belong to Satan or be willing to die a horrible death as a Christian," David said.

"The guillotine?" she asked in a whisper.

"That will be the quickest," Jeff said. "I'm certain there are going to be far worse ways, especially for someone in my position."

Amanda reached out to clasp the hands on each side of her. Everyone else followed her lead. No one spoke, no one prayed, everyone just held tightly for many minutes.

Finally, David stood, helping his wife up from the floor. "See you at breakfast." He and Gloria left the room.

"Good night," Bill said, walking from the room holding his wife's hand.

Amanda and Jeff remained where they were, looking at each other. "After everyone is settled for the night, okay?" she asked.

Nodding his head, Jeff lifted himself from the floor. Walking to the end of the hallway, he spent several minutes in the restroom before returning to her room.

She also made her nightly trip to the restroom in the opposite corner. Taking a shower, she arrived back in the room long after he did. He watched from the edge of the bed as she combed through her wet hair.

It seemed as if neither of them could find the words to tell the other what was going on in their minds.

By the time Amanda had dried her hair and polished her fingernails, Jeff had been silently and patiently watching for an hour. In his heart, he knew their time together was coming to a close.

Startled when she suddenly turned toward him, he stood quickly. The lump in her throat was too large for words to climb over; she tenderly touched his face before crawling into her side of the bed.

"Amanda," he said softly.

She looked at him as he knelt beside the bed.

"I have something for you." He held something wrapped in a towel.

Her eyebrows pulled together as she looked at the towel-wrapped package, wondering what he could possibly be surprising her with. Pulling herself up so that she was sitting in the middle of the bed, she began to unfold the towel.

"Jeff!" she gasped. "Where did you—"

"That doesn't matter," he interrupted. He had no intention of showing her the hiding place. "This is it, now what are you going to do with it?"

Reluctant to touch the weapon, she said, "Show me how to use it."

"Why?"

"Just in case," she said. "That's all, Jeff. Just in case."

Even though the weapon had been hidden for many months, it still looked almost new. Jeff picked it up, wiping it with the towel.

"It's simple," he said. It took only a few minutes to show her what she needed to know.

After the lesson was over, she carefully folded the towel around the weapon, padded over to her chest of drawers and covered the package in the third drawer under a layer of underclothes.

Returning to bed, she took his face in her hands, looked lovingly into his eyes and said, "Thank you," before kissing him on the lips and turning to her side of the bed.

For the second night in a row, Jeff lay on his back pondering how Bonnie's weapon would figure in to the days to come.

Although Jeff and Amanda heard nothing, everyone else in the building spent a frightened, sleepless night. Great rolling, rumbles of thunder shook the building. The night sky was continually split by blinding lightning. The wind howled as it crashed into the outside walls, threatening to cave them in.

Awakened by the alarm clock, still unaware of the night's storm, Jeff and Amanda began preparing for whatever they would have to face during the new day. Ten minutes before going upstairs for breakfast, Jeff gently took Amanda's hand and led her to the bed where they sat next to each other.

Taking a deep breath, Jeff said, "Amanda, this will most likely be the last time we're together. I am supposed to report for the implant as soon as I get to work. Of course, I won't take it which means I'll be arrested immediately."

"I can't go with you, Jeff," Amanda said.

"I have no intentions of taking you," Jeff said. "You survive the best way you can. I'll be with God soon so I'll be okay."

A sudden sob caught in her throat. "Oh, Jeff, I wish this could all be over with now."

"Me too, honey," Jeff said. "I don't want to die, but there's no other way. I'll witness to as many as will listen until I breathe my last."

"I love you, Jeff," she said.

Jeff stood, pulling Amanda into his arms as their bodies shook with desperate sobs. "I'll love you forever and I promise I'll be waiting for you in Heaven."

Jeff tried to pull away, knowing it was time for him to leave but Amanda clung to him. "Amanda, I have to go. I can't say any more goodbyes. Would you tell them that I love them?"

With his shirt clutched in her white-knuckled hands, she nodded her head.

As gently as possible, Jeff pried her hands from his clothing, not caring about the wrinkles or the tear spots on his hated uniform.

Deep, growling sobs echoed in the stairwell as he ran up the steps. Without looking back, he jerked open his truck door, revved the motor and spun out of the driveway, fishtailing his truck west on Woodville Road.

Everyone upstairs heard Amanda's heart rendering cry. "JEFF!"

Gloria and Alice ran down the steps as quickly as they could, finding Amanda collapsed on the floor.

Frightened, David and Bill followed. "Let's get her on the bed," David said.

Laying Amanda on her bed and covering her with a blanket, her friends placed their hands on her and began to pray.

Long, painfully intense minutes passed as all four foreheads continued to touch the edge of Amanda's bed which was dampened by their tears.

Amanda's eyelids fluttered for a moment before opening to see her friends kneeling by her bed. Stirring slightly, she reached out her hand and touched each of their heads.

Quickly raising their heads, they were surprised to see a sweet smile on her face.

"Thank you," she said weakly.

"Are you okay, sweetie?" Gloria asked.

"I'm going to be now," she said. "I need to get up."

Slowly, one by one, her friends stepped back as Amanda sat up on the edge of her bed. A renewed determination could be seen in her face as she looked at her friends.

"The others have to be prepared," she said in a stronger voice.

"Most of them should still be eating breakfast," David said. "We'll talk to them as soon as we know that you're going to be okay."

"I couldn't ask for better friends," she said. "I'm thankful that God brought us together. But the time has arrived that we were dreading. Any one of us can be taken at any moment. And from now on I will make every moment count."

"That-a-girl," David said.

"I'm okay. I need to take a shower then I'll be ready for breakfast," she said. When she stood up, Gloria had to steady her.

"Let me help you to the restroom," Gloria said.

"I know I'll be okay after my shower," Amanda said. Gloria wasn't so sure.

While Gloria helped Amanda, Bill and David went to speak with the rest of the residents about what was taking place.

Many questions were asked when David told everyone about the tiny computer chip that was going to be required of anyone in order to buy or sell anything. Several of the residents made the decision to move on, determined to find a more secure hiding place.

Just as David had answered the last question, Amanda walked into the fellowship hall and took a seat at one of the tables. Gloria brought her a plate of warm food and a cup of hot coffee.

Many of the frightened residents had left the room. Some of the women could be heard weeping. Others busied themselves with cleaning up the kitchen.

Suddenly, gasps rippled across the room, causing everyone else to look toward the doorway. Two large, male W.S.F. agents stood looking over the room.

"We're looking for Amanda Fountain."

"I'm Amanda," she said.

"You need to come with us, Ms. Fountain."

"Where are you taking her?" David said, quickly standing next to her.

"That is none of your concern, sir," the bigger of the two said. "Please, stand aside."

Amanda laid her hand on David's arm as she began to walk toward the agents. "Can I know where you're taking me?" she asked.

"Our captain would like a word with you, ma'am."

"I hope to be back soon," she said. "If not, I love you all."

Amanda's friends were thankful the agents did not put handcuffs on her. The first agent led the way with Amanda following and the larger agent behind.

FIFTY-TWO

Immediately upon arriving at headquarters, Jeff made his way to Captain Mercett's office where he was ushered inside by two agents slightly older than himself.

Jeff quickly checked out the rest of the room. Other than the captain and the two agents, Jeff saw only one other person.

Sitting behind a rather small table, a middle-aged woman with dyed red hair was watching him from behind dark-framed, thick glasses.

Her ample body spilled over the edges of a heavy duty, folding chair. She was wearing a white nurse's uniform with a bright blue W.S.F. logo on the left side of her grotesquely large chest. The hem of her skirt came to just below her knee caps, revealing large calves and ankles bulging through white nylon hose.

Fear seized him as he looked at the medical paraphernalia spread out on the table.

"Agent Howard, we were expecting you and your fiancée," Captain Mercett barked.

"She decided not to accompany me this morning, sir," Jeff said, hoping his voice wasn't revealing the depth of his fear.

"I see," the captain said. "This will only take five minutes. Are you ready?"

"No, sir," Jeff said, squaring his shoulders.

"Excuse me?" the captain exclaimed.

"Captain Mercett, sir, I am a Christian and I refuse to have that chip implanted on any part of my body, sir."

"Just as I thought," Captain Mercett exclaimed with a wicked sneer on his face. "Arrest him."

Without hesitation, Jeff held his hands behind his back before the two agents had the chance to touch him. As one agent placed the handcuffs on him, the other removed his weapon and placed it on the captain's desk.

Captain Mercett grabbed it, turning it over to check the tiny, digital readout window on the bottom of the weapon. Jeff smiled when he saw the look of disbelief on the captain's face.

"Get him out of my sight," the captain ordered.

"Sir, before I go, I'd like for you to know that I pray for you every day," Jeff said boldly.

No one in the room was prepared for the sudden, violent movement of the captain as he snatched up a glass paperweight and threw it in Jeff's direction hitting him on the shoulder. The force was so hard, the paperweight bounced from Jeff's shoulder into the face of the agent who had handcuffed him.

The agent grabbed the side of his face as blood ran through his fingers onto his uniform.

"Get him out of here," the captain screamed.

"I'm sorry," Jeff told the blood covered agent.

Jeff was placed in the back seat of a W.S.F. vehicle and transported to the Lawrence County Security Center where he was stripped of his uniform and given a gray and white stripped prison uniform.

"Don't bother getting comfortable, you won't be here long," the jailer said.

Warned to keep Jeff separated from the other prisoners so that he wouldn't have the opportunity to talk to them, he was taken to a tiny, pitch-black cell. Shoved violently through the door, his shoulder crashed into the back wall as the metal door clanged shut.

Jeff slid to the floor, feeling something wet and squishy under his feet and his bottom. Feeling the muck begin to seep through his thin trousers, he quickly stood back up. The stench was so horrible, he immediately began to gag.

"God, help me!" he cried out, just before covering his face with the long sleeve of his shirt.

FIFTY-THREE

Meanwhile, Amanda was just stepping out of the W.S.F. black SUV in front of the headquarters. *Who would have ever believed that our high school would be used for evil?* Entering the gymnasium, she gasped at the changes.

As she was led across the hardwood floor, she was certain she was being watched. Refusing to look up, she kept her eyes glued to the back of the agent in front of her.

Having climbed the long flight of stairs, they now stood in front of a door with a large golden W.S.F. emblem attached to it. After the slight knock and the ensuing gruffly shouted "enter," Amanda was pushed into the inter sanctum of Jeff's evil superior officer.

Using more self-control than she thought she had, Amanda stood with her shoulders back and her head held high as Captain Mercett sauntered up to her, shaking her un-offered, limp hand. He refused to release his grip until she was led to one of the chairs across from his large desk.

"Please, make yourself comfortable, Ms. Fountain," he said, sitting on the edge of his desk.

Amanda took her time looking around the room. Although they were the only two in the room, she did not miss the small white table covered with medical paraphernalia.

Clinching her teeth, she finally spoke, looking directly into the captain's eyes.

"I prefer to stand, thank you. Why have I been brought here?"

"Ah, a straightforward lady." An evil sneer crept across his face. "I understand that you are engaged to Agent Jeff Howard."

"Yes, sir, I am," Amanda said.

"Well, Amanda—I can call you Amanda, can't I?"

"No, sir, you cannot. You may call me Miss Fountain."

The heinous laugh that erupted from the captain caused Amanda's resolve to weaken as her heart began to thump in her chest.

"Amanda." He took vile pleasure in emphasizing her name. "I have brought you here as a courtesy because of Mr. Howard's position."

Amanda continued to look directly into the captain's face, all the while praying silently. *God, help me! Help me! In Jesus' name, please help me!*

"Did Agent Howard discuss anything about a computer chip with you?" Without waiting for an answer, he quickly stepped close to her and rubbed his finger across her forehead. "With a pretty face like yours, you will no doubt want it in your wrist." He grabbed her hand and began sensuously rubbing the inside of her wrist.

Amanda jerked back from him, trying to move out of his reach. "I would advise you, sir, not to touch me again."

She had no recourse but to grab her arms to control her trembling when the captain's evil laughter filled the room.

Despite her fear, her eyes shone with defiance as he scooted his large behind onto the edge of the desk.

"Please, Miss Fountain, have a seat. I have disturbing news to share with you," Captain Mercett gushed with false kindness.

"I will not sit," Amanda said. "Just say what you've got to say so I can get out of here."

"Your boyfriend has been arrested and will be executed within the next twenty-four hours." The captain's large, muscular body stood to his six-foot-five height.

Hearing Jeff's sentence and seeing the captain's menacing stance caused Amanda's knees to tremble. Even though tears began to trickle down her cheeks, she continued to stare at the captain with her jaws clinched.

"I can see how upsetting this news is to a beautiful young lady who had hopes of bedding a handsome young man every night for the rest of her life." The captain strutted over to her, stopping within inches of her trembling body.

"As his commanding officer, I considerate it my duty to fulfill the needs of my men." With the terrifying quickness of a cobra strike, his large hand grabbed Amanda's hair, pulling her against his body.

Struggling desperately until she realized it was futile, Amanda immediately went completely limp, causing his grip to loosen as she toppled to the floor. Her plan backfired when his body fell on top of her knocking the air from her lungs.

Angered, his words hissed in her face. "That won't work with me."

Amanda found a safe place in her mind to escape the duration of the long, painful ordeal.

As if nothing happened, the captain slowly walked behind his desk where he sat and began to shuffle the papers before him while Amanda carefully stood and straightened her clothing the best she could.

"It is in your power to give your boyfriend life—at least for now," Captain Mercett growled as she crept toward the door.

Amanda stopped in her tracks, turned to her mortal enemy and asked, "What do you mean?"

He crossed his huge arms across the desk, leering at her. "Every morning that you return here, I will allow Mr. Howard to live one more day."

Silently, she exited the most stifling, evil environment she had ever known existed. As she stumbled down the steps, the two agents met her, taking her elbows and leading her outside to the SUV.

Unlike the drive to headquarters, one of the agents scooted into the back seat with her. As she stared straight ahead, her hands clasped firmly in her lap, she prayed for the strength to do what she knew she had to do.

Seeing the familiar limestone covered church building caused Amanda's eyes to flood over with tears. Trying to scoot out of the vehicle quickly proved difficult.

Realizing her difficulty, the agent took her elbow gently and helped her step from the vehicle. As he did, he cautiously slipped a piece of paper into her hand. Confused, her hand clamped onto the paper as she allowed him to help her to the door.

"I'm sorry," he whispered hoarsely.

Stumbling down the steps, her feet slipping on the last three, Amanda fell to her knees just as Gloria walked around the corner.

"Amanda!" she screamed. "David, come quick!"

"I'm okay," Amanda said weakly.

"Sure you are, honey," Gloria said, wrapping her arms around her friend.

"What on earth?" David exclaimed, getting his arms around Amanda and helping her stand.

"I'm sorry, I just fell," she said as great sobs began to shake her body.

David led her to the edge of her bed, Gloria instinctively knew what horrible thing had taken place.

"David," she said, gently placing her hand on his arm. "Leave me alone with her for a while, okay?" She looked into his eyes, trying to convey silently what she didn't want to say out loud.

Watching him look more closely at Amanda, she saw the look of anger in his eyes and the redness creep up his neck into his face. He got the message.

"Let me know when you need me," he said, clinching his jaws.

"Do you think you can make it to the shower, honey?" Gloria asked.

Amanda nodded her head as she continued to cry. Gloria dug through her chest of drawers to find her something comfortable to wear.

Just as she reached for the third drawer, Amanda yelled, "No, I'll get those."

Startled, Gloria dropped the items she already had. "Okay, I'm sorry."

"No, Gloria, it's not you," she cried.

Gloria quickly picked up what she had dropped, walking over to her friend. "It's important that you cry, but let's do it in the shower, okay?"

Nodding, Amanda told her friend to go ahead and she'd be right there. When Gloria reluctantly left the room, Amanda reached into the third drawer for just what she needed before scuffing down the hallway.

Beginning to take off her clothing, Amanda said, "I'll call you if I need you, okay?"

"Not a problem," Gloria said as she reluctantly left the restroom.

Amanda stood under the steaming shower until there was no more hot water. During that time, Gloria had returned to pick up the clothing Amanda had dropped in the floor, finding a trash can to stuff them in.

By the time Amanda was dressed, had combed her hair and put on a little more makeup than usual, her plan was firmly formed in her mind.

Painfully kneeling beside her bed, she prayed, "God, I can't change what happened, so I'm putting it in Your safe place. Before I do what I have to do, please forgive me. And I ask that right now at this very minute, you allow Jeff to feel Your presence surrounding him."

Sitting on her bed, she remembered the little piece of paper she had shoved under her pillow. Reaching for it, she un-crumbled it and began to read.

> *Thanks to Jeff Howard, there are more of us. I apologize for what's happened to him and to you. If you ever need help, get a message to me.*
>
> *Tom Brooks*

FIFTY-FOUR

Shielding his eyes from the glaring light, Jeff's arm covered his face when the metal door was jerked open.

"Come out of there," the guard shouted.

With his eyes trying to adjust to the light, Jeff gingerly stepped across the slimy floor.

Immediately across the hall was another opened door. "Get in there and clean yourself up."

The guard shoved him through the door and flung a pile of clean clothes in after him before slamming the door.

"I don't blame them, I smell awful," he muttered as he peeled off his nasty clothes before stepping into the shower. Expecting hot water to cascade over his body, he yelped when a stream of ice-cold water gushed from the showerhead.

"Should have known," he said, lathering his hair and the rest of his body. Satisfied that he had removed the stench, he shivered uncontrollably as he dried off with the ragged towel he'd been given then donned his clean prison uniform.

"At least I have something for my feet," he said as he slipped his feet into rubber thongs. "I wonder what this is all about."

Heavy pounding on the door startled him. "You better be done in there." Without waiting for an answer, the door jerked open.

"Follow me. Your captain wants a word with you."

Captain Mercett! What would he want with me?

The guard shoved him into a well-lit room that held a table and one chair, which was presently occupied by Captain Mercett.

"Sir," Jeff said.

"Well now, Mr. Howard." Contempt oozed from the captain's voice. "Don't you look chipper in your new uniform."

"Sir."

"I hope your accommodations are suitable to you. Actually, you were supposed to be executed by now, but your beautiful fiancée talked me into giving you a little extra time."

"Amanda?"

"Ah, yes. Sweet, *tender* Amanda."

No! No! No! Not Amanda! Jeff's heart shattered into a million pieces.

"Yes, Amanda has agreed to visit me every morning just to give you one more day of life. Isn't that lovely?" His evil laugh bounced off the walls bombarding Jeff's senses.

Help me, God! PLEASE help me.

"Sir," Jeff began, as calmly as possible. "There's always hope, and I want you to know that I will not give up praying—"

Mercett's chair slammed against the wall as he jumped to his feet, rushing to stand in front of Jeff.

"If you ever say those things in my presence again, I will kill you with my bare hands," he hissed into Jeff's face. "Do you understand me?" His powerful hands bounced on Jeff's shoulders, causing Jeff to stumble backward.

As if nothing out of the way had taken place, the captain sauntered back to the table, pulling his chair under him. "Now, to the matter at hand. Even though I have enjoyed getting to know what a fine fiancée you have, I will make a proposition to you that could not only give you back your freedom, but you would still discover Amanda's pleasures for yourself."

Jeff's hands were clenched into tight, white-knuckled fists.

"I will give you this one last opportunity to have the chip implanted. In doing so, you can have your freedom and your well-used girl. What do you say?"

"Sir, my life is not my own. I've been bought by the blood of Jesus—" His words were cut off violently. The table sailed across the floor, knocking him against the wall.

Catching his breath, he looked into bloodshot, evil eyes.

"Every day you are allowed to live, you will do so with the knowledge that I am enjoying myself with your fiancée." Slapping his hand against the call box, he ordered, "Get me out of here."

Jeff shoved the heavy table away from his legs, moving away from the door before it smacked his head. Although his upper legs and middle section ached from the vicious blow, Jeff stood as straight as he could. Boldly looking Captain Mercett directly in the eye, he gained a slight amount of pleasure to see Mercett drop his stare first.

Jeff was surprised when the guard returned him to a cell with at least a dozen other men. He had no way of knowing the rumors the guards had been spreading.

Jeff nodded at the men. They all turned their backs to him.

Undaunted, he said, “My name is Jeff Howard. I’m a Christian, are any of you?”

Those words caused several heads to turn. “A Christian? Ha-ha. I’ve never known a Christian who took pleasure in brutalizing women as part of his job.”

“You’re a disgrace.”

“What are you talking about?” he asked. “I haven’t brutalized anyone, let alone women.”

“Just shut up. We’ve heard all about you.”

Realizing that the cards had been stacked against him, Jeff found a corner to sit in, not having the emotional fortitude to argue his case any longer.

If I can reach any of them for You, God, show me how.

FIFTY-FIVE

Amanda knew she had to keep up her physical strength to accomplish her plan. While she was eating, her friends gathered around.

"I don't think we'll have any serious problems until our supplies run out and we begin needing food," David said. "In two weeks our utility bills will be due, which means we need to find other accommodations."

"Any suggestions?" Bill asked.

As they had learned to do, David reached for the notebook and began to write. *I've been thinking about the caves at Spring Mill State Park. They're cold and damp, but we could be safe there, at least for a while longer.*

After passing around the notebook for everyone to read, David watched every head begin to nod.

"Could work," Bill said out loud.

"How soon?" Gloria asked.

"We have two weeks," David said.

Gently wiping her bruised mouth on her napkin, Amanda shoved back her plate. "I can't face anyone else today, but everyone here needs to be told about what's going on. Not this," she said, tapping the notebook, "but about our limited time here."

"I'll do that," David said.

Gathering her dirty dishes, Gloria gently placed her hand on Amanda's to stop her. "You sit still; I'll take care of those."

"Thanks," she said, giving her friend a sweet smile. "I'm going to spend the rest of the evening in my room. I would like for all of you to join me after dinner."

"Gladly," Alice said.

"I have the inventory list in my room of our supplies that we'll go over tonight," Amanda said, standing slowly and shoving her chair up to the table.

"That's an excellent idea." David said. "You get some rest now."

Her friends watched sadly as Amanda shuffled across the floor, her shoulders bent forward.

Waiting until she was certain Amanda could no longer hear, Alice said, "She didn't say anything about Jeff."

"I'm sure she'll tell us this evening," David said. Somehow he knew that his friend would no longer be joining them.

It was two hours after dinner was finished when everyone had vacated the fellowship hall. David shared with the residents the information having to do with their limited time together.

David smiled sadly when several of the younger residents said they just might hang around and see how long they could last before being caught.

At last the foursome gathered in Amanda's room where she already had music playing louder than normal. Sitting on the floor, she motioned for them to scoot in closer.

"This morning Jeff's captain informed me that Jeff would be executed in twenty-four hours. When I was finally able to leave his office, he had given Jeff another day."

"Did he say why?" Bill asked.

"I will say this only once, and I don't want any questions," Amanda said. "That vile captain raped me and then told me that Jeff would live another day for every morning I visited his office."

Alice covered her mouth as tears welled up in her eyes.

Bill shook his bowed head. "I am so sorry, Amanda. I didn't know."

Even though everyone wanted to ask the question, silence prevailed. They hoped she would voluntarily share what her plans were.

"I do know that Jeff is somewhere in the Lawrence County Security Center. How he is being treated is something that I am unable to find out. So, we need to pray for him." Reaching into her pocket, she pulled out a small piece of paper. "This was secretly given to me by one of the agents who transported me to and from headquarters this morning. Read it and tell me what you think."

Gloria, sitting closest to Amanda, read the short note before handing it to her husband.

David read and re-read the note before passing it to Bill.

Bill and Alice read the note together, looking at each other when they finished.

When Amanda had the note back in her hand, she looked at her friends, "Well?"

"Do you suppose he was telling you that he is a Christian also?" David asked.

Amanda shrugged her shoulders.

"How can we be sure it's not a trick?" Alice asked.

"I think this young man took a dangerous chance with this note. I say—I say you can trust him." Bill's eyes didn't quite portray the assurance that his words did.

"I think that I agree with Bill," Gloria said. "At this point, what can you lose?"

"My life."

"Oh, honey, I didn't mean—"

"I know, Gloria," Amanda said, taking her friend's hand in hers. "My life's over anyway."

"I can't accept that," David said. "We've still got much work to do."

With a sad smile, Amanda looked around the group. "What would I do without you?"

"We're hoping you won't have to find out," Alice said.

"I don't know what tomorrow holds, but if I should leave in the morning, please don't any of you try to stop me."

"But, Amanda..." David began.

"No, David, I mean it," she said. "I have a plan. I don't know just how it's going to play out, but I definitely have a plan."

Looking into her eyes, David could see fierce determination.

"Okay," he said. "But let's pray right now for Amanda and for Jeff."

The group filtered out of her room. Amanda lay across her bed, finally able to let her resolve melt as she cried into her pillow.

Having slept only two hours, she slowly dragged herself out of bed. Every part of her body ached as she tried to stand without wobbling. By the time she had finished her shower, her mind was clear.

She remembered every detail of the plan she had mentally laid out just before falling asleep in the wee hours of the morning.

"I wish I could take my Bible, but I suppose that's pushing it a little," she said to herself. Certain that she more than likely would not be returning, she took time to write a long letter to each of her fiends.

"One more thing and I'll be ready," she whispered as she pulled out the third drawer. Carefully unfolding the towel, she gingerly picked up the weapon, double-checking everything Jeff had taught her.

Carefully sliding it into the back of her slacks where it pressed against her spine, she pulled on a wool jacket, checked herself in the mirror and with infinite sadness left the comfort and security of her room.

Jesus, go with me.

Although her plan was to drive to W.S.F. headquarters, when she stepped outside she saw the familiar black SUV parked at the end of the sidewalk. The driver remained in the car while Tom Brooks held the door open for her.

Without speaking to either of them, Amanda scooted across the seat as Tom again sat with her. Was that concern she saw in his eyes or was it her imagination?

FIFTY-SIX

Jeff remained in the corner of the cell long into the night. He felt no need for sleep since he was certain his body would very soon have no need for anything. As his thoughts drifted to Amanda, he silently cried out to God to protect her from the evil clutches of Captain Mercett.

Long before dawn, he was aware of movement as three of his cellmates tiptoed in his direction. Fear began to creep up his back as they loomed over him.

God, I don't care if I die, I just don't want to be beaten up. Please don't let this happen.

The three men squatted close to him as he straightened his back against the wall.

"Are you really a Christian?" one of the men whispered.

Jeff nodded his head.

"You're a W.S.F. agent but you're still a Christian?" another asked.

"That's why I'm in here," he whispered.

"You didn't do those other things they told us you did?" the third man asked.

Jeff shook his head. "No, but I'll tell you what the real truth is. My captain raped my fiancée yesterday after he put me in here."

"Most of us are in here on trumped up charges just because we're believers," the first man said as he sat cross-legged on the concrete floor.

"The word going around is that executions will begin tomorrow," the third man said. "You know anything about that?"

Shaking his bowed head, Jeff said, "I'm afraid so."

"You mean it's true?"

"They've built a guillotine on the courthouse square that they intend to put into use tomorrow," Jeff said in a low voice.

"A guillotine?" exclaimed the second man.

Several of the sleeping inmates began to stir. "Shut up over there," one of them yelled.

"How can they do that? That's a medieval contraption," he whispered loudly.

"According to books I've been reading, the guillotine will be the tool of executioners from now on out."

"No. This just can't be," moaned the third man.

"If it's any consolation, I'll be first in line," Jeff said.

"You're volunteering?"

"Not exactly," Jeff said. "The captain has waited a long, long time for this."

Everyone was silent as they each dealt with this information in their own way.

"Are all of you scheduled to die?" Jeff asked.

"That's what they tell us."

Several more seconds of silence ensued before Jeff spoke once more. "If that's the case, why are we just sitting here? Do you remember what Peter and Paul did while they were in prison? They had a good old-fashioned hymn sing. Let's sing some hymns and quote some Scriptures; we still have our voices."

"But they'll..."

"What?" Jeff said. "Kill us? We're going to die anyway. Let's give God's Word one last chance to change hearts in this place."

"He's right," the first man said.

As the four men began singing one hymn after another and quoting the Scriptures they could remember, lights began to flash on throughout the jail. Most of the other men in their cell woke up and joined in the singing.

As predicted, the guards swarmed through the hall, screaming threats. Because men in every cell had joined in the singing, the guards realized it was futile to continue their ranting.

As quickly as they had swarmed through the hall, they disappeared through the metal door. In a matter of minutes, total darkness descended on the cells.

The guards became even more incensed in hearing the singing grow louder.

"Call the captain."

FIFTY-SEVEN

"If you want to wait here, I'll walk her up," Tom said to the driver who was glad he didn't have to leave the warmth of the vehicle.

Holding her elbow, Tom led Amanda into the gymnasium. In the stairwell, he stopped her.

"You don't have to do this, you know," he whispered.

"I know," she said.

"I can find a way for you to avoid this," he said. "Please let me help."

"Thank you, Tom, but I have it under control," she said. "I would be pleased to know that you will be praying for me."

"Consider it done," he said as he reluctantly led her to the captain's door.

Without knocking, Amanda bravely walked to the middle of the room where she stood facing the captain's desk.

Somewhat surprised at her boldness, he smiled wickedly at her, devouring her with his eyes. "I knew you'd be back."

"Is Jeff still alive?" she asked.

"For the moment." He slowly pushed his chair back when he saw her begin to remove her jacket. "Eager even." Moving quickly from behind the desk, he froze when he saw the weapon pointed directly at his heart.

"Whoa! What have we here?" The ugly, lustful look no longer lingered on his face. "That can't be Mr. Howard's. I have his. So, that must have belonged to Agent Summers."

Amanda saw no need to speak as she was taking great delight watching fear flash in his eyes as he tried to break her concentration with his chatter.

Boldly taking a step in her direction, she stated calmly and evenly, "It would be wise of you to not take another step."

"Listen, Ms. Fountain," Captain Mercett said, watching her carefully, deciding how he could remove the weapon from her. "We can work something out. This is not necessary."

"We can work nothing out," she said.

Trying to cause her to falter, he said, "It might be of interest to you to know that the security center authorities have orders to execute Mr. Howard unless they receive a call from me. I have not made that call yet this morning."

"So be it," she said.

Realizing that she had every intention of using the weapon, his face took on an evil sneer as he said, "He was going to die this morning anyway because of a disturbance he instigated in the jail."

"I have no worries about Jeff, I know where he's going," she said.

"You know where he's going?" Mercett asked.

"That's right. And it's certainly not the same place you're going," she said. "So, sir, I would advise you to begin saying your prayers."

Upon hearing that word, a deep growl exploded from his lips as he began to charge toward her. Without batting an eye, her finger pressed the trigger.

"Wow," she whispered. "That was awesome." Taking a folded cloth from her pocket, she carefully wiped every inch of the weapon before walking behind the captain's desk and pulling out drawers until she found one with enough room to hold the weapon.

After carefully wiping each drawer handle, she folded the cloth, shoved it back into her pocket, put her jacket on and left the room.

Agent Tom Brooks looked up in surprise to see Amanda walking toward him as he stood at the head of the steps.

Even though she could see the questions in his eyes, she said nothing until she was seated once again in the back seat of the SUV.

"Captain Mercett told me that my fiancé is to be executed at ten o'clock," she said as tears began to trickle from the corner of her eyes. "I need to be there. Could you take me?"

The driver immediately punched the captain's office number into his cell phone. When he received no answer, he tried the captain's personal number. Again, no answer.

"What do you think, Tom?" he asked. "The captain isn't answering."

Feeling Tom's eyes on her, Amanda refused to look in his direction. Instead, she dug the cloth from her pocket to dry her eyes.

"Let's go, we haven't much time," he said.

Miss Fountain, what have you done?

FIFTY-EIGHT

At nine-thirty, Jeff's hands were bound securely as he was being led from the security center across the street to the courthouse square where a crowd had already gathered.

"The Lord is my shepherd, I shall not want. Yea, though I walk through the valley of the shadow of death, I will fear no evil for Thou art with me. You promised to never leave me nor forsake me, God. You are my strength, my shield, my fortress. I will not fear what man can do to me. Precious Lord, take my hand, lead me on, help me stand. My God shall supply all my needs. Into Your hands I commit my soul."

Until he was led to the edge of the platform, Jeff continued to quote Scriptures and parts of hymns he had heard all his life while sitting in church beside his parents. His heart felt like it was going to pound through his rib cage. Even so, he continued to hold his head up high.

At the moment the guards grabbed his arms, he saw Amanda standing on the edge of the crowd. "No! No, please don't be here," he whispered.

"I love you, Jeff Howard, and I'll see you soon," she yelled.

Expecting to be forced face down, Jeff was startled when he was spun around and knocked backward. As the guards locked a metal bar across his knees, he looked up in horror at the waiting blade.

To keep from watching death plunging toward his throat, he squeezed his eyes shut. "Father, forgive them," he whispered as tears forced their way through the corners of his eyes.

Jeff heard the loud snap of the release mechanism and the whoosh of the blade rushing downward a mere second before Jesus' hand reached out for his.

As Jeff's beautiful blond head slid down the blood soaked chute, Amanda's knees gave way and darkness enveloped her.

Tom Brooks' partner ignored her limp body as his eyes stayed riveted on the horrendous scene before them. As Tom bent to pick Amanda up, his heart ached as he listened to her anguished moans.

"Jeff, I love you."

Tom was just setting Amanda onto the back seat when another identical vehicle screeched to a halt against Tom's bumper.

"We're placing that woman under arrest," barked an older agent, pushing Tom out of the way.

"On what charge, sir?" Tom asked.

"Captain Mercett is missing and we believe she was the last person to see him."

"I see," Tom said. "I'll be glad to transport her, sir."

"Not necessary," the older agent snapped.

Tom watched helplessly as the two agents dragged Amanda to their vehicle and roughly shoved her inside. Watching them speed away, he leaned against his own vehicle as his partner continued to stare at the guillotines, which were now in full use.

After vomiting at the back of the vehicle, Tom slumped onto the front seat as he waited for his partner. *If Jeff Howard could stand firm even up to the end, why can't I?*

By the day's end, thirty inmates, male and female, had been crudely and cruelly beheaded. Two of the guards puffed on cigarettes, laughing about the number of heads in the hoppers under the blood covered blades.

Before the night was over, every inmate in the security center had become Christians. The female inmates clung to each other knowing that the next day would be their last.

"Jeff Howard showed us how to walk into God's presence. If he could do it, so can we."

The words of "Onward Christian Soldiers," "We're Marching To Zion," and "Amazing Grace" echoed throughout the rows of cells all through the dark hours of night.

FIFTY-NINE

By four o'clock in the morning, Amanda could no longer speak coherently.

"I'll ask you one more time, Miss Fountain, where is Captain Mercett?" His putrid breath popping onto her face, a very large, burley W.S.F. agent shouted at her.

"Don't know," she mumbled.

His backhanded blow knocked Amanda to the floor. She did not move.

"Pick her up," he shouted.

"Sir, she is no longer able to respond," the fat, ugly nurse said. "Have her thrown into the lockdown room for at least a couple hours. If she's still uncooperative at that time, I'll give her something."

"Get her out of here." He turned his back on her.

The two agents who had arrested her, now dragged her to a small, dark room no bigger than a coat closet where they literally tossed her inside, locking the door.

Mental, emotional, and physical exhaustion kept Amanda from awakening during her incarceration in the tiny room.

Dark shadows were under their eyes as they pulled Amanda from her tiny cell. Dragging her back to Captain Mercett's office, they deposited her in the same chair they had hauled her away from two hours earlier.

Sudden jerking movements awakened her as she was thrust into the hard chair and intensely bright lights blazed into her face.

"Please, I can't do this any longer," she begged.

"Answer our questions and you'll be free to go," the older agent barked.

Amanda laughed. "Oh, I'm sure you will let me go."

"You were the last known person to see the captain. Where is he?"

"And I keep telling you that I don't know," she said with a deep sigh.

The nurse grabbed her arm, painfully jabbing a needle into it.

"What are you doing?" Amanda cried.

"Just a little truth juice."

"Truth juice? What's that," Amanda asked, rubbing her arm.

"Something that will put an end to your lies," the nurse said. "We're tired of your games."

After waiting in silence for the shot to begin its work, the older agent began to question her again.

"Amanda Fountain, tell us where Captain Mercett is at this time."

"In Hell," she said without hesitation.

"Excuse me?" the agent exclaimed.

"Why?" Amanda mumbled.

Restraining himself from striking Amanda with a killing blow, the agent asked her one last time. "Where is Captain Mercett?"

"He's in Hell," she answered loudly.

"What do you mean by that?" he asked.

"Captain Mercett raped me and threatened to kill Jeff Howard if I didn't return so he could do that to me every day. I used one of your fancy weapons on him, so I can safely say that Captain Mercett is burning in Hell as we speak."

Speechless, the agent stared at Amanda. The nurse's eyes widened as her mouth hung open in disbelief.

Finally, the agent straightened and ordered the guards to transport Miss Fountain to the Lawrence County Security Center.

Just as they lifted her from the chair, he changed his mind. "On second thought, take her to the church where she's been living. Throw her inside the door with the message that everyone there will receive the same unless they agree to have the computer chip implanted before the week is over. First thing tomorrow morning, pick her up again and transport her to the Security Center for execution."

Amanda's drugged, exhausted brain could not decipher what was being said. As she was shoved into the SUV, she fell over in the seat and remained in that position until she felt the pain of being thrown onto a carpet-covered concrete floor.

Immediately after delivering their message, the agents sped out of the parking lot, leaving Amanda in the care of her friends who hardly recognized her bruised, swollen face.

With broken hearts, they carried her to her room and cleaned her up as well as they could. Blankets were gently draped over her as they watched her thrash around in her sleep.

Just before daybreak, Amanda lay quietly trying to open her swollen eyes. Sensing someone near her, she whispered, "Who's there?"

"It's us, honey," Gloria said, placing a cold, wet cloth on her eyes. "This will help with the swelling."

"Jeff's dead," Amanda whispered.

"We heard," David said quietly.

"Are all of you okay?" she asked.

"So far," David said.

"They'll be back for me soon," she whispered again.

Gloria hugged herself tightly with one arm while the other hand clasped her mouth tightly to hold in her sobs.

Alice held both hands over her mouth.

"From the reports we've been given, Jeff started a revival in the jail before he died. Isn't that wonderful?" David wanted Amanda to know as much as possible before she had to leave again.

"I wish the same could be said about me," she whispered hoarsely as hot tears slipped into the cold cloth.

"What are you talking about, girl?" Alice exclaimed. "Look at all of us. And Jeff wouldn't be with Jesus right now if you hadn't witnessed to him."

"And have you forgotten that it was your idea to make an empty church a refuge for all of us; and your idea to stockpile supplies for our future?" David added.

Amanda smiled. Removing the cloth from her eyes, she held out her hand. "Please, help me up. I'm not going to waste any more of my time here."

Gloria grabbed her hand, gently pulling her to an upright position. It broke her heart to watch the grimace on Amanda's face.

"If this truly is your time, you just remember that all of us living in this building will continue what you have started," she said.

"We'll use the rest of our time to help others become Christians, we promise," Bill said.

Amanda had just nodded her head when loud banging sounded from the foyer door.

"I feel like the Apostle Paul," Amanda said. "I have fought a good fight—even though it has been short—I have kept the faith. I'm ready to go. Please, keep the faith."

After everyone hugged her, David wrapped his arms around her as if to give his strength to her. His heavy tears dripped onto the top of her head.

"Let me help you up the steps," he said, wrapping one arm around her waist. When they made it to the foot of the steps, he picked her up in his arms and carried her the rest of the way.

Tom Brooks and his partner waited at the door holding two documents. His partner began reading the first. "Amanda Fountain, you are under arrest and will accompany World Security Force agents who will transport you to the Lawrence County courthouse square where you will be executed promptly at twelve o'clock noon today."

Tom stepped forward and took Amanda's arm, intending to handcuff her.

"Please, sir," David said. "Her shoulder has been dislocated. Could you please not handcuff her? Please?"

Instead of pulling her arms behind her, Tom brought her wrists together in front and as gently as possible clasped the metal bands around her bruised arms.

"The following order has been given for David Patterson, Gloria Patterson, Bill Short, and Alice Short. You are hereby ordered to report to the Lawrence County courthouse square as witnesses to Amanda Fountain's execution today at twelve o'clock noon."

David's fists were tightened into white-knuckled knots and his jaws were clinched so tightly that stabbing pains radiated from his ears to the base of his neck.

Spasms in Gloria's stomach were the only indication of her agony as she resolved not to give these agents the satisfaction of watching her fall apart. Even though she could see the remorse in Tom's eyes, at this moment in time she hated him for what he was taking part in.

Alice's fingernails dug into Bill's arm as they clung to each other.

"I love you all and I'll see you in Heaven," Amanda said as she was led away.

Immediately upon their departure, David turned to the others and said, "Help me move as many of our supplies as possible before we have to leave."

"Where?" Bill asked, stunned that this had to be done immediately.

"Honey, why do we have to do this now?" Gloria asked.

"I can't explain it," David said, walking swiftly to the closet that led to the attic. "I just know that we have to move as much as possible."

Without argument, everyone began to move quickly. The women ran into the kitchen to get sacks to put the items in. Within an hour they had cleaned out the supplies in the attic. None of the other residents seemed to notice what they were doing as they carried full trash bags into the fellowship hall.

"What now?" Gloria asked. "Do you have another place to store all of this?"

"As a matter of fact, I do. We just don't have time to hide them right now," David said, pulling two large sacks onto each shoulder. "Grab what you can carry and follow me."

Hoping that any watching eyes would think they were getting rid of trash, David walked quickly to the parking lot. With his pocket full of keys, he opened the first trunk and tossed in the trash bag. He quickly opened several more trunks for the rest.

"Everybody, remember which vehicle you put your sacks in," he said. "We've just got time to clean up and drive to Bedford."

"Can we all ride together?" Alice asked.

"Yes," David answered. "We'll take one of the cars that hasn't been used before, just in case we're being watched."

In their apartment, as they hurriedly changed their clothes, Gloria asked her husband, "Honey, can you tell me what this is all about?"

"I honestly don't know." His trembling fingers tried for the third time to fashion a knot in his tie. "I just feel that it's imperative that we get the supplies out of the building."

Selecting a bronze colored Toyota, the foursome began the grievous journey to watch their friend's execution.

"How can we do this?" Gloria asked, wiping the tears from her face with tissues.

"I don't know, but they're going to be watching us closely," David said.

"We'll just have to remember that Amanda will truly be in God's hands," Bill said, holding his weeping wife close to his side.

Arriving at the already crowded courthouse square, they were directed to an empty parking space at the bottom of the square directly in front of the guillotine.

"David, I can't do this," Gloria moaned as both her hands seized his arm.

After wresting his arm from her death grip, he wrapped her in both his arms. "God promised to never leave us or forsake us, Gloria. If Amanda can do this, so can we."

It took several minutes, but she finally gained enough control to stand free of his arms. After taking a deep, ragged breath, she blew her nose, wiped her face, and applied a thin coat of lipstick.

"Alice, we have to do this," Bill said, trying to gently pull his wife from the back floor board where she had thrown herself. Her weeping was almost more than he could endure.

"It's either do this or we'll be the next in line." The commanding tone in his voice reached through the grief. Ever so slowly, she moved back onto the seat next to her husband, refusing to look at him or at the scene in front of them.

"Take several deep breaths and blow it out slowly," David said to everyone. "Remember, God knows we need His strength."

Alice's first several breaths were too shallow and ragged to do any good. But with Bill's encouragement, she was finally able to breathe in deeply enough to blow out enough pain and fear to function once again.

Looking into his wife's face, David recognized the glazed look in her eyes. *She's found her place.* He remembered that same look when her baby disappeared from her body.

Slowly exiting the vehicle, the two couples were led by a uniformed guard to the middle of the front row. It was obvious that their every move was being watched.

Amanda was the first to be led to the guillotine. As the charges of her crime echoed across the square, she was shoved to her knees; her head was rammed downward until her neck was in the clutches of the darkly stained indention.

Straining for one last deep breath, she shouted, "Our God is an awe—" The thundering blade released her soul into the waiting, loving arms of Jesus.

"Amen," David said quietly. Gloria remained in her safe place. Bill and Alice, with hands clasped and bodies trembling, agreed with David. "Amen," they whispered.

As nonchalantly as possible, the four remaining friends slowly walked back to their vehicle, with full knowledge that at any second they too could be arrested.

Riding back to Mitchell, Gloria's mournful sobs shook her body. Alice's face was buried in her husband's chest as she wept bitter tears. David's vision was blurred as he kept checking his rearview mirror.

"I wonder what's burning," Bill asked, seeing black smoke billowing high into the sky.

With a sick feeling in the pit of his stomach, David pressed his foot down on the accelerator. Before he made the turn onto Woodville Road, they all knew exactly what was burning.

Speeding into the front lawn, David slammed on his brakes, skidding through the wet grass. Jumping from the car, he ran as close to the building as possible before being driven back by scorching flames.

Watching in horror, a handful of people stood nearby as black-edged, red flames engulfed the entire church and the storage shed.

"Where is everybody?" David shouted. "Did they all make it out?"

"We're the only ones," a young man answered. "The doors were nailed shut from the outside before the fire started."

"You mean, they're still in there?" David yelled in desperation as he grabbed the young man by the shoulders.

"Yes, Mr. Patterson. They're still in there."

David sank to the ground crying as he clutched the top of his head with both hands.

Seeing her husband bent over with his forehead on the ground, Gloria jumped out of the car and ran to him. Bill and Alice followed.

Screams pierced the air when one of the burning vehicles exploded.

A young man, whose face was blackened by smoke, dove onto the ground beside David and Gloria.

"There are only ten of us left," he rasped, staring forlornly at the inferno.

Another vehicle exploded.

"David, we have to move," Gloria cried, grasping her husband's arm.

Ever so slowly, David rose from the ground with his face speckled with mud and soot. Gloria watched as he squared shoulders, his eyes shining with resolve. Holding out his arms, he ushered everyone far away from danger.

"They can not stop us. They can burn the building down but they will not win. We are on God's side, and He will prevail."

"Amen!" Hearing the determination in David's voice gave the small group the will to fight to the end.

Digging into his jacket pocket, David's hand closed around a handful of keys. Holding them out, he said, "Here are the keys. Move our designated vehicles where they'll be safe."

Each person snatched a key and began trying to find which vehicle it belonged to. Working feverishly, they were able to save each vehicle that held their supplies.

"Well done. Well done," David said when they had all gathered around him once more. "Our shelter has been destroyed, but our faith holds strong."

"The supplies," Bill exclaimed. "That's why you felt so strongly about moving them."

Nodding, David watched sadly as limestone walls crashed into the flames.

Looking around the small group that was left, David tried to assess their immediate needs.

"Some of you don't have jackets or coats, but we know there's extra clothing in the vehicles, thanks to Amanda. We only have a few blankets so we need to find some kind of shelter before nightfall."

"How about the caves in Spring Mill State Park?" Bill asked.

"The caves! We can stay in the caves," Gloria said with excitement.

"Good idea," David said. "However, if all of us drive in at the same time we will attract too much unwanted attention. Gloria and I will drive in first? We'll park in the Donaldson area and carry our supplies down into the cave.

Bill, you and Alice come next with yours. By that time I'll have our cars moved farther back into the picnic area.

Half an hour after Bill leaves, you guys join us," David said pointing to four young men. "The rest of you wait another half-hour before driving out to meet us. Just make sure you get there before dark."

"Sounds like a plan," one young man said.

David checked around the area, making certain no one was watching their movements.

"God, our Father, we will not give up the fight for Your kingdom. As we leave here today, we ask that Your heavenly warriors keep watch over us and protect us. Until we're with You in Glory, we give ourselves totally to Your service. In Jesus' name, Amen," David prayed before they began their ten-minute trip to Spring Mill State Park.

"Father, God," Gloria prayed. "I want to give you thanks for saving us, even though we were stupid enough to be left after Jesus came. I want to thank you for Amanda and Jeff and their witness to us. I want to thank you for giving us shelter and supplies so that we can survive long enough to lead others to You. Amen."

"We have to leave now," David said softly.

Gloria nodded her head, gave Alice a hug and climbed into her car.

Spring Mill State Park, snuggled into forest covered cavernous hills in southern Indiana, is only a few miles east of Mitchell. Although there were several caves in the park, Donnelson Cave is the largest.

As dusk arrived, all supplies were stored in Donnelson Cave. Each vehicle was parked in different areas of the park. Silently, everyone moved far back into the damp, inky blackness of their new home.

Fueled by unquenchable, holy fire burning in their breasts, the fourteen totally committed Christians confronted their uncertain futures with fierce determination to use whatever they had been left to not only survive, but to help others become Christians before it was eternally too late.

That time was close.

Their ears yearned to hear Christ Jesus' words, "*I am the Alpha and Omega, the beginning and the end. I will give unto him that is athirst of the fountain of the water of life freely. He that overcometh shall inherit all things; and I will be his God and he shall be my son.*"

The End

SLEEP TIGHT

by Barbara Wagner

Paperback, 289 pages
6" x 9"
ISBN 1-60610-096-3

Attractive Caryl Stewart, a western artist, has inherited a fortune and fallen in love with David Eagle, the confident and sensual man of her dreams. When her flamboyant, oil-rich great-aunt, Savannah Buckman, dies, the young redhead travels from Scottsdale, Arizona, to manage her great-aunt's estate in upscale Winter Park near Oklahoma City. After a disturbing secret from Savannah's past is revealed and a manipulative friend, almost Caryl's exact twin, becomes the third victim, Caryl knows she is the target of a cunning killer, an unknown murderer who is slowly going insane. Tormented by Oklahoma wind and trapped in the eerie atmosphere of a mysterious mansion, she struggles to escape from a maze of terror, revenge and murder. When her Native American lover is accused, Caryl makes a startling discovery and a cruel psychopath prepares to combine her death with his pleasure.

About the author:

Both a writer and an artist, Barbara Wagner lives with her husband in a suburb of Kansas City close to their grown children. She grew up in Oklahoma, has a degree in fine art from the University of Oklahoma, and studied creative writing at Butler University in Indianapolis. An award-winning artist, her work was marketed in Scottsdale, Arizona, for many years. Though *Sleep Tight* is entirely a work of fiction, the artistic life of the novel's protagonist, Caryl Stewart, is drawn from Barbara's own experience and adds a strong framework to the suspenseful story.